Instinct

The Coven, Volume 1

Jennifer Noel Dennis

Published by Jennifer Noel Dennis, 2023.

INSTINCT

First edition. March 1, 2023.

Copyright © 2023 Jennifer Noel Dennis.

ISBN: 979-8215038741

Written by Jennifer Noel Dennis.

Dedication:

Most people would probably make a dedication out to their significant other or their children, but this one is different. Because I am making this book out to me. So, this one is for the fifteen year old girl who wrote the very first draft of the book you are about to read. And, though it has gone through many changes since it's conception in 2009, I couldn't have done this without you.

I am so proud of you.

Prologue
Phoebe

There are things in this world that are far more sinister than even the darkest minds can comprehend. Edges of the world so black that even the shadows dread them. Those places, in the darkness, are where the secrets are kept. Those things that go bump in the night. The stories mothers tell their babies to keep them tucked into bed. But what nobody ever seems to question is where those stories come from. Who would think up such horrible things? An even better question is why would mothers tell their precious little children about them?

Because, not so long ago, they weren't just stories to be told.

The media loves to cover dramatic stories about children going missing and homes burning down in the night. When you're a kid, it seems like a lot of bad luck. When you're a teenager, you don't see the horror. And when you're an adult, you look away in fear. But what about those few who know? Those few who have seen the dark corners of the world, who see what lurks beneath the false security of sunshine and flowers. They watch. They listen. They know.

Things are not the way they seem. Of course, everyone always says that, don't they? I was one of those who believed the pretty lie.

The world isn't what we thought.

The world is a much darker place.

And now I belong to that world. There is no going back.

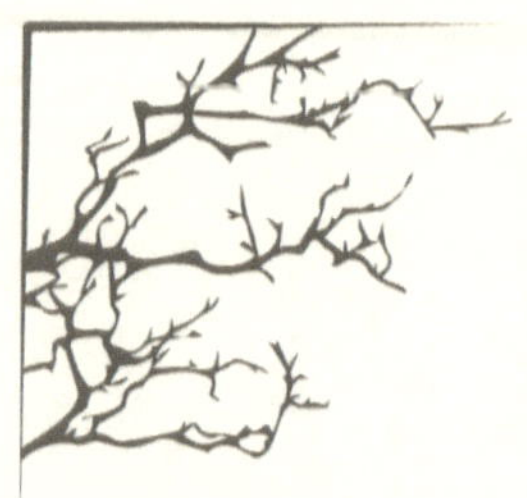

Chapter One
Phoebe

"Phoebe, you have to come." The words were spoken with a whine, coming from my best friend since grade school. "Everyone is going to be there."

I shot her a dark look and rolled my green eyes. "Angie," I said. "You know I can't. I'm busy tonight. I have to work." I propped my feet up on the beat up coffee table and hoped that she would drop it. But we both knew that she wouldn't.

She sighed and pushed her fingers through her brown hair. "Call in sick," she told me. "You never go out anymore."

I shrugged my shoulders and glanced around the room of our shared apartment, avoiding her eyes. I knew every nook and cranny, from the peach colored walls to the beige carpet. The kitchen sink leaked, the shower never got hot, and the neighbors blasted music all hours of the night, but it was home. "You know why," I said quietly, refusing to even glance in her direction.

Angie fell silent, and I knew she was cursing herself for saying anything. "Phoebe," she whispered. "I'm sorry. I meant nothing by it, I promise."

I finally turned to look at her and could see that she really meant it. Her brown eyes were wide, and she looked like she thought I was about to cry. But I wasn't. I had cried enough in the last few months since the accident. "I'm fine," I said simply. I didn't want to get into it, but I figured it was going to happen anyway, regardless of my wishes. Things never really seemed to go my way.

"If you were really fine, you wouldn't lock yourself up in this place all the time. You only ever go out for school and work, Phoebe. I'm worried about you," Angie told me, sitting forward slightly. She sighed, and I saw her shoulders slump. "Ever since your parents—"

"Don't," I interrupted quickly, my feet finding the floor in case I needed to make an escape from this conversation. "Please." I didn't want to talk about it. She *knew* I didn't want to talk about it.

She snapped her mouth shut and sighed, standing. "I really wish you would come," she said softly. "Even if just for a bit, just to get out and get some fresh air."

I watched her walk toward the door and bit my lower lip. I was never big on parties, but Angie may have been right. For months, I had done nothing but go to school and work. Maybe I just needed one night out to loosen up. A few drinks couldn't hurt. I stood. "Okay."

She looked at me, and it broke my heart to see the doubt in her eyes. She wanted to believe me, but she didn't. Had I really become so unreliable? "Okay, what?" she asked.

"Give me a second to call work and get changed," I said. "I'll be right back. Wait for me?" I asked, forcing a smile. I felt a pit in my stomach the size of a baseball. My anxiety threatened to have me take it all back. To laugh it off and say I was only joking. I was too responsible to call out of work for something so trivial as a party. But I knew, in that moment, that Angie needed me more than work ever could. She needed me to be okay, and I guess she was right. I needed to be okay.

Angie grinned. "Of course!" she exclaimed, suddenly bouncing back to her bubbly self now that I had given confirmation of her wishes. I briefly wondered if it was all a ploy to get her way, but shook the thought from my head. Either way, she was right.

I turned and headed to my room, fishing out my cell phone as I went. I dialed the number for my crappy waitressing job and held my breath. It rang four times before someone answered. I managed a weak cough. "It's Phoebe," I said, trying to make my voice a little scratchy. "I can't make it to work… I'm really sick." I paused a second and waited for the manager to call me on my bluff. But she didn't. She sighed loudly and told me to feel better. I dropped the phone on my nightstand and shifted through my closet for something appropriate to wear to a party while counting my blessings that she had let me get away with that. There was no way my illness was believable. It had sounded fake to my own ears.

I ended up choosing a pair—my favorite pair—of dark skinny jeans, a black tank top, and the leather jacket Angie had saved her money to buy me for my last birthday. I turned and headed to my makeup station—also known as the top of my dresser. I ran a brush through my wavy blonde hair, swiped on some mascara, ran a tube of red lipstick over my lips, and called it good. I would not go all out. Too much makeup coupled with the amount of black I was wearing wasn't really my style. I felt bad for ditching work for a party, but as I stepped into a pair of four-inch black stilettos, I actually found myself getting excited. It had been a while. Maybe I was ready to live again.

I gave myself a practice run, walking across my room a few times to make sure I still remembered how to function in high heels, and grabbed my purse off the bed on the way to the door. I went through the checklist as I returned to the living room. Keys? Check. Wallet with a credit card and some cash? Check. Tampons? Check. I looked up at Angie and smiled. "I'm ready."

She whistled and winked at me, and I just laughed. "Looking foxy," she commented, making a show of giving me a once over.

I grabbed her sleeve and pulled her toward the door. "Nobody says that. Nobody has said that for a long time." The two of us took the elevator to the lobby and strode out to our shared car. It was old, it was dented, and it ran—mostly. Angie got behind the wheel with little trouble, but I had to wrestle the passenger door open. She glanced at me when I finally took my seat.

"We need a new car," she said with a sigh, turning the key in the ignition.

"We can't afford a new car," I told her. "Maybe a new *used* car," I suggested. "But that's a pretty big maybe."

She shrugged her shoulders and pulled out of the lot, turning the car toward the party. "I'll take what I can get," she said with a smile. "But I want something cute. Sporty."

"How about we get what we can afford?" I asked, quirking an eyebrow. The thought of what the insurance would cost for something *sporty* made my wallet cringe.

Angie gave a long sigh. "Fine," she said, flicking the radio on without looking and turning it to her favorite station. "Ruin all my fun. Take everything away from me."

Being a smartass, I turned the station on the radio, and she shot me an outraged look. "*Now* I've taken everything," I said with a laugh. My laughter died in no time, however. "Eyes on the road," I blurted. It was a habit. Call it a side effect of being the only one to survive a car accident. If that's truly what it even was.

Angie's eyes snapped back to the road, and I witnessed her hands tightening on the wheel. I should have offered to drive. Angie didn't enjoy driving with me in the car anymore. It made her nervous anytime she was reminded of what had happened to me. I turned my eyes away from her and looked out at the slowly darkening sky. I knew; however, that she never would have let me drive. If one of us hated driving more than the other, it was me. Ever since the accident, I just didn't like getting behind the wheel.

"I think you should talk about it."

She had spoken so quietly that I almost wasn't sure she had said anything at all. I slowly turned to look at her, but her eyes were fixed firmly on the road ahead of her. "What?" I asked, blinking.

"You haven't talked about the accident since it happened," Angie said rapidly. "To anyone. I think you need to talk about it. You need to get the guilt off your ch—"

"Guilt?" I interrupted. She had no idea what had actually happened, and yet somehow she hit the nail on the head. I *did* feel guilty. I barely knew what happened. Or maybe that wasn't right. Maybe I knew *exactly* what had happened, and I just didn't want to admit it. Because it was crazy.

I saw her wince, but I also saw the clench of her jaw. She would not back down. "You were driving." She said nothing else, and she didn't have to.

"You don't know anything," I mumbled, turning to look out the window again. I didn't want to have this conversation. She would think I was crazy, just like the police who had arrived at the scene. Maybe I *was* crazy. It was impossible.

"Because you won't talk to me," Angie said in exasperation. She pulled the car up along a sidewalk, wedging herself between a truck and a little Pontiac. I stared at the house we had arrived at instead of looking at her. The lawn was freshly mowed, and the flowerbed was tended to. The windows were clean, and the porch light was already on, even though it wasn't very dark yet. Chances were high that the house belonged to a nice family, and the parents were away for the weekend. Of course, the responsible kids would *never* throw a party. I wondered for the first time at the age of our gracious hosts, worried Angie had dragged me to a high school party.

I rocked my foot back and forth on the heel and finally spared her a quick glance. "It's crazy," I said with much effort. I didn't want to talk about it, but maybe she was right. Maybe she would believe me and tell me I wasn't off my rocker. Maybe she would have a plausible explanation for it all.

She killed the engine and twisted in her seat to look at me more fully. "Phoebe," she said. "I am your best friend. You can tell me anything. I know you're not crazy, so you have nothing to worry about. Please, you have to get this off your chest. You can't keep it bottled up inside forever. Talk to me."

I heaved a loud sigh and closed my eyes, pressing my fingers to my temples. "There was a man," I said, my heart beating in my chest so hard I was certain she could hear it. It sounded deafening to my own ears.

Angie frowned. "A police officer?" she asked, tilting her head to the side slightly, trying to piece together the puzzle with too few pieces.

I was already shaking my head by the time she finished her question. "No. There was a man in the road. He just... appeared out of nowhere." It was like he materialized or moved so fast, none of us had seen him coming.

Angie was silent for a moment. "And you swerved," she supplied gently. Still not enough pieces to make the picture form. She thought she knew what had happened. Of course, Angie had heard the same story everyone else had. It was easier than the truth. I had been driving the car that night, my parent's passengers. It didn't matter where we had been headed because it was all a lie, anyway.

I winced. "No," I whispered, wrapping my arms around myself. I hadn't been driving, and I hadn't known where we were going.

She looked at me, startled. "You hit him?"

I clenched my teeth together so hard it hurt. "No," I said again, my fingers biting into my arms. "Angie, listen to me. I wasn't driving the car." I don't know why I needed her to believe me so badly. It wasn't like it made a difference. The police reports would stay the same, regardless of what Angie believed.

She stared at me, confusion etched into every feature. "But the reports—"

"Are wrong," I interrupted. Now that I was talking about it, I just wanted to get it all out there. I didn't want to hold it inside of me any longer. I needed someone else to hear the absolute absurdity of it all and tell me I wasn't crazy. I needed to hear someone tell me I wasn't insane. At least, I hoped I wasn't. "The reports are wrong, Angie. I wasn't driving that night. And I know for a fact that a car accident isn't what killed my parents." Saying the words out loud for the first time made my stomach hurt. The anxiety was back in full force, growing in size, gnawing at my insides.

I could feel the air in the car thickening with tension. It was getting hard to breathe and suddenly I didn't want to do this anymore. I couldn't. I shook my head and grabbed the handle of the door. "Phoebe," Angie said quietly.

I started opening the door, and she grabbed my wrist. "What?" I asked through clenched teeth. My parents died in a horrible car crash. That was all there was to it. So why could I taste the lie on my tongue?

"Tell me what happened. Everything, from the beginning." I looked back at her and saw no judgment in her eyes. I sighed and closed the door, sitting back in my seat again.

"I didn't understand what was happening," I said quietly, folding my hands into my lap, my eyes blurring, staring blankly out the windshield. "Mom was acting strange. Dad wasn't much better. She was packing a bag, and he kept telling her to hurry. They wouldn't tell me anything. Every time I asked what was happening, they just told me to pack a bag. To hurry up."

"Phoebe," Mom said quickly. "Just grab the necessities. Please, sweetheart, hurry." Her voice was nearly frantic. I had never seen her so scared. But what was she scared of?

Dad grabbed a duffle bag and slung it over his shoulder. "We are running out of time," he said gruffly. "Whatever you've got, grab it and let's go."

"*Where are we going?*" *I demanded, grasping my backpack in my hand, filled with a few haphazard outfits. "What is going on? Why won't you tell me anything?"*

"There is no time," Mom said softly. She took my hand and pulled me toward the door. "We will explain in the car." She gave my hand a squeeze, leading me swiftly out the door.

The three of us left the house, leaving the door unlocked. Dad got behind the wheel, Mom in the passenger seat, and me in the back. He started the engine and looked at me in the mirror. "No matter what happens," he said gravely, eyes full of a steel I had never before seen. "We love you."

Tears pricked my eyes. I didn't know what was going on and that just made everything worse. Maybe if I knew what was happening, I could understand better. "You're scaring me," I whispered. I had never seen either of them like this before. They were scared, too.

Mom sighed sadly, turning in her seat to look at me. "You should be scared."

Dad pulled out of the driveway and turned onto the road, driving much too fast. "Would Kathleen take her?" he asked, shooting Mom a look.

She was already shaking her head before he had finished his sentence. "No, she wouldn't. Not after what I've—"

"Stop it, Jas," Dad said, shooting her a stern look. "You haven't done anything wrong," he added, voice softening.

"Perhaps," Mom muttered to herself. "Others might not see it that way."

I gripped the seats tightly, not sure what they were talking about. Mom was practically a saint and wouldn't hurt a fly. What could she possibly have done wrong? "Dad, you're speeding," I said weakly. He didn't respond.

He whipped down the road well above the speed limit, taking turns so sharply the tires squealed. Tears leaked down my cheeks and my heart beat painfully against my chest. I wished I knew what was going on. Maybe it would make more sense if they would just talk to me. Why were we leaving so quickly? Why didn't we say goodbye to anyone? Why were they talking about my Aunt Kathleen? I had only met her once, and she didn't like me very much.

"We'll figure it out," Mom said, rubbing her temples. "It'll be okay."

Through my tear-filled eyes, I looked forward and screamed. "Dad!" A man was standing in the middle of the road. Where had he come from? It was like he had just appeared.

"Bradly...?" Mom asked, voice full of resignation.

Dad ignored both wife and child and pushed his foot down on the pedal harder, barreling toward the man. Mom closed her eyes, and I grabbed the back of my dad's seat, breath caught in my throat. Time seemed to slow.

The impact was harder than I expected. It was more like slamming into a brick wall or a tree. The front fender crumpled. Metal crunched and glass shattered, the airbags deployed, and I was thrown back against my seat; the seatbelt cutting into my flesh. A loud ringing sounded in my ears, and I tasted blood. Black spots danced before my eyes as everything settled. I could hear something that didn't belong. My mind didn't comprehend it. Snarling. It sounded as if we had come upon an animal attack, but that didn't make any sense.

A hand touched my face, and I blinked. "Mom...?" I asked weakly, trying to focus on her blurry figure leaning over me.

"Phoebe," Mom said rapidly. "Darling, we have to go." She was checking me over swiftly, making sure I was alright.

"Where's Dad?" I asked as she unbuckled my seatbelt and helped me out of the car. We had slammed into a tree when we skidded after hitting the man, and the passenger side of the car was destroyed. Mom had blood running down her temple where she must have hit her head on impact. I stumbled out of the car, and she slipped her arm around me. "Mom?" I asked, eyes unfocused. I must have hit my head too; it

was really hard to concentrate. "Where's Dad?" I asked again, looking around.

"Don't look, baby," Mom said, reaching to cover my eyes, but I had already seen.

The man that had been standing in the road appeared to be perfectly fine. But that wasn't what brought the scream to my lips. In the middle of the road, just before the wreckage, my father and the man who had been hit were fighting. Mom pulled me against her and gave a squeeze. I think she knew there was nothing she could say to fix it. I couldn't unsee the blood. I couldn't unsee the way those two men went after one another, not with fists, but with teeth.

"Phoebe," Mom said suddenly. I could hear the urgency in her voice. "Get in the car. In the driver's seat." Her urgency unnerved me.

"What?" I asked, uncomprehending, as she shuffled me to the wrecked car and got me into the driver's seat. She reached over and clipped the seatbelt, grabbing my face in her hands.

"I love you," she said fervently, pressing a kiss to my forehead. "You were driving, baby. Okay? Say it."

"I... I was driving?" I asked, shaking my head slowly. What did that have to do with anything? Why did it matter who was driving?

She nodded her head and kissed my forehead. "That's what you tell them, sweetheart. You were driving." She left my side and went to the passenger seat. She climbed back into her seat and winced. Before I could say or do anything, she threw a hard punch, her fist slamming into the windshield. The glass cracked even more right in front of her, and her blood smeared across the glass. I yelped, and she looked over at me apologetically. "I love you," she said. "I promise we will explain everything later. You have to trust me." She reached over and caressed my cheek. "Do you trust me?"

"What?" I asked. "Mom, what are you saying? Of course, I trust you. What's going on? What's happening? D-dad?" She didn't answer me but pressed her fingers down on my neck and I began to feel dizzy. I

slumped forward, my head resting on the steering wheel. Before I passed out completely, I heard her scream. "No, please!"

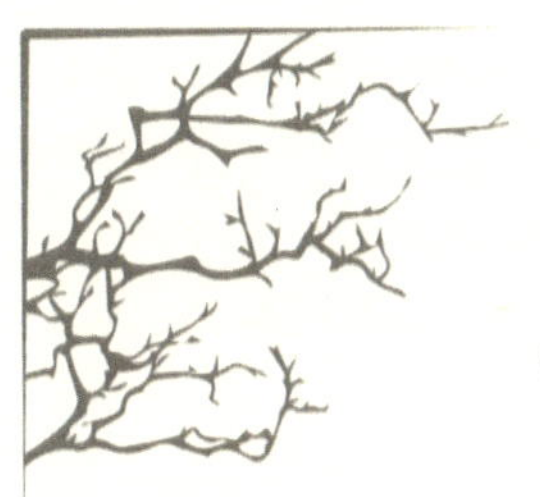

Chapter Two
Phoebe

Angie stared. She shook her head once and stared some more. "Phoebe," she said after a painfully long moment. I knew it sounded crazy.

I sighed sharply and shoved the car door open. "Forget it," I said. I knew she wouldn't believe me. I slammed the car door before she could say anything, but she quickly scrambled out after me. I could hear the furious clicking of her heels as she practically ran after me as I stalked up to the house. I wasn't mad at Angie, not really. I was more angry at myself for telling her. Nothing about what actually happened that night made any sense to me, so why should anyone else buy it?

"I didn't say I didn't believe you!" she exclaimed. "But you did say you hit your head."

"So, you don't believe me. Like everyone else I ever told," I said, slamming my finger down on the doorbell. "So, forget it. You're right. I was driving. I crashed the car when a wild animal ran into the road and after the crash, the wild animal dragged my parents away but left me untouched."

Angie didn't say anything, and I turned away from her. The door opened and a guy a little younger than us looked out. He smiled. "Come on in, ladies."

Angie and I stepped into the house and thanked him. I headed off in one direction and, after some hesitation, Angie went the other way. She knew I needed my space. I already regretted coming. I should have just gone to work and ignored Angie's pleading. I could have continued on pretending like everything wasn't completely insane, but now that I had told her the truth, she would never just let it go. We would have to talk eventually, and I would have to make the choice. I would either dig my heels in and insist on the story I had told her, the truth about what happened. Or I would recant, and claim I was confused, remembering wrong. I wasn't sure which was the better choice.

I found an unoccupied couch and sat down heavily, folding my arms across my chest, hoping to appear unapproachable. I didn't really want to talk to anyone after that fiasco. I just needed some time to get out of my own head. I wondered if I could just call a cab and go home. Angie wasn't going to leave, and I didn't want to leave her without a car. I wasn't that mad at her. But at the same time, maybe I would be doing her a favor. What if she drank and then got behind the wheel because I wasn't there to drive her home? I would never forgive myself if something happened to her.

I was so lost in my own thoughts that I didn't notice when someone sat down beside me. He cleared his throat, and I lifted my head, startled. I guess I wasn't doing a very bang-up job looking unapproachable. "What?" I blurted, less than welcoming.

He smiled regardless, and I stared. He was good looking, tall, and I could see a lean and muscled chest beneath his black t-shirt. I had never seen him before, but then again, it wasn't exactly a small town. His blue eyes seemed guarded, and he ran a hand through his longish black hair, his lips quirking into a half smile. "I said hello."

"Oh," I said, my cheeks heating with a blush. "Sorry. I was in my own little world." Truthfully, as lost as I was in my own thoughts, I wouldn't have noticed a herd of elephants traipsing past.

"To be truthful, I don't know why I came over here," he said. His words sounded planned. Carefully articulated. Had he been nervous about coming over and speaking to me? I couldn't wrap my head around that and shoved the thought away. Doubt crept in and I felt the cool touch of suspicion dance along my spine.

I instantly went on alert and sat a little straighter. "Well," I said. "The seat was open. If you'll excuse me." I stood and started walking away, half expecting him to grab me or something horrible. I found it hard to trust people after the accident. My parents had kept something from me and look what happened. I trusted them more than anyone. I didn't know what it was about his eyes, but something had seemed off. He seemed too stiff, like he was putting on an act. And maybe he was a really nice guy, but I wasn't going to take that chance. He let me go, and I went in search of Angie. It occurred to me that being apart wasn't a good idea when we didn't really know anyone. I wasn't so much worried about leaving Angie alone as I was about being alone myself. It was one thing in the comfort of my own home, but somewhere unfamiliar with a whole bunch of strangers was a different story. It put me on edge. I remembered why I didn't like parties, even before the accident.

I scanned the room for her familiar brown head but didn't see her. I sighed and started snaking my way between people, looking more closely for her. There were a lot more people present than I had expected and everywhere I turned, there was someone standing there. I heaved a sigh, beginning to feel trapped. I whirled around, thinking to check upstairs for her, and slammed into someone. My eyes snapped up, and an apology formed on my lips, my cheeks heating. The apology died on my tongue as I looked at him. This man looked to be a little older than most present. He was handsome, for sure, but something about him unnerved me. His eyes were almost unnaturally green, and I wondered if he was wearing contacts for the creepy effect. I swallowed and took a step back, managing a smile. "Sorry," I said. "There's so many people here." I forced a laugh.

He gently grabbed my arm and flashed a smile at me that seemed too predatory for my taste. He pushed his free hand through his short blond hair and gave me an obvious once over that left me feeling as if I was standing naked in the middle of the room. I felt very unnerved and just wanted to find Angie and get the hell out of there.

"No harm, no foul," he drawled, a hint of a southern accent peeking through, lips curved upwards. "No blood was spilled." He laughed suddenly, as if he had told a great joke, startling me. I tried to slip free of his grasp, but his hand tightened almost painfully around my arm, and I winced, looking up at him, trying not to let my fear show.

"I'm such a klutz," I said, forcing a chuckle. "It's the shoes," I added. "I haven't worn heels in a while." I motioned down to the offending things, taking in slow, deep breaths. I didn't want to have a panic attack here in a potentially dangerous situation.

His green eyes traveled down to my shoes. "I see," he said. It sounded like he couldn't possibly care any less about my shoes.

"Well, it was nice talking to you," I lied. "But I really should be going. I was just looking for my friend." At least that wasn't a lie.

"Richard," a hard voice said from behind me, causing me to jump noticeably.

The man grasping my arm—who was evidently named Richard—looked over my head and his lips pulled back slightly. "What?" he demanded, as if the interruption annoyed him.

I turned to look over my shoulder and blinked. "Hello again," I blurted.

His blue eyes flicked to me, and, for a moment, I saw amusement there. "Hello," he said, tipping his head slightly. His arms were folded across his chest and his eyes were flat as he looked at Richard once more. His lips turned down into a scowl, and I subconsciously found my eyes tracing his lips. He wasn't what I would classify as my type, but I found myself a little drawn to him, regardless. He seemed strong and sure, but I didn't know a single thing about him. All I had to base that on was the brief interaction we had and what I could see with my eyes. And what I could see was a straight posture, muscular arms crossed over a strong chest, and an admittedly nice mouth set in a frown.

Richard chuckled and pulled me against his chest, twisting me around so that I was facing the other man and my back was against his chest. "He's alright," he drawled, his lips brushing my ear, as if he had read my mind.

I squirmed and tried to break free, but he had a powerful grip. I was almost positive I would find a bruise come morning. "Let me go," I demanded, deciding that being amicable was getting me nowhere.

"Richard," the other man said again, taking a step toward us. "No," he warned. "Not her." What the fuck did that mean, exactly? Not me? I had to assume the two knew each other, and I took back anything nice I had thought about the blue-eyed stranger. I was scared, and confused, and getting angrier by the second.

Apparently, Richard was in the same boat. I peeked up at him and saw him blink his green eyes slowly before he cast a scowl down at me. "Come on," he said. I could have been wrong, but it sure sounded like he was goading the other man. "Seems like fun. What's one time?"

The mystery man's eyes suddenly became troubled, and he flicked his gaze to my face as if this was completely my fault. His eyes trailed over my every feature, making me blush without my consent, and finally rested on Richard's arm securely around my waist. "You know why," he said, clenching his jaw.

"Enlighten me," Richard said with a smirk, his breath tickling the side of my neck. I felt so very exposed and everything in me screamed to get away from him, away from *them*. I was prepared to scream and make a scene when there was another interruption to this nightmare.

"Richard!" a female voice snapped. "What do you think you're doing?" A young woman who couldn't have been older than early twenties walked toward us, her almond-shaped hazel eyes furious. She had gorgeous, silky, chocolate-colored hair that grazed her shoulders. I would have felt envy for her if I weren't so scared that this was going to turn into some kind of fight, and I was going to get stuck in the middle of it all. I could only guess that she was Richard's girlfriend and she would be pissed at me.

"What does it look like I'm doing?" Richard asked, resting his chin on top of my head. From where I was standing, it sounded like Richard was all sass and attitude, but I didn't want to go with the assumption that he was all bark and no bite. I felt his chest rumble, and I figured out that he was laughing, but I didn't know why.

"You're scaring her half to death," the new woman sighed, standing hands on hips. She looked annoyed, but like she was used to this sort of thing. Her hazel eyes turned to me, and she flashed a smile full of sunshine, leaving me even more confused. "Hi," she said brightly, as if this was a normal situation.

"Kalene," Richard muttered, sounding more annoyed than angry. "Back off."

"I have to go," I said, forcing a smile into my voice. "As much fun as this has been..." My heart was thundering in my chest, and I was almost certain it was going to jump right out and splatter on the floor.

"Go where?" Richard asked, pressing his face close to my neck. I heard two sharp intakes of breath and I cringed away from Richard, twisting my body, trying to put as much space between us as I could.

My mind was running in a million different directions, trying to figure out the best course of action. "My boyfriend," I blurted.

"Let me guess," Richard said conversationally. "He's a football player. No wait, a cop."

I was growing angry with the whole situation. Was this a game? Did he just like toying with people? "Let go!" I hissed, balling my hands into fists. Not caring about the consequences, I slammed my fist backwards and felt a tiny bit of sick pleasure from the yelp of pain he gave as my hand connected with his crotch. It was just enough for me to slip free of his grasp. I moved back out of his reach and glared. "If this was some kind of game," I said, glaring at all three of them. "You're sick."

"You don't understand," Kalene started, but the man who had not given his name lifted a hand to stop her.

"Go," he said, his voice not unkind. "I'm sorry for your trouble."

I ignored his apology and turned on my heel, striding away as quickly as I could without appearing to be running. I glanced back over my shoulder and witnessed Kalene smacking her hand against Richard's head and the other man watching me. He had a troubled expression on his face, and I felt like he was the kind of guy who usually was in control. And that whole thing had been anything but under control.

I found Angie in the kitchen, sitting on the counter with a bag of chips in her hand and a group of boys around her. The second she saw me, she hopped off the counter, the swarm of boys stepping back to allow her room. They shuffled away quickly and left just the two of us and a few stragglers behind. "Phoebe?" she asked, looking me over. Angie had a way of knowing when something was wrong. It was like some kind of freaky intuition, and this time was no different.

"I want to go," I said. "I just wanted to let you know. I'm going to take a cab and leave you the car, but I need you to promise me you'll call me to come pick you up if you drink. Even one drink, Angie, you call me, okay? I'll be here."

"Okay, fine, but why are you leaving? Last I saw, you were talking to some hot guy," Angie said with a confused frown. "What happened? Are you alright?"

I nodded quickly, not particularly wanting to get into it. I just wanted to go home and curl up on the couch in front of the television. I knew that if I told Angie what had happened, she would insist we both leave, or go find that Richard guy and give him a piece of her mind. I wasn't sure why, but something told me that was the last thing that needed to happen. Besides, she was way more into the party scene than I would ever be. "Yeah," I lied. "Everything is fine. I'm just not really feeling it, that's all."

She looked skeptical. "Well," she mused, glancing me over as if she would find something amiss. "I guess I should be glad you came out at all. You never come out with me anymore. I miss you, you know?" she asked me, tilting her head to the side. She reached out and rubbed her hand down my arm, a bittersweet expression on her face.

I nodded. "I know, Angie," I said. "I'll try to hang out more. But you know how busy I am."

We both knew I wasn't that busy.

"Yeah," Angie nodded. "Sure." She was disappointed. I kicked myself for hurting her feelings again. She was like a sister to me, and that was the absolute last thing I wanted to do. I needed to be a better friend. I promised myself then and there that I would do better and be better for her.

"Excuse me?" Angie and I both jumped at the polite words, turning to look at the intruder. I stared, folding my arms across my chest and Angie flashed a smile, unaware.

"Can I help you?" she asked, just as sweet as can be.

He ignored Angie and looked at me for a long moment. His mouth opened and closed, and he gave me a frustrated look, but never got around to actually speaking. "I'm fine," I finally said bluntly. I figured it was a good tactic. If he was actually trying to ascertain whether I was alright, then it put him out of his misery. And if he wasn't, it put him in his place. I didn't know what the entire ordeal had been about, and I didn't care. At the end of the day, Richard hadn't hurt me. He had just scared me a whole lot. I would leave the party and put it out of my mind. I would never see any of them again.

His blue eyes locked onto mine and he smiled, but it seemed as if he were forcing himself to do so, was forcing himself to check on me. "Richard," he began, taking a pause, rolling his eyes slightly. "He's..."

"It's not important," I interrupted. I didn't want Angie to cause a scene, and that was exactly what she was going to do if she found out that someone had terrorized me at this stupid party. She looked confused already, as if she were trying to piece together what we were talking about, but didn't have quite enough information.

The man seemed relieved to hear me say that. I supposed he didn't want to have this conversation just as much as me. His eyes glanced around the room once, and I came to the realization that it was just the three of us in the kitchen. Evidently, he came to the same conclusion. He cleared his throat, and I reached up, rubbing my neck. I remembered the feel of Richard's breath on my skin and shivered. The stranger noticed, and I couldn't help but see how his eyes slid to my neck for a moment.

"Am I missing something?" Angie asked, looking back and forth between the two of us. "Did you want to be alone?" she wondered, eyebrows pulling together.

"No," the stranger and I said in unison. We both shot each other startled looks, but quickly averted our gazes.

A third voice suddenly interrupted, startling me. "What's going on in here?" a crisp voice asked. My eyes lifted to find a woman standing in the kitchen doorway, her long fiery locks curled elegantly, falling over her shoulders. She stood with one hand on her hip, peering into the room. She glanced at Angie and then her eyes landed on me and I felt like I would shrivel up and die on the spot. She was the definition of 'if looks could kill', only I didn't know what I had done to warrant her hostility.

"Fee," the man sighed, halfway turning his back to me, motioning halfheartedly in my direction. "Richard—"

"Honestly," the woman interrupted, shaking her head. She sighed softly. "I don't really care what Richard has gone and done this time." She stepped into the room and took his hand in hers, entwining their fingers. "Let him clean up his own messes." She flashed a smile, but it quickly vanished when the man untangled his hand from hers. She looked hurt for only a moment before she schooled her features into a neutral expression. The man shot me a look, almost as if he were saying 'it's not what it looks like.'

I managed a weak smile. "Well," I said, forcing cheer into my voice. "This has been fun, but I've got to go." I turned to give Angie a hug, squeezing gently. "See you back home," I said softly.

She shot me a look. "We'll talk later," she said. And I knew she meant it. "Be safe."

I skirted around the couple in the middle of the room. "You too," I called to her before slipping quickly from the room. I bolted for the door, praying that I didn't run into Richard again. My fingers grazed the doorknob when I felt the hairs rise on the back of my neck. I paused and glanced over my shoulder, only to find the man standing in the kitchen doorway, his blue eyes drilling holes into my back from across the room.

I had no idea what darkness had just entered my life.

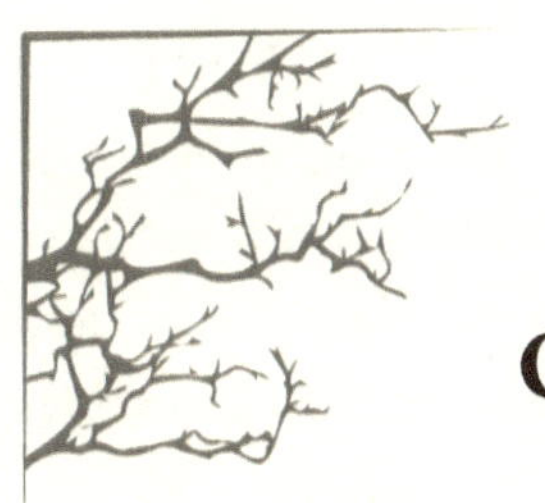

Chapter Three
Levi

I watched the girl practically run away from me. It kind of bothered me to see her fleeing, like she knew I was a monster. There was something about her that just seemed so damned familiar, but I couldn't put my finger on it. I felt like I knew her, or maybe she just had one of those faces. She stopped at the door and glanced back, catching me staring at her. I wanted to look away from her, embarrassed at having been caught staring, but couldn't. She captivated me with her intense green eyes, her blonde curls settling around her shoulders gently. She was beautiful, but that wasn't what drew me to her. I just... couldn't name it.

I watched as her eyes suddenly shifted away from me, darting to my left. I glanced in the same direction, expecting to see Richard pulling some stunt, generally just being a menace to society. Instead, I felt my undead heart give a painful thump. I stared, dread washing over me. Had it truly been a hundred years already? How time flies when you don't die.

Avatrice Loughlin. The name rolled through my head, and I was sure it sounded like a scream to Richard. Why, of all people, would he be drawing the pretty blonde's attention? And why would he be *here,* of all places? There was really only one explanation: me. I started moving without even thinking. I needed to get out before he saw me. If he saw me, things might get very bad, very fast. Probably a lot of blood. Innocent blood.

It wouldn't be a friendly reunion. It would be a little hard for me to believe he didn't hold a grudge against me. After all, I was one of the few who put him in prison for the last century. I did not have such great luck. I was nearly at the blonde's side when I felt a chill race down my spine. I turned to look and saw his cold, black eyes staring right at me, as if he could see into my soul. If I even had one.

The blonde was right by my side, her eyes locked on the same man. It was like she couldn't see anything else. She didn't even seem to notice my arrival. A horrified expression crossed her face, and she began to shake. I tore my eyes away from Avatrice long enough to look down at her. Without so much as a glance in my direction, she turned and threw herself out of the house. The door hung open slightly, and I hesitated. Stay and confront Avatrice, or flee like the girl had? Why had she disappeared so quickly? My mind began working furiously, trying to piece together the puzzle with so few pieces.

Was she working with him? Was he using her to get to me? Flaunting a pretty girl in my face, trying to get me alone or vulnerable? I realized I had spaced and looked up quickly, but Avatrice was gone. Startled, my blue eyes quickly scanned the bodies standing around me. A million heartbeats filled my ears, but I couldn't find him. Gone?

I looked to my side at the door. It was closed now. I hesitated before grabbing the handle and almost ripping the door off its hinges in my haste. The door slammed behind me, and I felt the last rays of sunlight hit my skin. The feeling was a little uncomfortable, but bearable. Nothing like the feeling of the full-blown sun on my skin. And certainly nothing like how it was when I was first Turned all those years ago.

My eyes found the girl walking briskly down the street in the distance, her high heels clicking loudly in the quickly descending night. She rounded the corner, and I heard her heels stop clicking.

Frowning, I began forward. Maybe I needed to stop her and talk to her. Maybe I needed to find out what she knew about Avatrice. If she were working with him, maybe I could warn her about his nature and save her before it was too late. She was only human, after all.

I was halfway down the sidewalk when I heard her scream.

P*hoebe*

The scream tore from my lips, shrill to my own ears. The man I had seen at the party–the same man I had seen months ago, standing in the middle of the road before the accident–now knelt on the cement before me, a young woman in his arms. How had he gotten ahead of me so quickly? How had I not seen him? Her eyes and mouth were open wide, as if she, too, had tried to scream. Blood smeared along her neck and soaked into her pink top. The man lifted his head and looked at me, his mouth coated in red.

Blood.

I took a step back, heart beating frantically. What in the fuck was going on? I needed to get away from him, that much I knew. It was about the only thing I knew. The man was on his feet and in front of me before I could even take a step. I nearly swallowed my own tongue in fright. It was impossible for him to move so fast, but then again, I had seen him get hit full speed with a car and yet here he was, alive and perfectly healthy. He grabbed me, dragging me into an alley, and slammed me against the wall of a brick building. My teeth clacked together painfully, and stars swarmed my vision. I heard a low growl, like I recalled hearing that night months ago. "Please," I begged, "let me go."

He smiled, the sight unnerving, and closed a hand over my upper arm. His touch was light, but there was no mistaking the power behind it; it was both chilling and repulsive. "Now, where's the fun in that?" he asked, his black eyes locked onto mine, the red around his mouth in stark contrast to his pale skin.

I struggled against him, trying to break free. "Shh," he said, pushing my blonde curls away from my neck. I felt his fingers gently trail along my throat and shivered. I didn't understand what he was doing. He was being gentle, and yet there was no mistaking the strength he possessed. He leaned forward, and I felt his teeth graze my skin. They felt so sharp, and in my panicked frenzy, I had an insane thought. *He's going to bite me.* An image of the woman he had held in his arms flashed through my head. The blood that covered his mouth. The only logical assumption I could make was that this man was either a cannibal or a vampire. And I wasn't sure if either were actually logical, or if my brain was overloading. I stilled out of fear, but there was something else there, too, hidden beneath all the fear and anxiety.

Defiance.

I would not beg with him. No, I would not tell him that I wasn't going to tell anyone about him. Hell no. I was going to tell anyone and everyone that this psycho had attacked me. Maybe I would omit the fact that he was a vampire cannibal, but assault was assault, right?

And then he bit down on my fragile skin and pierced flesh. Lightning fast, before I had even processed the first bite, I felt his teeth pull free and then he clamped down again, locking me in place. I stood there, frozen. It stung, initially, but then there was just... nothing. I felt paralyzed. I could not move, unable to scream as he drained my life blood away. The ground underneath me spun, and I clung to him instinctively. I needed to stay upright. My head swam, but I still managed coherent thoughts.

Was it supposed to go this quickly? Was it supposed to be this... peaceful?

Peaceful?

INSTINCT

The man growled against my neck, one hand curling painfully into my hair, wrenching my head further to the side. It almost wasn't so bad dying this way. If I had ever given a single moment of thought to what it would be like to die to a vampire cannibal, I probably would have said it sounded painful and messy, but this wasn't. Even though I *knew* he was biting me, it felt warm. Almost like a gentle caress. I almost didn't mind.

But I did.

I was going to die if I didn't do something, if I didn't come back to myself *right now.*

This was *not* okay with me.

An inarticulate sound gurgled in my throat, and my eyelids dropped in an involuntary reaction as I clutched his shoulders. In the brief moment between life and death, when my body fought but my mind knew there was no hope, an odd sense of calm washed over me. That calm was shattered when I forced myself to think, to *think,* damn it! I tried to keep breathing, to keep myself alive. Some sort of self-preservation system kicked in and I knew I had to do something now or it would be too late for me. I felt his hand slide from my hair and land, feather light, on the side of my neck that he wasn't latched on to and I could feel his lips against my skin. It didn't hurt, but knowing what was going on made it hard for the sensation to feel pleasant. Was this some sort of trick? Some sort of magic to make me feel lethargic and comfortable?

I was *dying!*

The sharp thought sent a jolt through me, and fear snaked down my spine, golf balls hurtling haphazardly around in my stomach. I thought I might throw up. I shifted my body ever so slightly that he didn't notice. Or if he did, he didn't care. It must have been awfully empowering to know he was stronger and faster than his prey, namely me. Then I brought my knee up hard and fast and shoved his gonads halfway up his throat. The man groaned and jerked his fangs free of my neck but didn't back away. He rested his forehead against my shoulder, breathing hard. Did vampire cannibals need to breathe? I was slowly leaning more toward *just* a vampire, but my brain wasn't ready to make that leap just yet.

I was in complete panic mode now, and I gave a hard shove. He stumbled back in surprise, his eyes widened in shock. I wasn't sure if I had just gotten lucky and caught him unawares, or if I truly didn't know my own strength. I've heard adrenaline can do crazy stuff to a person. I turned and launched myself toward the street, a scream bubbling up in my throat. I took about three steps and then my heel snapped—lovely—and sent me sprawling to the ground, ripping my jeans, and tearing flesh from my palms. I skidded a few inches and then there was a man there, crouched next to me, touching my face lightly.

The man from the party. I never did catch his name.

I wanted to get up, to run, to fight, to scream, but I was just so damn tired. I just wanted to rest for a few seconds. My eyelids fluttered and everything grew fuzzy. I was a goner. I was so completely done for. He was here to finish off the job; I was sure. I'd never get to see Angie again, would never get to apologize.

"Avatrice," I thought I heard the man say, his hand trailing to my throat. This was it; he was going for the kill. They were double teaming me now. How could I have been so stupid? He leaned down, and I felt his lips brush my ear. "I'm sorry," he whispered.

I was fairly certain I had imagined that last part as I slipped into unconsciousness. I faded in and out, and in those brief moments when I was somewhat cognizant, I tried to take in everything I could.

I felt something wet and sticky on the side of my neck, seeping into my shirt.

Blackness.

There were muscular arms wrapped around me and I was pressed against someone's chest. Rhythmic breathing, a slow, but steady heartbeat.

Blackness.

I was lying on some kind of leather seat. In a car, perhaps? I could feel the vibrations beneath me.

Blackness.

A car door slammed, and then I was being lifted into strong arms again. The gentle sway of careful, measured steps.

Blackness.

Lips pressed against my ear, whispering fervently in words I couldn't understand.

Blackness.

Voices, raised and angry and a hard surface, pressed against my back. Somehow, I managed to remain conscious and clung to anything I could to keep myself grounded. The cool hands touching my arms, the feel of the wet fabric of my shirt clinging to my skin, I clung to those things. I tried to make out the voices, but I couldn't force my eyes open. It took too much energy and so I just lay there, focusing on breathing and listening. Focusing on living.

"What the hell were you thinking?" A harsh voice demanded. It was a male, that much I knew, and it caused a chill of anxiety to run through my body. I knew that voice very well. I had heard that voice not too long ago against my ear. Richard.

"I don't know. I wasn't. I just... reacted. She was in trouble." I could imagine him shrugging his shoulders and peering at me quickly, as if to make certain I hadn't stopped breathing. I hadn't. The man from the party, with the blue eyes.

"Why didn't you just kill her and put her out of her misery? Look at her—she's a mess," Richard said. I wasn't sure if that was a nice thing to say or not. It was like he thought I was some kind of dog that had been hit by a truck, not a human girl who had been mauled by a vampire.

"I don't know that either."

"Well, what do you plan to do with her?" Richard asked, a sigh of frustration breezing past his lips.

There was a long pause in which I could feel the man frown as if I were looking right at him. "I want to keep her here," he stated suddenly, as if he would not allow an argument on the matter. I would have laughed at the absurdity of it all; that is, if I could laugh. "It's not forever. I just need to know what she knows and how she knows Avatrice."

"Just think about this for a minute," Richard said, sounding almost as if he were defeated, knowing he had lost already.

"I'm not killing her. Is that completely understood?" the man continued, his voice holding a ring of authority with it. He sounded very in charge, and I wondered who the leader of the pack was.

I managed to open my eyes slightly, to thin slits, and took in as much as I could without moving my head. Richard stood directly in front of me, arms crossed over his chest. He seemed to be ignoring me, giving all of his attention to the blue-eyed man. He wasn't moving, and he looked like he was thinking of killing me and getting it over with. The amount of pain screaming through my body made me almost welcome it, but I hadn't fought this hard to just die now.

The red-headed woman from the party was standing closer to me than Richard was, and she looked furious. Her eyes were flashing, and she kept pulling her lips back in a sneer, though she didn't speak. She was with Richard on this—she didn't want me around, either.

Then there was another man—one I hadn't seen before—standing back a way. I hadn't heard him speak, and I wondered if he was simply listening as I was. He was handsome—He had brown hair that he wore in a short ponytail at the nape of his neck and assessing brown eyes. He seemed to find it difficult to look at me for any length of time, and I wondered if my bloody appearance was bothering him. Did I look that bad? I suppose Richard thought so if it was enough to kill me over.

"She can't stay," the brown-haired one said suddenly. "She has family, and they will come looking for her. We can't run that risk." He sounded confident and practical.

"She stays." I could hear a rumble deep in the blue-eyed one's chest, and it was actually kind of comforting. At least I had one person defending me, even if I wasn't sure I could trust him. But I was still alive, wasn't I? If he had wanted me dead, I would have been so a hundred times over by now.

There was silence; Richard was still unmoving, while the other two were glaring, and the man whose name I didn't know was standing over me with his arms crossed tightly over his chest. I thought perhaps they were going to argue, to kill me right there on the spot. They didn't. No one moved.

Finally, a very feminine voice I recognized said softly. "She's your responsibility, and I'll expect you to get rid of her if she causes problems." It sounded as if saying the words caused her physical pain, and I irrationally liked her, even though I knew nothing about her. I tried to conjure up her image from Angie's party, but my mind was so fuzzy that I could only catch glimpses that weren't enough to tell me anything about her. Brown hair and kind eyes...

"She won't cause problems." I felt his cool hand on my cheek and could feel his breath against my face, as if he were leaning very close to me. "I won't let her."

"Levi," someone sighed. The other man that I didn't know the name of.

"No!" Levi snapped. I cringed, thinking about trying to scoot off the table that I was on and making a break for it, but then remembered that there were others in the room who wanted me dead and inched closer to him. "She won't cause problems." He enunciated each word carefully and precisely.

"But she's *human.*" I was fairly certain that it was Richard. That confused me. Yes, I was human. Weren't they? I remembered the feeling of sharp teeth sinking into my neck and my earlier notion of vampires flashed through my mind. Maybe not so crazy after all.

"I know," Levi answered. "But... she's more than that."

"This is foolish. She won't last," a sharp female voice said. Not at all like the softer one from before. The red-headed one. She had been called Fee at the party. I suppose she didn't like me much, though I still was unclear on what I had done to warrant her hostility.

"We'll see," Levi said, scooping me up and cradling me to his chest. I could practically feel him smile. He turned and started walking, but the ride was so smooth I could tell he was trying to be careful with me. After all, I was so breakable. I could feel some rising and falling of his chest and became fascinated. I pressed my head closer to his chest and listened intently, holding my breath. There was a steady heartbeat, but it was much too slow. Not at all like my erratic and racing heart.

"Hey?" Levi whispered against my ear. "Are you alive?" I thought about playing dead. Perhaps he would toss me out and leave me be. Maybe I could get away. My heart sped up at the thought, and I could hear him laughing. "I'll take that as a yes."

I cursed my damn heart and sulked, refusing to speak—if I even could. I wasn't entirely sure either way. I heard a door open and close, and then I was set down gently on what I could only assume was a bed. Did vampires sleep? And that was the last thought I had before it became too much for me, and I faded into the blackness once more.

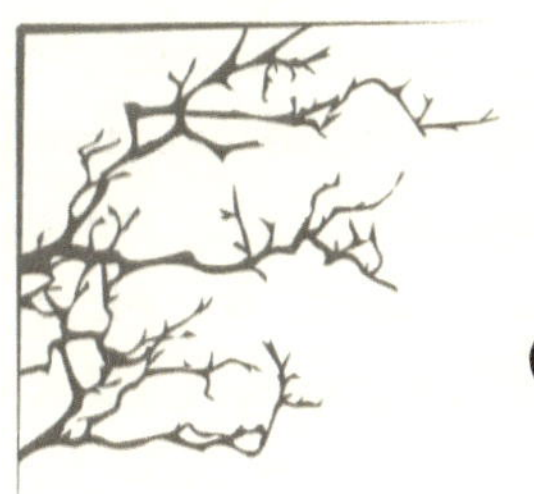

Chapter Four
Levi

I really had no idea what I was thinking. I stared at the girl sleeping soundly on my bed, my blue eyes scanning her slight frame. At first, my eyes avoided the carnage on her neck, but it wasn't long before I couldn't help but look. Avatrice hadn't been particularly gentle.

Avatrice.

My mood soured at his name flitting through my mind. At first, I had thought he was using the young woman to get at me, to get under my skin. I wouldn't really blame him, I supposed. After all, it was partially my fault they had locked him away for a hundred years. Charged with endangering us and attempting to create an army. For what purpose had never been discovered, but nothing had come of it.

How long had he been free?

But seeing the woman on the concrete, covered in blood, heart beating weakly, I knew that wasn't likely. But how else would she know the malicious vampire? It didn't seem plausible that she would just happen to be in his circle after being locked away for one hundred years.

I turned and walked to the bathroom adjoined with my bedroom. I gathered a few supplies and returned to the woman. She looked almost peaceful sleeping there. If she weren't covered in blood, clothes torn, I could almost pretend she had simply fallen asleep there, soft and delicate. How was I going to explain my way out of this one? I sighed and went to work, carefully cleaning her wound. I worked as gently as I could, cleaning the blood away from the mess of her flesh. Her blood smelled heavenly, making my mouth water and my teeth ache. It wouldn't take but a second to sink my fangs into her throat and take a sip, but I stood quickly, recognizing my wayward thoughts. I returned to the bathroom to rinse the bloodied supplies and gathered some bandages. I returned to the bedside and knelt beside her, brushing her hair away.

"What?" I asked aloud. My fingers traced what was left of her wound. It was already healing. Mere moments had passed since I had cleaned her wound and yet, there it was, seemingly healing before my very eyes. My eyes darted to her face, confusion clear in mine. My mind was slow to work, digging up memories long since forgotten. Memories of the research in Avatrice's home.

Hybrids.

His home was raided and writings of a race of human and vampire hybrids—he called them dhampirs—were found. Supposedly, they were superior to both humans and vampires, in that they got the best of both worlds. They could move about in the sun without pain. They were stronger and faster, but did not require blood to live. And they had remarkable healing abilities, better even than the vampire, because they simply healed. They did not require blood to enhance the process.

Suspicion entered my mind again. Could it be possible? I narrowed my eyes at the woman, my mind racing. Was she one of the dhampirs from Avatrice's writings? Was she truly working with him, one of his creations? I shook my head. That made little sense. Why would he attack one of his own? And I was fairly certain her age didn't line up. Avatrice had been gone a long time, and she didn't look to be over a hundred years old. Although, I mused, I didn't know what the aging process was like for a dhampir, if that's truly what she was. I needed to know more before I passed judgment, but that would have to wait until she awoke. I finished getting her patched up and left the room, closing the door behind me to allow her to rest.

I found the others in the kitchen still. Kalene looked at me first, her brown eyes kind. "Levi?" she asked, clearly sensing my confusion.

I shook my head. "I don't know," I said, answering her unspoken question. "I saw Avatrice at that party. She saw him too, and she had a… a reaction. She left and I think he went after her. I followed."

"Why?" Caleb asked, cocking his head to the side. "Are you looking for a fight with him?"

"No," I answered automatically. "I want to avoid him if I can, but I am afraid we may be past that now. He saw me there. We… spoke. Sort of. He didn't attack me, but he wasn't exactly giving off friendly vibes."

The room was deafeningly quiet. Felicity spoke first. "And?" she asked, prompting me to continue.

"He attacked her," I said, a sigh escaping my lips. I rubbed the back of my neck and regarded my family. "I came upon the attack. She had tried to escape from him, and he was coming back for her and, I don't know what happened. I stopped him. I stood in his way and told him to leave her."

"Wow," Richard drawled. "And how did that go over?" He leaned against the counter, hands shoved in his pockets.

I shrugged. "He just looked at me for a long time and said nothing. Then he just… left. He never said a word to me."

"We can't keep her here," Caleb said finally. "It's too dangerous. What if he comes looking for her?" Caleb was always looking out for his family, and this was no exception.

"Why would he?" Felicity asked, crossing her arms over her chest. "She's just a human. He can find another. They're a dime a dozen."

"I don't think she is," I mumbled. Of course, they all heard me, and I felt all four of them turn to look at me. They were going to think I was crazy. But then again, none of them had been around when it all went down. We hadn't known each other, then. "She's already healing," I explained, motioning to my own neck as if they had forgotten.

"How is that possible?" Kalene asked, shaking her head. "She's not a vampire—besides, when would she have had the time to feed? She wouldn't have been in the state she was in if she had."

"She's not a vampire," I said, growing frustrated. And so I told them. I went into detail about the day we captured Avatrice. I told them about how we—myself and about eight or nine other vampires, including the Council—busted into his home and took him down. I told them about how we had to lock him up with inhibitors in order to take his gifts from him. I told them of all his research and what we found down there, and none of them spoke the entire time. When I had finished, Richard was the first to speak.

"A dhampir?" he asked, rubbing his jaw. "How... unusual."

"But what does that mean for her?" Kalene asked. "Does she know?" Her kind eyes traveled to the staircase, glancing up toward my room above us.

"I don't know," I said simply. "She is still asleep."

"Where did you put her?" Caleb asked, flicking his eyes to the stairs. He was a little more wary than most of the unknown. It was probably stressing him out having a stranger in the house. I felt badly. I hadn't meant to make my family uncomfortable, but bringing her here had seemed like the best thing to do. At the time.

"She's in my room," I supplied. "I will talk to her when she wakes up, and I guess we will go from there."

Kalene was shifting from foot to foot nervously. "What if she freaks out? She was attacked, Levi. What do you plan to tell her?" Of course, she was worried about that. We all were. Explaining away what happened was going to be nearly impossible and any sort of explanation would simply be gaslighting her into believing she had imagined the whole thing. If I was smart, I would simply Compel her to forget everything. I would find out where she lived and deposit her safely in her own bed and wipe her memory of everything. But if Avatrice *was* after her, that was doing her a disservice. And I still *needed* to know the truth.

I shook my head. I hadn't thought that far ahead. The truth, I supposed, would be the easiest course of action. "I'll let her do the talking. I'll ask her what happened and get her memory of the events. And I'll just go from there. If she doesn't remember much, I'll spin a tale and send her on her way, none the wiser. But if she remembers what happened—she was *bitten* —I don't see how I can keep it from her. There are things I want to know, too."

"And if she tells others?" Richard asked quietly. "She could expose us, Levi. The Council is pretty lenient about a lot of things, but they get a little touchy about exposing ourselves. It tends to start wars."

"You would have me consult the Council on it?" I asked, surprised. Richard wasn't generally the type to ask for permission.

"Better to ask forgiveness than permission," Felicity said with a shrug, mirroring my thoughts. "If she seems like she's going to bolt or tell, we kill her."

"I don't know," Caleb said thoughtfully. "Should we not send word to the Council that Avatrice is here? I would think they would want to keep their eyes on him. Perhaps one hundred years in prison chilled him out, or perhaps it made him worse than ever." He rubbed his chin, looking lost in thought. "You know him better than any of us," he added after a while. "What do you think?"

I pursed my lips. "I think that she is already here, and it will take at least a week to reach the Council. And then who knows how long before they reach a decision? I agree with Fee on this one. I'll ask the forgiveness."

"Be careful," Kalene said softly, her eyes finding mine. "Just..."

I held up a hand. "I will," I said. With that, I turned and headed back upstairs to wait for the mystery girl to awaken.

P*hoebe*

I felt like I had been hit by a truck. I pried my eyes open and groaned. My knees ached, my neck throbbed, and my ankle was on fire. I tried to sit up and felt tears sting my eyes. Then the guy from the party was in front of me, and I screamed, cringing away from him.

He held his hands up, his eyebrows furrowing. "I'm not going to hurt you," he said, suspended there, hands raised, half crouched to be in my line of sight.

Yet, I thought bitterly. My head swam. *What* had happened to me? I lifted my head and rubbed my forehead, trying to remember. I had left the party early. Why? It all came back so suddenly that I gasped. My eyes went wide, and I looked around the room rapidly, not really seeing anything. Where was he?

"It's just us," the man said slowly. "My name is Levi..." He trailed off, waiting for me to respond.

"Phoebe," I choked out, my heart pounding. I wasn't sure if 'just us' was any better, but I was still breathing, so I supposed that was something.

"Phoebe," Levi said cautiously. "What do you remember?"

I looked at him suspiciously and pulled myself up into a sitting position, despite the pain. I winced and wrapped my arms around myself, acutely aware of the fact that I was sitting in a bed in a strange place. "I went to a party with my best friend. I met you there. And the other man - Richard, you called him. I decided to leave the party after that," I explained. I looked away, feeling ashamed. "Before I left, I saw someone else there. Another man."

"A man?" Levi asked. "Did you know him?"

"Yes," I answered automatically. "No... I don't know. I don't know his name or anything about him. I just know his face. I could never forget it." I shivered. I felt a tickle in my mind and found myself continuing. "He killed my parents."

Levi looked startled for just a moment. "Then?" he prompted, schooling his features into a neutral expression.

"I left. He followed me, but somehow, he was in front of me. I don't know what happened. He was there on the ground in front of me with a... a woman in his arms. She was... dead." I choked on a sob, my hand coming to cover my mouth. "He attacked me," I whispered. My hand lifted to my neck, fingers brushing gauze, and I fell silent. I didn't want to say anymore. He would think I was crazy. But there was that tickle in my mind again and my mouth opened, seemingly without my permission. "He bit me. I didn't want to believe it. The night he killed my parents, I had suspected, but it's crazy. After what happened to me, it's hard to ignore it now. He's a... a vampire."

Levi stared at me, not saying anything for a long time. I was appalled. Why had I said that? Why had I blurted out that word? I was going to get thrown into a mental hospital; I could see the headlines now. **GIRL CLAIMS VAMPIRES ARE REAL.** "Is there anything else you want to tell me?" Levi asked carefully.

No. "Yes." I pursed my lips, trying to stop the words from coming out, but I couldn't. It was like he had forced me to speak with that simple question. "I think my father was a vampire, too. But if my father was a vampire, what did that make my mother? What does that make me? And I really don't want to think about that, actually." He held up his hand, and I felt like I could control my mouth again.

"Understood." Levi sighed and pushed his hair back. He looked at me and then away, only to look back at me again. "I don't want to scare you," he said after a minute. When I didn't speak, he sighed again and faced me fully. "You're right. That man - his name is Avatrice - *is* a vampire. What I don't know is why he attacked you, and I don't know anything about your parents. I'm sorry."

I stared blankly. "How could you know anything about my parents? I've never met you before and you can't be more than a couple of years older than me."

"When did they die?" Levi asked quietly.

I shifted uncomfortably, noticing that I was in a little less pain. "A few months ago," I whispered. "We were running from something or someone. My parents were scared. My dad died defending us and my mom died defending me, I think. It's all kind of blurry after a certain point. I don't know why he left me alone." I also didn't know why I was telling this man, this stranger, anything.

"I guess there is no going back," Levi said, clenching and unclenching his hands. "Phoebe?"

I stared, nerves building rapidly, making me feel sick. "Levi?" I asked, his name feeling foreign on my tongue.

"I'm also a vampire."

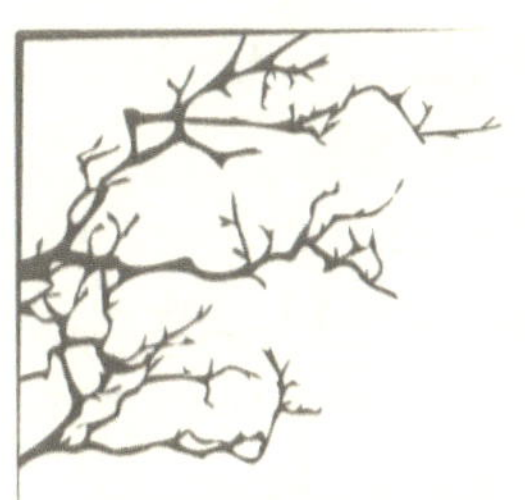

Chapter Five
Phoebe

I think I passed out. I don't remember what I said after that revelation, and when I opened my eyes again; I was alone. I sat up and rubbed my head. How insane. Vampires? I almost laughed. I swung my legs over the edge of the bed and stood wobbly. My ankle hurt a little, but it was so small I could ignore it. I was glad I hadn't messed myself up trying to escape from...

The vampire.

The room threatened to turn sideways, so I forced myself to walk forward. I paused at the closed door and rested my hand against the cool wood. "What have I gotten myself into?" I whispered, pulling the door open. I surveyed the hall in front of me. It was empty and quiet. I turned and looked to the left and saw a flight of stairs. Carefully, prepared to scream or run, I crept down the stairs. I stopped at the bottom, unsure of where to go.

"If you are planning to escape, I strongly recommend you don't." The voice came from my right, and I almost screamed. I turned to take in the man standing there. I didn't recognize him. His brown hair was held at the nape of his neck in a ponytail, and his eyes were warm and chocolate. "Caleb."

I stared. My mind caught up with what was going on. "Phoebe. Are you a vampire, too?" I must have lost my mind to just be blurting things out like that.

He looked startled for a moment before clearing his throat. "So, he told you." It wasn't a question. "I wondered if he would." I distinctly noticed he didn't actually answer my question, but I could guess at the answer.

"I kind of suspected." It was only partially a lie. I had suspected—no, I *knew*—my attacker was a vampire. I hadn't really lumped Levi in with all of that craziness until he announced it to be so. And as far as my dad went, it wasn't like I could ask him about it.

"So... when do I die?" I asked, a little more offhandedly than intended. Really, I think I was just in shock and the realness hadn't soaked in yet.

Again, he looked startled. "I'll let Levi answer that." And with that, he disappeared down a hallway. I turned to find a kitchen. I was weirdly calm as I walked into the room, seeing Levi sitting in a kitchen chair backwards and the girl from the party sitting on the counter, her legs dangling. They both looked up when I entered.

"You're up," the woman said perkily. "I'm Kalene. I heard you talking to Caleb, and I know you've already met Richard at the party. I promise he's not all that bad. Just likes to mess around too much." She grinned at me. I stared at her blankly.

"I'm sure you have questions," Levi said warily, not looking at me. "Ask. Or scream. Whichever."

I blinked. "Scream?" I asked, dumbly. "You give yourself too much credit. You're not that scary." I was mostly all talk. I was pretty freaked out, but I had to admit it. Levi *wasn't* scary. He had done nothing to harm me thus far and had taken care of me when I was hurt. I had to give the guy the benefit of the doubt. And Kalene seemed nice enough.

That drew a laugh from deep in his chest, and he finally looked at me, seemingly more at ease. "You're strange. Few people would take finding out vampires are real so well."

"Yeah, well..." I muttered, rubbing my arms. "Not entirely normal to be attacked by a vampire twice in your life, I guess." In a weird way, it was comforting to know. It gave me some answers about what happened that night, but also brought up so many new questions.

Levi pushed to a stand. "Does it really count if it's the same vampire, though?" he asked, a smile threatening to spread across his face. I took a moment to look at him. He was handsome. I allowed myself to really look at him and take in everything. His hair was black, just brushing his cheekbones. He had a strong jaw, a straight nose, and his eyes were the bluest I had ever seen. And he was a vampire. Which meant he wasn't entirely safe, no matter what my wayward mind tried to say. I found myself wanting to get closer to him and wondered if it was because he was a vampire. Maybe they had some kind of magnetism that drew humans in? *But am I even human?* The thought came suddenly, and I bit my lip to keep from crying.

"What do I do now?" I asked, choking back a sob. "I don't even know what I am."

Levi walked over to me and hesitated before pulling me into a hug. I watched Kalene raise an eyebrow behind him, but she didn't say a word. "I can help you," he said. "Avatrice... we have history. And I think I know why he was after you."

I looked up at him, my heart lodged in my throat. He smelled like lavender and mint Old Spice, and I felt weirdly calm in his embrace. It was probably the lavender, I reasoned. "You do?" I mumbled into his chest. I didn't care that we barely knew each other. He was offering comfort, and I was willing to take it. No one had tried to hurt me yet, but my guard was still up. It was just crumbling.

"Forgive me," Levi said sheepishly. "I know little about it. But... I know Avatrice once researched a thing he called dhampirs. A hybrid, if you will..."

"Half human and half vampire." The words left my mouth without me realizing I had even thought them. And I felt like that was right. I had suspected my father was a vampire after that night, but my mother remained a mystery. Could she really have just been a human?

Levi nodded slowly. "I can... *we* can protect you," he said., gaining another raised eyebrow from Kalene. "If you stay here, with us. We can help you learn more about who you are and what Avatrice wants and keep you safe from him."

I was already shaking my head and stepped back from his embrace. "I can't. I have a life, a job, and Angie. Angie!" My eyes went wide. "Oh fuck. She's going to be so worried I didn't come home. What time is it? Is it tomorrow?" I realized all the shades were pulled shut and looked between the two vampires in the room.

"Yes," Kalene said with a small chuckle. "It is, indeed, tomorrow."

I had lost my phone in the scuffle with Avatrice. I felt something slide into my hands and looked down to see a cellphone. "I found your purse," Levi said simply.

I smiled my appreciation and dialed Angie quickly. She answered on the first ring, and I wondered what I was going to say. I was *not* going to tell her I was in a house full of vampires. I could barely comprehend it myself, let alone expect someone else to and for her to accept it and not think I was nuts. Definitely too much to ask.

"Where are you?" The words came out in a rush, almost accusatory the second the call connected. "You left the party, and you never came home. I thought I was going to have to call the police! Are you okay?"

I took a deep breath, acutely aware of Levi's eyes on me. I could almost feel him threatening. *Don't say a word.* "I'm fine," I said. It was technically true. I was alive, anyway.

"Well, what happened?" Angie demanded again. I could almost see her pacing the room, picking at her fingernails anxiously.

My brain scrambled to come up with a suitable lie. "I... met someone," I said slowly, eyes on Levi. "A guy." I knew that would be enough to throw her off. She would be so surprised she would forget her worry and maybe even be happy for me.

"That guy from the party? Tall, dark, and handsome?" Angie asked, a hint of excitement entering her voice. Levi chuckled beside me.

"Yeah," I admitted begrudgingly. "That guy."

"You went home with him?" Angie asked loudly. Was she always so boisterous? I felt so embarrassed, positive the two vampires in the room, and maybe all the vampires in the house, could hear her. How many were there?

"Yeah..." *Sort of.* I felt my cheeks growing warmer and shifted from foot to foot. Was it hot in the kitchen, or was it just me? I felt like I was burning up.

She screamed on the other end of the phone, and I had to pull mine from my ear, wincing. "Did you do the nasty?"

I choked on my response. "What?" I asked, coughing. A glass of water slipped into my hand, and I shot a glare at Levi, who wasn't even trying to hold back his grin. I noticed his teeth were distinctly normal looking. No fangs. "No, Angie. I didn't sleep with him. We just... talked."

Angie snorted like she didn't believe me. "Okay, sure. Wait...is he there?"

Levi laughed out loud, and Angie squealed. "He is! I can't believe you—still there at this hour." She clicked her tongue at me. "Don't do anything I wouldn't do!"

I needed to wrap this up, and fast. "Okay, Angie. I just wanted to check in with you. I won't see you until later tonight, probably. I have to work." That was a good excuse. Especially since it was true. I could hear her question over the line. *How are you getting there?* "I'll find a way there," I said. "Okay, gotta go. Love you, Angie. Bye!" I hung up before she could talk and let out a *whoosh* of air.

Levi fairly cackled. "You've known me a day and already I'm ruining your reputation." He leaned back against the kitchen sink and folded his arms across his chest, regarding me.

"I didn't have a reputation before you," I muttered, thinking.

"Even better," Levi said with a smirk. "What do you need?" he asked, watching me look around.

"I wasn't lying," I said. "I do have work tonight. So, unless I'm being held captive..." I motioned around us to the house and Levi looked contemplative for a moment, tilting his head to the side.

"No," he said finally. "You are free to go. I want you to know that you are welcome to come back anytime. I'm serious, Phoebe. Avatrice is bad news, and if he is after you, it isn't for anything good. We can protect you and maybe you can learn more about your parents and this dhampir stuff." He sounded almost like he was pleading. Like he wanted me to stay, and I felt a strange pang in my chest. Almost like *I* wanted to stay.

"I can't, Levi," I said, hating how his name came out so softly. "I have a life, sort of. I just want to forget all about this vampire stuff. Your secret is safe with me, I promise. Even if I told someone, they would think I was crazy, anyway. I appreciate what you did for me, truly. I can't thank you enough. But I don't think I want to step into this world... your world." I wasn't ready to dive headfirst into this insanity. I just wanted to forget this ever happened.

Levi bowed his head, his smile gone. "I understand," he said simply. He brushed past me. "You can use the shower attached to my room to get cleaned up. I'm sure Felicity or Kalene have something you can wear to work. I can take you if you'd like."

"But the sun..." I trailed off, not actually knowing if vampires could go out in the sun or not.

"The car has tinted windows. And besides, vampires don't burn up in the sun, per se. It is very uncomfortable and is downright excruciating in bright sunlight, but it won't kill me." Good to know.

He led me back to his room and motioned to the attached bathroom. "I'll leave you to it," he said, exiting quietly.

I sighed and closed the bathroom door behind me. What had I gotten myself into? I stripped my clothes and let them fall in a heap on the floor. I didn't spare them a glance as I quickly found a towel, turned on the shower as hot as I could stand, and climbed beneath the spray. And for a while, I just stood there, letting the water wash over me. It felt nice to take a shower that could actually be classified as hot. The best I got at home was lukewarm. I hadn't realized until that moment how dirty I felt. The memory of the vampire touching me - Avatrice - made me shiver. The feel of his teeth on my flesh. I lifted my hand to my neck and found no wound. I sighed loudly, glancing to my left. I saw shampoo and body wash. The source of Levi's heavenly scent, I realized. I scrubbed at my hair, determined to get it shiny and full of life. Then I moved on to the rest of my body and lathered up with Levi's body wash. I sniffed it appreciatively. At least, if nothing else, I would get to smell like a hot guy. It could even add credence to my story with Angie if she got even a whiff of it.

I winced. Had I really thought that? I glanced around as if Levi would just appear in the shower with me. That was a scary thought, and I didn't want to entertain it further. I rinsed myself off and remained under the warm spray for another moment. I reluctantly shut the water off and wrapped myself in the towel. I shivered and padded across the bathroom, pausing when I realized I hadn't figured out what I was going to wear. I stared at the torn and dirty clothes and grimaced, saddened by the state of my leather jacket. I picked up my top and inspected it. There was a splotch of blood on the strap. I groaned and quickly got dressed, deciding I would ask Kalene if she had anything to wear.

Towel drying my hair, I exited the bathroom to find her already in the room. She turned and smiled, holding up a few options. "I'm not sure where you work or what you want to wear, so I brought a lot." She laughed, and I looked at the bed behind her. She wasn't kidding.

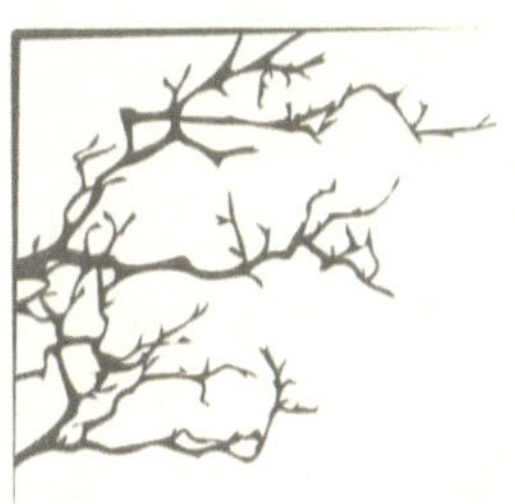

Chapter Six
Phoebe

"I am sorry for what happened to you," Kalene said gently, as we sorted through the clothes she had laid out for me. Her style was a little more preppy and cuter than anything I usually wore, but we were able to find a pair of dark wash jeans and a light blue t-shirt that fit pretty well. She had a bigger chest than me, so the shirt fit a little loose, but it would do the trick for the night.

"Thanks," I said, looking away from her. Everything had happened so fast, it was mostly just a blurry memory. In the moment, it had seemed to stretch on forever, but I knew that it had only been seconds. Attacked by a vampire only to be rescued by another. Certainly not your average evening.

She offered me her hair styling tools and makeup, bringing me to her room to help me get ready. While I didn't *need* the help, I gladly accepted. If I pretended she wasn't a vampire, the whole interaction made me feel like I was just hanging out with a girlfriend. Like I was hanging out with Angie back in the day, before everything got weird after the accident. I applied simple makeup, wondering if it was smart to be sharing makeup with a vampire, but I shook the thoughts away and swiped on some neutral brown to my lids and a touch of blush to my cheeks. Kalene ran a flat iron over my wavy hair and swept it up into a high ponytail that simply put to shame any pony I had ever achieved.

"Here," she said, turning back to her closet for a moment. While she rooted around, I surveyed her room. It was perfectly placed, everything in order. Her bed was made with pastel pink bedding, a huge, fat stuffed fox resting in the corner. I made no comment on it because it was cute, and I still had my stuffy from when I was a kid, so who was I to judge? Kalene turned back to me and presented a silk scarf in a blue that matched the borrowed shirt nicely. She helped me tie it prettily around my throat, hiding the remnants of the attack. When I looked presentable enough for my waitressing job, I headed downstairs. Levi glanced up at me and I saw the briefest of smiles flit across his face. I shifted a little uncomfortably from foot to foot, not knowing what to say. I felt too done up for work, but then again, maybe it would garner me more tips and more tips was always nice.

"I guess I'm ready," I mumbled. I had a spare apron at work and a pair of beat up tennis shoes I could use for now.

"Good," Levi said, walking toward me. "I'll take you." He motioned to the front door, and I turned, waving at Kalene.

"Thanks for the help. It's been... weird." I chuckled nervously, still not sure my brain was comprehending the whole vampire thing. Maybe someone had slipped something into my drink at the party and this was all some kind of drug-induced dream. Except I knew that wasn't true. Something deep in my gut was telling me they were for real, and we had set something in motion. I just had to figure out how to keep up.

I hadn't thought about being alone in a car with Levi until we both shut our doors, the thud deafening in my ears. I swallowed and glanced over at him. Alone with a vampire. Alone with a stranger. I sighed and fidgeted with my phone in my lap. "I understand why you declined to stay," he said, startling me out of my thoughts. "I wish you would reconsider. At least until we find out what Avatrice is up to and what he wants with you."

I was already shaking my head. "Angie will worry and know something weird is going on. It wouldn't be like me to just leave her on her own. We live together—she would notice my absence. And coming up with a plausible reason for being gone all the time will go about as well as that phone call. I appreciate the offer, really, but I have to pass up on it. You have to admit, it would be weird. We don't even know each other."

"True," Levi mused. "A fact that would easily be rectified if you moved in, but I concede. The door is open to you if you ever need it," he added, turning toward my job. I felt a little uneasy thinking about how he now knew where I worked, but pushed it out of my mind. Levi seemed like a good guy. Vampire or not, I had the strangest feeling that he could be trusted.

"Thanks. I'll make sure to keep that in mind," I said as he slid the car into a parking space out front. My heart skipped a beat when he killed the engine. "Are you coming in?" I asked a little too quickly.

"Of course. I want to ensure you start your shift without a hitch and thought I could, perhaps, get a bite to eat..." He looked at me expectantly, as if waiting for me to object.

"Vampires eat actual food?" I asked, almost in a whisper. It wasn't something I had ever thought about. Then again, until recently, the thought of vampires hadn't exactly been prevalent in my thoughts.

Levi chuckled, climbing from the car. I followed suit, awaiting his answer. "Occasionally," he responded. "It does nothing to help the... hunger..." he said carefully. "But it can be enjoyable, nevertheless."

My hand went to my neck involuntarily, brushing against the little blue scarf. The hunger. I could only assume he meant for more than a good steak and shuddered. I had to forcibly push the thoughts from my head and turned toward the front door. "Well, I have to clock in. The hostess will seat you shortly. Thanks for the ride, Levi." I waved as I entered the building, Levi trailing slowly behind me, as if trying to give the impression we were not together. I didn't have time to think about it because my shift was starting. I quickly grabbed my spare shoes and apron and threw them on. I clocked in and stepped onto the floor after learning what part of the dining room would be my section tonight.

I barely paid any attention to the people at the tables, but when I realized Levi had been seated in my section, I felt my heart flutter a little and a million questions flitted through my mind. Was it hard for him to be around so many humans? Was he thinking about the girl in the next booth, her pretty neck exposed for any vampire to sink his fangs into? What was he planning to order? I walked over and smiled faintly. "Hi, again," I said, notebook poised in my hand to take his order. "What are you having?"

Levi looked at me for a long moment, an almost troubled look on his face. "A cheeseburger," he finally answered. "Medium rare, please. And... a chocolate shake."

I lifted an eyebrow. "A sweet tooth?" I asked, scribbling his order down. He chuckled, and a shiver raced down my spine. I didn't give him the chance to answer, turning away. "It'll be right out." I hurried away, but another customer caught my attention.

"Excuse me?"

I turned and plastered a smile on my face, regarding the man. He was handsome enough, but I was too busy to really notice. "Yes?" I asked pleasantly. He simply motioned to his drink, and I nodded, making a mental note to bring him a refill, and walked off to finish out Levi's order.

The night went by quickly and I was glad; I didn't have time to think about vampires. And even better, I was going to get to go home tonight and sleep in my own bed without having been brutalized by a vampire. I cursed mentally, irritated that, at the tail end of my night, vampires slipped back into my mind. I guess it was inevitable, with one sitting in my dining room slurping on a soda. My eyes flicked to Levi, and I found him looking at me. Heat flooded my cheeks, and I looked away quickly. I wanted this all to be over. I didn't want to learn about vampires and dhampirs and that guy—Avatrice. He killed my parents, but had spared me just to try to kill me months later? It didn't make sense, and I didn't care to figure out the puzzle.

Levi remained through the rest of my shift, slowly sipping his drink I brought after he downed his meal and milkshake. His eyes followed me around the room as I worked, and I almost felt like he was stalking me. Not like a creep, but like a *predator.* The idea was chilling. I rubbed my arms, despite it actually being kind of warm in the restaurant, and went to clock out. Levi was waiting for me by the door, an easy smile on his lips. "You didn't have to wait for me all night," I said automatically.

He tilted his head to the side. "Who else was going to give you a ride to your home?" he asked.

Good point.

I cursed silently. Not only would he know where I worked, but he would know where I lived, too. Crap. I was really dropping the ball tonight. I climbed into the car, feeling exhausted. It had been a long night, though undemanding. I rested my head against the cool window and lazily directed Levi toward my apartment. He was unusually quiet as we drove, but I didn't mind the silence. It felt comfortable. I was sleepy and ready to crawl into bed. When he finally spoke, we were in front of the apartment building, and I was half asleep in the passenger seat.

"You have my number," Levi said slowly, his eyes on the building in front of us.

"Hm?" I mumbled, rubbing my eyes with the back of my hand.

He slid a glance in my direction. "I programmed it into your phone while you were out. Kalene is in there, too. If you ever need anything—I mean it. Call." His eyes swiveled back to the apartment. "I don't sense any vampires inside."

"You can sense each other?" I asked, looking at my phone. I found his name and almost smiled. I shook my head to push out any thoughts that might have been trying to creep in about him being sweet. He was a vampire. *And you're half.* The thought hit me hard, and I winced. Maybe. I didn't know that for sure. I wasn't sure I *wanted* to know.

"Yes. If there was a vampire in there, I would know. Trouble is, I suppose, it could be a neighbor just as easily as it could be someone in your apartment." His words were stated matter-of-factly, but I was just coming to a realization. I could have been living in an apartment with vampires and wouldn't have ever known. I found a measure of relief knowing Angie wasn't a vampire, though. Small victories, I supposed.

"So...do *I*... feel like a vampire?" I hedged, chewing on my lower lip as I watched him contemplate my question.

"No," he finally said, glancing at me. "I think you are human enough that you don't read *vampire.* I don't think we can sense halfl—" He stopped himself. "I don't think we can sense dhampirs." He smiled almost apologetically, and I sighed. Time to move on.

I climbed from the car, leaning down to address him. "What, not gonna walk me up?" I teased, half hoping he would. The irrational part of my brain was telling me that there could be a dhampir in my apartment and he wouldn't know it. And the even more irrational part of my brain wanted him to come up and stay a while.

Levi chuckled and put the car in gear. "If you need anything, call me. I'll be here." I took that as a no and shut the car door, turning and walking up the path to the apartment. Levi stayed in the parking lot until the door closed behind me. I fished my keys out of my purse and climbed the stairs to my second-story apartment. I found; however, that it was unnecessary. Angie had left the door unlocked. I mentally told myself to chastise her for that when I saw her sleeping on the couch in front of the TV, running old reruns. I snuck past her to the bathroom. I wiped off my face and had just started getting undressed, ready to put on pajamas and go to bed, when I heard a noise. I froze, my shirt halfway over my head.

I tried to tell myself that it was just Angie. She must have woken up at my noise and was making her way to her bedroom. But I knew it couldn't have been Angie. I would have heard her moving around, probably would have heard a yawn and her clicking the TV off. But the TV continued to drone, and I heard nothing more. The hair on my arms stood up, and I yanked my shirt back down, grabbing my cell. Levi's name was on the screen and my finger hovered over the call icon. What if I was overreacting? What if I wasn't? I licked my lips and pressed *Call.* Better to be safe than sorry. Besides, I mused, almost embarrassed, maybe he would stay after all. I heard another sound, and ice flooded my veins. There was *definitely* someone in my apartment. The phone rang twice, and Levi's voice filled my ears as I ambled out of the bathroom. *"Phoebe?"*

"Levi..." The word came out in a whisper. I heard footsteps, carefully measured. Someone was taking every precaution to be as quiet as possible.

Levi was talking on the phone, but I didn't hear a word he said because suddenly I could see a figure at the end of the hallway that had just emerged from my bedroom. My heart stopped. The figure turned, and we locked eyes. I screamed and practically flew back down the hallway and into the kitchen; the phone clattering to the floor at my feet. I skidded into the kitchen, my mind working in overdrive. A weapon. I needed a weapon. I heard the man pounding after me and I whirled around. He stood in the doorway, looking mean and pissed off. And it took me a moment too long to realize that I knew him. Well, I didn't *know* him, but I had seen him tonight. He had been sitting in my section at work. Had he been watching me? I shuddered at the thought, wondering how I hadn't noticed. I already knew the answer. I was too busy worrying about vampires, and one vampire in particular.

He looked bigger than I remembered, and I felt panic rising in my chest as I realized he was about three times my size. He took a step toward me, and I jumped back, bumping into the counter. I swallowed and shifted my eyes around wildly, trying to find some way to escape. He took another step forward, and I grabbed the toaster, ripping it out of the wall socket, and launched it at him. He dodged it and kept coming. I flung cupboards open and started throwing glasses, bowls, and plates. Glass shattered everywhere, but he just crunched over it, still moving toward me. Where was Angie? I whirled and wrenched a knife out of the block and jumped behind the kitchen table. It put something between us and made me feel somewhat safer. My heart was racing, and my brain was barely functioning. I was so scared. He was prowling my kitchen, eyes trained on me. He lurched to the side, but I was too smart for that; however, and when he jerked to the right, I ran that way, too. I felt arms around my waist anyway, and my victory was short-lived. I screamed and swung the knife wildly. The man made a startled noise, and his arms left my middle. I whirled around as he dropped to his knees, pressing his hands to his throat. Blood spurted out between his fingers, and I gasped, a scream lodged in my throat as I stumbled backwards.

I was sitting on the floor; the knife lying beside me, blood smeared over my hands when Levi came crashing through the door. He found me shaking like a leaf against the cabinets, trying to figure out how to breathe again. The man was lying face down on the ground, blood and glass surrounding him. His head was turned in my direction, his open eyes staring at me, accusing. *You did this.*

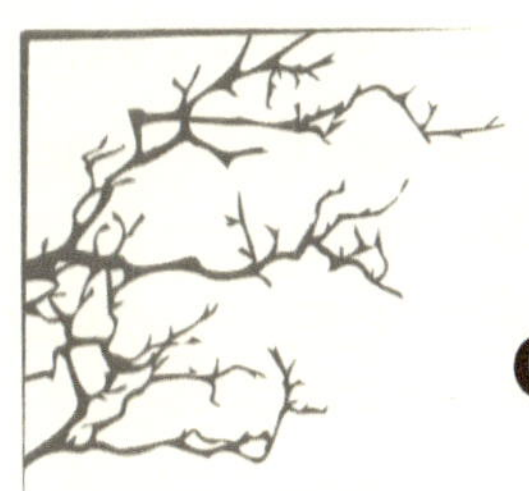

Chapter Seven
Levi

How could I have been so stupid? I should have known Avatrice would not let her go, just like that. I had felt an icy grip on my heart when I heard her scream over the phone. I had slammed on the brakes and whipped the car around so fast that I had nearly wrecked. When I reached her apartment, I hadn't even stopped to think. I flew through the door, following the sounds of a struggle. When I burst into her apartment, she was on the floor, sobbing. It took a moment too long for my brain to catch up. Blood filled the air and made my head swim, making me dizzy. I steadied myself using the wall and stumbled toward her.

"Phoebe." I knelt in front of her, and she looked up at me, her eyes red. She looked at me for what felt like an eternity, almost as if she didn't know who I was. And then relief washed over her face and before I could even comprehend what was happening, she was in my arms. I wrapped my arms around her gently, my eyes straying to the dead man in her kitchen. I should have known better. I held her a little longer before helping her to her feet, keeping her eyes turned away from the death. I called Richard. He would probably bring Felicity. They were pretty good at the cleanup part when something went wrong. And something *had* gone wrong.

I had failed to protect her.

"I'm sorry," we both said at the same time.

I looked down at her, startled. "What have you got to be sorry for?" I asked, incredulously. Surely she must have been joking.

"I don't mean to be such a baby." She stepped back, out of my arms, and I felt a profound sense of loss at her absence. Then her eyes widened, and her heart thumped loudly. "Angie..."

She turned and ran from the kitchen. I followed just in time to see the look on her face as she looked down at her friend. I wished I hadn't witnessed it. Wished I hadn't heard the heart wrenching scream of agony that fell from her lips. I wished I hadn't seen her drop to her knees, screaming. Her eyes locked on the stain of red dripping down the side of the white couch. I walked over to her and sat on the floor with her, pulling her into my lap. I cradled her and turned her head away, my eyes meeting who I had to assume was Angie. I remembered her vaguely from the party. Her eyes were unblinking and accusatory. It was as if she blamed me for her untimely demise.

I blamed myself.

I was still sitting on the floor, rocking Phoebe back and forth, when Richard and Felicity walked in. Their eyes swept the carnage, and Richard found me. He lifted an eyebrow, but wisely did not speak. "So are we here for the stiff in the kitchen or the dead chick on the—" Felicity was cut off with a dangerous growl from low in my chest. She nodded and backed off. Phoebe shuddered but did not pull away. She had stopped crying, but her body still shook. I stroked her hair and sighed softly. This was already turning into a mess.

"Phoebe," I began cautiously. "We need to go."

She lifted her head and looked at me. "Go?" she asked, eyes sliding to Angie slowly. "What about...?" She choked on a sob.

"Richard and Felicity are taking care of the intruder. They will scrub the apartment clean of any sign he was here. We will leave Angie here and make a call to the police when we are further away. They will find her and probably want to interview you and find out what happened. They won't get the closure for her death, but... she will get a proper funeral." It surprised me she hadn't passed out on me yet. She was strong.

"Okay," Phoebe said, sniffling. "Can I pack a bag?"

"Of course," I said, pulling her to her feet. "I'll help you, but we have to be quick. The longer we stay, the more likely we are to be caught." She led me to her room, and she silently packed a bag with some essentials, a photograph, and a handful of clothes. She tossed the bag over her shoulder and wiped at her eyes. "Let's get you out of here," I whispered.

She didn't speak, and she didn't look at either dead body as we exited the apartment. I helped her into the car, and we simply left. A few blocks away, I called the police and said I had heard screaming coming from her apartment. When we reached the house, we both sat there silently, lost in our own thoughts. I gently pushed into her mind, encouraging sleep. I climbed from the car and scooped her into my arms. Her head fell against my chest, and a soft sigh escaped her lips as her eyelids fluttered closed. Clenching my teeth against my rising anger, I carried her into the house and up to my room. I laid her on my bed, gently removing her shoes. I tucked her hair back behind her ear and brushed a kiss across her forehead before slipping from the room to speak with Caleb and Kalene.

I found them in the living room, seemingly waiting for me. "What's the word?" Caleb asked, watching me.

I sighed and rubbed a hand down my face, leaning against the doorframe. "I didn't sense any vampire," I said. "But I don't think he was. Not as easily as she took him down."

"She killed him?" Kalene asked, startled. Her eyes shifted upward, toward my room, and I saw a bit of pride in her eyes. "Good for her."

"Yeah, well, she's traumatized," I said, following her gaze. "I mean, how could she not be? Her parents died a few months ago in a vampire attack. She gets attacked by that same vampire just yesterday, and today she finds her friend dead in their apartment after killing the intruder in the kitchen."

"Pretty rough Tuesday, if you ask me," Caleb said dryly. "I don't suppose you'll ever give up the notion of her staying here now, will you?"

"No," I answered. "This only proves that Avatrice didn't attack her randomly. He wants something from her. I don't know if he just wants her dead or if there is something more, but I will find out," I said.

"She's peaceful," Kalene said quietly.

"I may have encouraged her to sleep," I said sheepishly. "I knew she would never settle without a little help."

Kalene sent me a chastising look, but it soon softened. She climbed to her feet and came to stand in front of me, lifting her hand to my cheek. "You're kind," she said. "You showed up in that girl's life precisely when you were supposed to."

I felt that her life had gotten distinctly more complicated since my arrival, but perhaps it would have happened, regardless. Would Avatrice still have found her if I hadn't been at that party? The one Felicity insisted we go to? Or would everything simply have played out as it would have if I had been removed from the equation, the girl long dead? I wasn't sure, but there was no sense dwelling. I needed to find out what was going on, but for now, I was exhausted. I hadn't slept a wink since bringing Phoebe into my home, and it showed. My mouth unhinged in a yawn and Kalene stepped back, motioning for Caleb to follow her.

"Get some sleep, Levi," she said gently. "You need it."

"My bed is a little occupied," I said with a chuckle. "But I'll crash on the couch." I knew Richard and Felicity would arrive home soon, but I could get perhaps a few minutes of shuteye. I sprawled out on the couch, my long frame barely fitting. I was so tired that I simply didn't care. I threw my arm over my eyes and sighed, drifting asleep quickly.

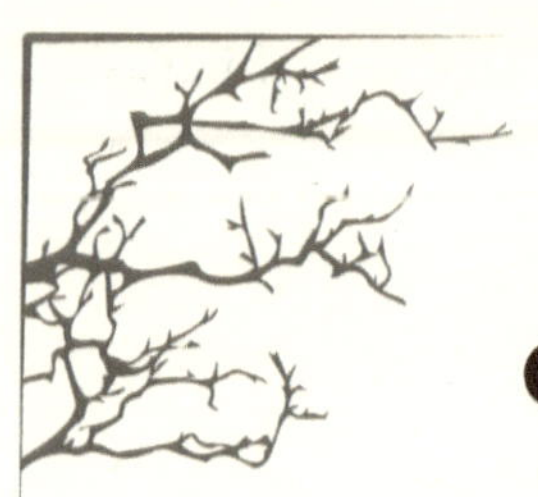

Chapter Eight
Phoebe

I could feel something in the back of my mind, like a worry long since forgotten, trying to rear its ugly head. I pushed it away and shook out my blonde locks, a smile crossing my face. I was standing in the middle of a beautiful field with trees surrounding me. I must have traveled through the forest to find my way here, though I wasn't sure why. There were wildflowers all around me and little butterflies fluttering about nearby. It was beautiful. I held my hand out and one white butterfly landed on my palm. I smiled and slammed my fist closed, crushing the creature.

The beautiful field started to rumble, as if an earthquake were beginning. I looked down at my bare feet, my white dress swishing in the wind, and saw thick, dark, lash-like vines twisting and writhing out of the earth. I opened my hand and watched the crushed butterfly drift to the ground and took a step back. The vine whipped out at me and curled around my ankle. I stumbled back, falling as the sky above me opened up and rain began to pour, soaking through my thin summer dress quickly and plastering my curls to my face and neck. I reached out and used my nails to tear at the vine, twisting it savagely and scrambling away. I turned and ran, not bothering to think about where I was going.

I winced as twigs slapped me in the face, creating little cuts in my flesh. Rocks jabbed me in the feet and every little thing snagged on my dress, ripping and tearing, slowing my progress. I could hear someone's harsh breathing and realized with a start that it was not my own.

"Phoebe!"

I ran faster, panic building in my chest.

"Phoebe!"

It was Avatrice, and he was chasing me. I had to push myself to go faster. I came upon a felled log and scrambled to get over it. Arms clamped around my waist in a vice-like grip and I screamed, trying to claw Avatrice in the face.

"It's me!" Levi hissed against my ear. I went limp in his arms, an overwhelming sense of relief flooding my system. "Come on," Levi whispered, hoisting me over the log. He took my hand, and we ran through the woods together. I was able to keep up with him surprisingly well.

Suddenly, my foot caught on a twisted root and Levi's hand was ripped from mine as I went down to the ground on my face. "Come on, Phoebe, get up!" Levi hissed, moving toward me to help.

I tried to untangle myself from the weeds, but they were twisting themselves around my legs, holding me captive. Levi crouched next to me and began snapping at the offending things, but we could both hear Avatrice coming, crashing through the trees. We didn't have the time. "Just go," I whispered, tears stinging the backs of my eyes.

"I'm not leaving you," Levi growled, working harder to free me, but for every vine he snapped, another wrapped around my legs. I was trapped.

"He'll only kill you too," I said, sadness making my chest ache. The idea of Avatrice getting his hands on Levi caused me a great deal of pain.

"Then we will die together," Levi said, pulling my head toward him for a kiss that stole my breath away. I clung to him, never wanting to let go.

"Cute," Avatrice snarled, his teeth bared at us in the dark. I glowered at him, not showing any sign of fear. I had learned long ago that it was better to stand up to him and risk injury than to let him do whatever he pleased.

"Avatrice," Levi snarled, standing in front of me, hoping to shield me.

"Levi," Avatrice returned, a lazy smile spreading across his face. This was all a game to him, and he was certain he had won.

Before I could break free and perform some kind of daring—and probably stupid—rescue, Avatrice flicked his wrist, and the wooden stake flew through the sky and pierced Levi through the heart.

I screamed as he fell to his knees on the rain soaked earth.

I awoke with a start, lurching up in bed, panting. Sweat dampened my clothes and my throat felt raw. Had I been screaming? The dream had felt so real and so very confusing. My question was answered when the bedroom door swung open loudly and Levi walked briskly into the room, eyes sweeping the area. Finding nothing wrong, his eyes landed on me. I sat in the middle of the bed, knees pulled up to my chest. I looked at him, my eyes already watering. Why was this happening to me?

"Phoebe," Levi spoke quietly, regarding me from the other side of the room. He held one hand up, as if to show me he meant me no harm. I almost laughed at the thought. Levi was about the only thing I felt safe around anymore. The idea of going out into the world was terrifying. What if I ran into more of those things? I shuddered. I was one of those things.

"I don't know anything about this world," I whispered. I wrapped my arms around my knees and tried to keep my tears at bay. "Vampires and dhampirs and this... this Avatrice guy."

"We can help you," Levi said softly. "I don't know everything myself, but we can help you find the answers you seek."

"Who was that guy?" I asked, not looking at him. I already had my suspicions, but I wanted to hear him say it. To confirm what I already knew.

"He was a dhampir." Levi spoke almost flatly. He folded his arms across his chest and scowled. "At least, we think. As of now, we don't know of any surefire way to test that theory unless they are alive and since he... wasn't..."

I flinched, remembering. I had killed a guy tonight. And Angie was gone, dead, when I walked into the apartment. That guy must have been inside already, just waiting for me to get home from work. How had I not noticed him watching me at the restaurant? "What now?" I asked, looking up at Levi. "What am I supposed to do now?"

Levi finally came into the room fully and approached the bed. He sighed and pushed his hands through his dark hair, looking troubled. "I, of course, won't force you, but I really think you should stay here with us. We can work something out. You can bunk with Kalene, if you want. Or if you prefer my room, I can sleep on the couch..." He trailed off, looking a little uncomfortable. "We don't have any spare rooms. We aren't often graced with visitors."

"I agree," I said softly. "I think my hand has been dealt, and I don't think I have any better options. I'll stay if you all will help me figure out what is happening. I need to know who I am and what I am. I need to know where I fit into this whole thing. Who this Avatrice guy is, and I know you can help me with that. At least a little." And I couldn't bear the thought of going back to the apartment after what had happened.

Levi nodded. "Yes. But for now, you should rest. You've been through an ordeal. Just take some time and get yourself comfortable. I can leave you to—"

"No," I interrupted. "I mean, yes, I think resting is a good idea, but I don't... I don't really want to be alone right now." I looked away from his blue eyes, almost embarrassed to admit that weakness. I had never been the type to need someone. Everyone I had in my life was there because I wanted them there, but I felt like, if I let Levi walk out the door, I was going to collapse into a mess of tears and confusion, and I didn't want that right now. He was keeping me grounded. He was someone to talk to and someone to distract me from the horrible evening.

Levi grunted, and I glanced at him. He was looking at the bedroom door, a pensive look on his face. Finally, after what felt like an eternity, he sat on the edge of the bed. His bed. I felt terrible all at once and shifted uncomfortably. "I can sleep on the couch," I blurted.

He threw a look at me and chuckled. "No," he said simply. "You will not."

I narrowed my eyes at him. And just why not? "Oh?" I asked, lifting my chin a little higher.

Levi leaned a little closer to me. "If someone tries to get to you here, they have to go through me first." He said it like it was just a simple fact. Like he had no problem putting himself in danger for me. Was it simply because he was a vampire, and he was a little sturdier than me? Someone who only just found out she was a dhampir and that vampires are a thing? I sighed and laid back on the bed, folding my hands across my stomach. I looked up at the ceiling and chewed my lower lip thoughtfully.

"Tell me about them," I said softly. "Your family."

Levi shifted. "I don't really remember much about my family," he said. "My blood has been dead for... years," he said with a rueful smile. "The Coven is my family."

I shrugged one shoulder as he laid beside me, mimicking my posture. "Tell me about the Coven, then," I prompted, turning my head to regard him.

Levi sighed, twirling his thumbs around each other over his stomach. "Well... Richard is... Richard. He isn't as bad as he may seem. He likes to push the boundaries a little too much, so he may seem cruel, but I have never known him to do anything truly reckless. What he did to you at the party was unacceptable, but it would not have gone further than giving you a thorough scare. I am, by no means, condoning his behavior. And, as I am sure you have begun to suspect at least, he can read minds. Most of the time, he tunes everything out unless someone is thinking a particularly loud thought. How one controls the volume of their thoughts is beyond me, but he frequently gets irritated with Felicity for her loud thoughts."

I wasn't sure how I felt learning that Richard could actually hear my thoughts. That was pretty terrifying. "I'll try to keep it down then," I mumbled.

"Then there is Kalene," Levi continued. "She is younger than most of us, older only to Felicity and by only a few minutes. She is a very kind and gentle woman, always looking for the nicest way of doing something, even if it is unpleasant in nature. She is Felicity's older sister, though not by blood. I believe Kalene's parents adopted Felicity, but you would have to talk with her to learn more. Kalene does have a temper, though it is typically slower to show. However, I don't recommend getting on her bad side." Levi glanced at me before continuing. "She is an Empath." At my confused expression, he continued. "Meaning she can read emotions like Richard can read minds. You can be the best liar on the planet, but they will be able to call you out."

"Sounds like you know from experience," I teased.

Levi snorted. "You could say that."

I nudged him with my elbow. "You said Kalene was Felicity's older sister? Tell me about her." This was serving to give my mind something to focus on, as well as allowing me to learn more about the people I suddenly lived with.

Levi sighed softly, closing his eyes. I thought for a moment he wasn't going to answer. "She can be quite standoffish to put it nicely. She is fiercely protective of those she cares about, so that can make things a little uncomfortable for newcomers." He slid a glance in my direction. "She doesn't open up to others very well, and sometimes she can be misunderstood. She comes on a little strong, but underneath all of it, she really isn't bad."

"And she's got a thing for you," I blurted. Why had I brought that up?

Levi laughed out loud. "That obvious?" He sighed. "Yes, she has a bit of a schoolgirl's crush, I suppose." I almost snorted. She had seemed a little territorial at the party, but then again, I hadn't seen much of her since. When I didn't say anything, he continued. "She likes to keep it pretty hush-hush, and she doesn't use it around us generally, but Felicity has a bit of her own gift. She can cast illusions. Hyper-realistic ones," he said, glancing at me. "Caleb is the oldest," he continued on, as if he hadn't just dropped that bomb. I hoped it was something I never had to witness. "But that doesn't mean he is the wisest. He is charming and witty, and he has a protective streak a mile long. We are his family, and he would die to protect us. All of us."

"So how come some of you, like Richard and Kalene, have special powers, but others like Caleb don't?" I asked, my eyes growing heavy.

"I don't have an answer," Levi said simply, turning to look at me. "We think it has to do with your human life before you were Turned, but it is pure speculation. For example, Kalene was a very empathetic person and when she was Turned, it simply amplified." Levi reached up and rubbed his forehead, and for the first time I noticed he looked exhausted. He continued speaking; however, silencing anything I had been thinking of saying. "Although I wouldn't say Caleb isn't talented in his own way. He's the fastest vampire I've ever seen, second only to Avatrice himself. Perhaps not as exciting, but useful nevertheless." He shrugged and closed his eyes briefly.

"What about you?" I wondered. "Do you have any special powers?" I waited for a response of some kind, but none came. After a moment, I realized he had fallen asleep. I smiled to myself and rolled over, getting comfortable. I wasn't going to wake him up just to send him to the couch and he would be angry with me if I went to the couch, so I simply closed my eyes and went to sleep, feeling just a bit better.

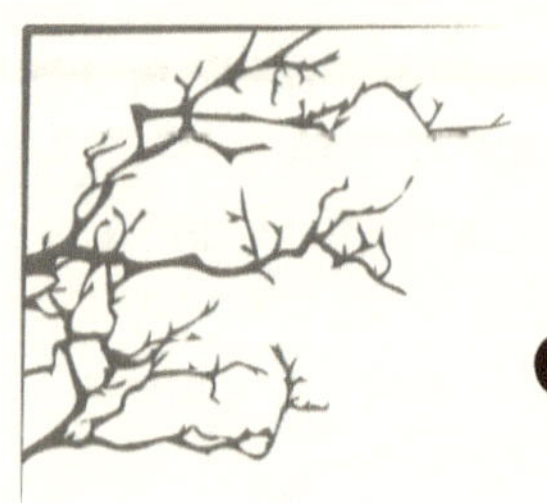

Chapter Nine
Phoebe

I awoke with a start, my heart jumping into my throat. I couldn't breathe. "Phoebe?" The word was spoken softly, but it startled me, nevertheless. It took a moment for my sleepy brain to realize what was happening. Levi had rolled over in his sleep and must have draped his arm across my chest, making it hard to breathe. He lifted his head and looked at me in the dark. I could barely make out his features in the moonlight, but he looked like he had also just woken up. He slowly lifted his arm off me and groaned, rolling to his back and sitting up. He rubbed his face with both hands and sighed loudly.

"Levi?" I whispered into the dark.

"My apologies," he responded, voice husky from sleep. "I must have fallen asleep." He started to stand, but my fingers closed around the hem of his shirt, seemingly of their own free will. He stilled and glanced back at me as if I were a frightened animal he was trying not to spook. "Are you alright?"

I hesitated. I didn't know the answer to his question. I didn't know why I had stopped him from leaving. The thought of being alone was terrifying, but the idea of continuing to sleep in the same bed as a practical stranger was equally scary. "Will you come to the kitchen with me? I need a drink." That seemed reasonable.

He chuckled. "Scared to move around a house of vampires on your own?"

I let go of his shirt and sniffed. "Something like that." I was trying very hard not to think about what had happened lest I fall apart again. I climbed to my feet and carefully maneuvered around the bed and headed toward the door. "You coming?" I asked over my shoulder, hand resting on the doorknob.

He grunted in response; the bed creaking slightly as he climbed to his feet. He stretched his arms above his head, his shirt lifting slightly to show a flash of skin. I quickly opened the door, averting my eyes, and we made our way downstairs and to the kitchen. He settled himself in a chair at the table and watched me move around the room silently. I didn't know what I was looking for, but I was kind of operating on the assumption I would know it when I found it. I opened the fridge and sighed. It was pretty sparse, but considering the residents didn't actually have to eat or drink, I supposed it wasn't bad. I suppose I was lucky that there was a fridge at all. I scanned the interior and chewed my lower lip, finally grabbing the milk, checking the expiration date, and some cookies I had found in one of the cupboards. I went in search of a glass but found I couldn't reach them. I turned to ask for help and came face to chest with him. I blinked, and he looked down at me as he reached up and plucked a glass from the top shelf.

"We can move these..." He said slowly, watching me, his eyebrows pulled together in a look of uncertainty.

I realized I wasn't breathing and took in a lungful of air as quietly as possible. He was much too close, much too quickly. But the counter was at my back, and I couldn't slide past him. The kitchen seemed charged with electricity all of a sudden and goosebumps sprung up along my arms. Levi seemed completely oblivious to whatever was happening to me, and the sound of the glass clinking on the counter brought me back to myself. I took another deep breath, and everything went back to normal. A second clink had me glancing behind me.

"May I join you?"

"Oh... uh... yeah," I managed to stutter out. He took the glasses and stepped back. And it was like nothing ever happened. I brought the milk and cookies to the table and poured two glasses and we sat across from each other, the cookies in the middle. Neither of us spoke for a few moments, each taking our cookie. "What about you?"

Levi lifted an eyebrow. "Pardon?"

"You were telling me about your family... the Coven. But I don't know much about you," I said. And I found myself wanting to know more about him. I leaned forward, cupping my cheek in one hand, dipping my cookie into my glass of milk with the other. I swished it around a moment and took a bite, watching Levi expectantly.

He shifted in his seat and sighed. "What is there to know?" he asked. "I already told you I don't remember much about my family. A few scattered memories, but it has been a very long time." He smiled a little ruefully, turning the cookie over and over in his hands as if he didn't know what to do with it. After a moment, he took a bite and followed it up with a sip of milk. I wrinkled my nose but said nothing. "When you don't have a support system there to guide you, it can be difficult after the change." He got a faraway look in his eyes, and I got the feeling he wasn't really sitting across from me anymore. "I did not make the choice to become...this. I was a lost soul trying to find my way in the world and someone took advantage." He scowled. "I was out that night, alone. I remember...there was someone waiting for me. A woman. But I had been drinking and was not my best. I stumbled into the gutter and just stayed there, looking up at the sky as it rained on me. I felt...alone. I felt...defeated. And that's when he emerged, as if he could sense my despair."

I frowned and started to reach across the table to touch his hand, but thought better of it and pulled back. For someone to have claimed they didn't remember much, he sure seemed to remember this. Though, I supposed I would probably remember the moment my life changed forever, too. No matter how long ago.

"He came to me and knelt by my side and just bit me. There was no pretense or lead up. It was simply an opportunity, and he took it. He nearly killed me, but I guess he changed his mind because, as I lay there, nearly dead, he forced his blood into my mouth. And I stayed there in that gutter for I don't know how long. He disappeared without ever speaking a word. I didn't know what was happening, but I was in agony for what felt like hours. And then suddenly it stopped, and my mind was clear. I pulled myself out of the gutter and went home."

The way he said it made a knot form in my stomach. "You don't have to-"

"The woman was there, waiting up for me. How horrible is it that I can't even remember her name?" He scoffed. "She hugged me and I... I could smell her blood and it made my mouth hurt. It made everything hurt, and I couldn't stop myself. I bit her, only I didn't stop. Not until she was dead."

I hadn't realized I was out of my seat until my arms were wrapping around him. Tears stung the backs of my eyes, but by sheer force of will, I held them back. I held onto Levi tightly, like somehow, if I just squeezed hard enough, I could make it all better. I wished I hadn't asked about him. I wished he hadn't told me about his past. It was obvious it was painful for him to remember, and I felt terrible for bringing it out of him. His arms slowly went around me, and he held me just as tightly. And we stayed there for a long time, just holding each other. Neither of us spoke, and when he finally let go, I peeled myself off of him and sat back in my chair. "I'm sorry," I said. And I meant it. It was a sad story, and he was right—he had been taken advantage of and didn't know how to control himself when he emerged on the other side of the change. I didn't know how anyone could see it as anything but an awful situation for all involved.

At the same time, he said, "Thank you."

We both fell silent again. Anything I could think to say just didn't seem right. What was I supposed to say after learning he killed someone important to him? She could have been his wife, a sister, his mother. I had never stopped to think about what it must have been like for him. For all of them. They all had a story, and I had a feeling most vampires didn't have a very feel-good beginning. Finally, Levi stood. "We should get back to sleep. I'll stay down here. Go on up to bed, Phoebe." He turned his back to me, but his shoulders were stiff, and I noticed as he left the room, he did not head to the living room, but to the front door. Against my better judgement, I followed.

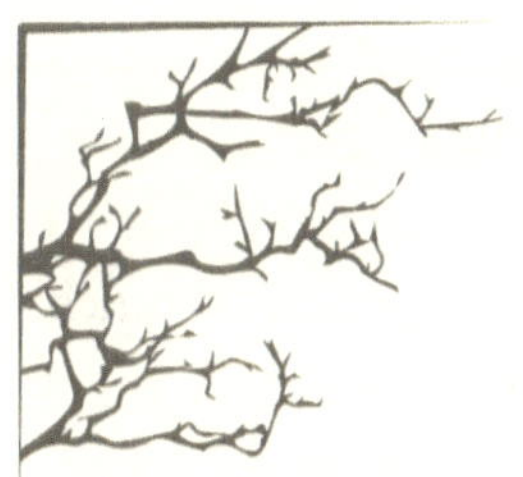

Chapter Ten
Levi

I knew she was following me. She wasn't exactly quiet about it, but I didn't turn to tell her to leave me alone. In fact, I wanted nothing more than to spend more of my time with her. And that scared me. I had never wanted to spend time with another person as much as I wanted to with her. Something about her just seemed... right. But I had just unveiled my darkest secret to her. She had to think me a monster. I stopped walking and just looked up at the moon, trying to make sense of my thoughts and feelings. I shouldn't feel like this about her. I turned to look at her and scowled. I shouldn't want to get closer to her, to hold her, to kiss her. But I did. God, I *was* a monster, after all.

She stared at me. Her green eyes were striking in the moonlight, and her hair was tousled from sleep. She had been through something terrible and the last thing she needed was a vampire who wanted... what? I wanted everything she made me feel was possible. I wanted her. I must have been making a terrible face because she began to fidget. "Are you... mad at me?" she asked softly.

I blinked. That's what she was worried about? "No," I answered quickly. "I'm not angry with you, Phoebe. I'm just... a little in my feelings right now, as they say." I chuckled. That couldn't have been a more accurate statement. I had a lot of feelings about a lot of things, and I was having a hard time processing everything all at once. I was glad Kalene wasn't around. But she was here, even after everything that had happened in such a short time. She was here, even after hearing about my past. That had to mean something. But it was not the time for *feelings*. The poor girl had been through hell recently, reaching back as far as the death of her parents mere months ago, to the last several hours of her life. Things were happening so quickly for her, and I was not going to add to her distress.

"I'm sorry if I overstepped or if I upset you in any way. I promise it was not my intention. I just...don't know anything about this stuff. And I know I said I didn't want to, but it seems like I don't have much of a choice. So... I wanted to learn a little bit about the people I will be spending so much time with. I wanted to learn a little more about you." She was fidgeting again. The words tumbled out of her mouth so quickly, it was as if she thought if she simply spoke rapidly enough, she could fill every silence and there would be no time for discomfort.

I walked over and rested my hand on her shoulder, wanting to touch her but not allowing myself to embrace her. "And you shall. But it is late—or perhaps early—so why don't we retire for the remainder of the darkness? It is a big day tomorrow."

Phoebe scrunched up her nose and looked up at me. "Why?" she asked.

I gave a slow smile; the wheels turning in my mind. "You'll see," I said, walking back to the house. She followed without hesitation, and my chest tightened slightly as we crossed the threshold. "This is where I leave you," I said, stopping in the living room. I reached for her hand and kissed the back of it gently, cursing myself the second my lips touched her skin. She felt warm and inviting and she had not run from me. It was a gift she would never know she had given me. "Goodnight, Phoebe. If you need me..." I motioned to the couch, and she sighed.

"If you get uncomfortable down here all by yourself," she began, but seemed to think better of it. She shook her head and turned. "Goodnight, Levi." I watched her walk up the stairs and flung myself down on the couch. I doubted I would sleep much more. I had a lot of work to do and a lot of thoughts to sort through. I laid there for a few minutes, contemplating, before I finally climbed to my feet. I would be exhausted come morning, but I recalled the look of disappointment on her face upon opening the fridge.

In all fairness, we didn't need to eat, so anything we had on hand was purely for the enjoyment of taste. Most of the stuff in the house belonged to Kalene, anyway. I grabbed the car keys and slipped out the door, ensuring I locked it behind me. I knew it was early. The clock had been blinking 5:30 when I started up the car, but there were a few shops in town that were open all hours of the night.

I pulled into the parking lot of one of them and climbed out, stuffing my hands in my pockets as I entered. I hadn't gone shopping for food in ages, but I knew Phoebe would need to eat and it was one less thing for her to worry about. I grabbed a cart and began gathering supplies. I placed eggs, bacon, biscuits, cereal, chips, and more in the cart, knowing this was going to be a sizable hit to the bank card. I wasn't concerned. Between the five of us, we had more than enough.

Richard found me in the kitchen come morning. He clicked his tongue and sat at the table, propping his feet up on another chair. "Went shopping?" he asked. I could hear the raised eyebrow in his voice. I threw a look over my shoulder, the food on the stove sizzling.

"Yes," I said simply. "She has to eat." I knew he would go searching my mind for further motives, but I was far too busy reciting the steps in my head to give him much of anything.

"And you're cooking for her?" he asked, cocking his head to the side, peering across the room at the breakfast I was making. I had to admit, I hadn't cooked in *ages,* and I had resorted to my phone and the internet to recall how best to cook eggs. At least I remembered the basics. *Don't burn the food and don't burn the house down.* Richard chuckled, and I scowled. "She's been through a lot in not a lot of time. The least I can do is breakfast." I slapped some raw bacon into a pan with one hand and scraped eggs off the bottom of another, crinkling my nose, certain I was doing something wrong.

The others migrated into the room as the smell of bacon permeated the house. "Someone's got it bad," Caleb snickered, shoving Richard's feet off the chair and taking a seat. He leaned back, resting one arm over the back of the chair, watching me. Embarrassment flooded my system as the room filled with my family, all watching me work. I shoved it down, cutting a quick glance at Kalene, hoping she hadn't noticed.

I snorted, hoping I sounded convincing. "I've known her, what, two days?" But I couldn't help but feel a little rattled by the woman in my room.

"You've been around a while," Richard goaded, his grin in full evidence. "You know what you like."

"What's that supposed to mean?" Felicity asked sharply, cutting her eyes to him. She wore her thick red hair loose around her shoulders and reached up, twirling a few strands between her fingers anxiously.

"It means that she is some eye candy when she's not mangled," Richard said with a sigh, waving his hand. "Not particularly my type, but you know. If she was down…" He trailed off suggestively and I nearly snapped the spatula in my hand in half.

"Don't talk about her that way." The words came from my mind but came out of Kalene's mouth. She folded her arms across her chest and threw a dirty look at Richard. "She's a person, not a hunk of meat."

"Hey, a guy could really...sink his teeth into her." Richard began to laugh, but it was cut off abruptly when everyone came to the realization that I was nearly shaking, gritting my teeth so hard it hurt. Anger built up in my stomach, and a low snarl escaped my lips before I could squelch it. I'm certain it surprised me just as much as everyone else.

The door upstairs opened, and everyone fell silent, but I was still shaking. Richard knew what I was thinking. *Touch her and you're dead.* Light footsteps preceded Phoebe walking into the room, rubbing her face with one hand, her hair even messier than it had been in the wee hours of the morning. My eyes drifted to the two glasses in the sink. "Morning," she muttered. She glanced around the room, her eyes lingering on me at the stove. "You're... cooking." The surprise in her tone was not lost on me.

My anger dissipated in an instant, the embarrassment creeping back in. "You have to eat," I grumbled, returning my attention to the food, hoping I hadn't overstepped.

"No, I mean... thank you. It's very sweet of you. I am starving." She laughed a little, and I felt the tension in my shoulders ease up. Her laughter was like magic. "I suppose it is too much to ask that there's coffee?"

I winced. "Uh... I forgot about the coffee. Didn't think about it. Sorry."

She waved my apology away, walking toward me. She stopped at my left and tapped my shoulder and pointed up. I chuckled and reached over to open the cupboard and pulled her down a glass. She smiled and peeked at the food on the stove, her eyebrows crinkling for just a moment before she smoothed her expression again. "Can I help?"

"Translation - you need help," Caleb said with a low chuckle.

I scowled, but Phoebe was sliding her glass into my free hand and taking the spatula from me. Her hands were gentle but firm. She was kicking me out. I watched her flip and stir effortlessly, as if she did this all the time. Then again, she ate a lot more often than me, so she probably did. She requested plates and Caleb fetched them for her and she plated everything up nicely and set it all out on the counter. She pushed her hair out of her face and smiled, seemingly proud of herself.

I was getting her a drink when I felt her hand lightly touch my arm. I glanced at her and smiled faintly. "Thank you," she said with a smile. "It was a very nice thought." She glanced at everyone in the room. "Are any of you going to eat? There's no way I could eat this all myself."

Kalene perked up. "I won't say no to a home cooked breakfast." She grabbed a plate and found a seat at the table.

Richard held up a hand. "Pass," he said, pushing to his feet and leaving the room.

Caleb took a plate, and, after some hesitation, Felicity did, too. They found their seats, and I watched Phoebe, letting them all grab food before she even made a move to make her own plate. Kalene looked up suddenly, and we both realized at the same time that Phoebe was quietly crying, her hand over her mouth. What had I done? I inched toward her, nervous. I glanced to Kalene for help, but she shook her head, uncertain.

Phoebe suddenly wiped her face and grabbed a plate, quickly filling it with food. She wouldn't look at me as she sat down and silently began to eat. I thought about saying something to her, anything to make her smile, but didn't know what to say. I didn't want to upset her further. Then, seemingly out of nowhere, Caleb glanced at her. She was looking down at her plate, looking glum. He reached over and took a strip of bacon off her plate slowly. She looked up at him, and he purposefully took a bite, staring her down. "Yours looked better," he said, blinking at her, completely deadpan.

She stared for a moment before chuckling. "Can't fault a guy for stealing some bacon," she said, a tiny smile on her face. It was such a simple moment, but it seemed to lighten her spirit just a little.

I walked over and, on a whim, brushed her hair behind her shoulder. "I'm going to go get changed," I told her. "Then, when you're ready, we can get started."

She looked up at me, eyes searching my face. "With?" she asked.

I smiled and backed away. "You'll see."

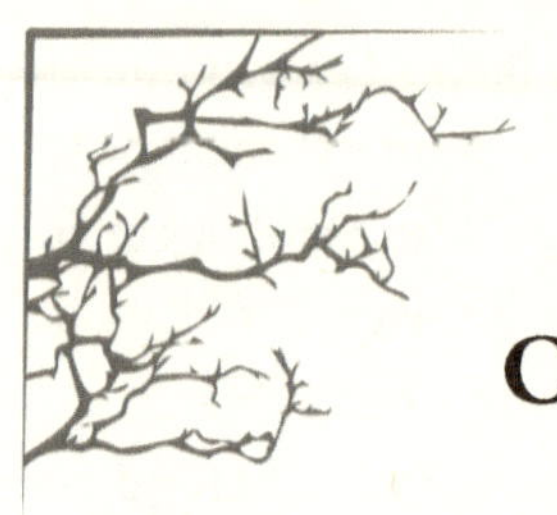

Chapter Eleven
Phoebe

I finished breakfast and washed everyone's dishes before Kalene shooed me out of the kitchen, chastising me for taking care of them. I went upstairs to Levi's room and found my bag. I pulled out a pair of jeans and a tank top and threw them on after searching the room and checking the adjoining bathroom for Levi. I borrowed his hairbrush and tossed my hair into a messy ponytail before heading back downstairs in search of him. I found him in the living room; the others milling about casually. Too casually.

The fact that they had rearranged the living room was another clue that something was amiss. They had pushed all the furniture to one side of the room, leaving an open area in the center. I glanced at everyone, but they were paying me no mind. Unease washed over me, but I reminded myself that Levi had told me repeatedly that he wanted to help me.

"What's...going on?" I asked after an awkward silence.

Levi lifted an eyebrow slowly and beckoned me further into the room. I wasn't sure I trusted what was going on, but I took another step, nevertheless choosing to trust *him*. As soon as my foot hit the floor, I was airborne. Strong arms lifted me up and swung me around like I was a rag-doll, depositing me just a little roughly on the couch. I blinked and let out a long breath, staring up at the ceiling, my heart hammering in my chest. Levi's face entered my vision, grinning. "You should always be prepared," he said. He held out his hand to me and I took it, only to find myself face down on the carpet next. I groaned and pushed up on my elbows. Caleb offered his hand, and I shoved it aside, standing. I whirled around to snap at Levi, but my feet were knocked out from under me. I heard a giggle from Felicity and scowled, my head bouncing off the floor. I growled and clenched my hands into fists.

"You make me breakfast and then abuse me?" I snapped, climbing to my feet, feeling the anger bubbling up in my chest. Just what was he playing at? I was trying to brace for an impact, but I didn't know where it was coming from, or from who. So, when an arm wrapped around my waist and dragged me back against a strong chest and my head was pulled to one side, exposing my neck more thoroughly, I gasped. We stayed suspended like that for what felt like an eternity. My heart was beating painfully in my chest, threatening to explode. I swallowed hard and tried to remember how to breathe. He wouldn't hurt me, not really. Right? Finally, Levi spoke.

"Not abuse," he said quietly, much closer than I had anticipated. I could feel his breath, soft against my neck. I jumped and felt the rumble of his laughter against my back. "Teach."

"Easy for you to say," I said, hating that I sounded a little breathless. "You're a lot stronger and faster than me. And I didn't know when I woke up this morning I was going to get my ass kicked."

Levi still held me but had released my head, allowing me to right my vision once more. I saw Richard hide a chuckle inside a cough and narrowed my eyes at him. "True," Levi said simply. "You have to learn to use that to your advantage. I am stronger and faster... however, you are smaller and have the added advantage of knowing about vampires. Learn the weaknesses and learn your strengths. Strength is not always physical." The idea of getting physical with Levi flashed through my mind without my permission and I quickly shoved the thought from my mind, but it was too late.

Richard chuckled. "Keep it down in there," he said.

I blushed straight to my roots, and Levi pushed me away from him. Though he was gentle, there was a bit of force behind it. He turned quickly, facing away from me, and rubbed his jaw. "Hm..." he muttered. "Might have to put this off for another time."

"Why?" I asked, avoiding eye contact with everyone. I busied myself with counting the polka dots on my socks.

"Vampires don't... hunger for other vampires the way we do humans," Caleb supplied, as if I was supposed to know what that meant. He shrugged when I looked at him, but was unapologetic. "We can feed off each other if there is need, but it is not as satisfying. Robbing Peter to pay Paul and all that. Humans replenish their blood supply, but vampires only keep what they consume. It doesn't go anywhere, unless we are injured or another drinks from us, and so drinking from each other will only benefit one, while the other has to go refuel, so to speak." It was the most I had heard Caleb say since arriving and I felt grateful for the knowledge, even if I didn't particularly understand it.

"Drinking directly from the source is... wonderful," Felicity said, a wistful smile on her face. "It is a very intimate thing. Honestly, the experience is kind of intoxicating. And the fact of the matter is, some blood is just better than others. What I like, Richard might not. And what tastes good to Richard may be less appealing to Kalene and so on."

"Of course, we don't drink from the source these days. It's far more humane and, quite honestly, simpler, to go to a local blood bar and just order a glass. And even animals, or as Caleb said, each other, can do in a pinch. But there is the idea that each person—vampire or no—has that someone special. Their Destined is what I've always heard it called. A soulmate, if you will. That person who is perfect for them. And should a vampire find their Destined, I have heard the blood is... on another level," Kalene spoke simply, as if she were telling me about the weather and not talking about the merits of eating a person versus drinking blood on tap.

"Okay," I said slowly, trying to wrap my brain around it. "But what does that—"

Richard sighed loudly, obviously tired of everyone beating around the bush. "Honestly," he said. "Levi wants a nibble."

Levi made a sound like he was choking and threw a dirty look at Richard. "Well," he muttered. "That's not a very nice way to put it."

"You want to bite me?" I blurted, pursing my lips. I said it matter-of-factly, surprised to find I wasn't embarrassed. I had never thought I would say those words, and given the circumstances, it had a whole other meaning for us. Of course, that thought had crossed my mind. He was a vampire, after all. I supposed he was just as likely as anyone to want that. And given the fact that I was the only human-ish person around, it made sense. It freaked me out how practical it all sounded.

"I won't," Levi assured me. "I just... might need to keep my distance until I can go feed. I didn't account for your human half to be so..."

"Dude, gross," Richard said, shaking his head. "Take it from me—don't say those words out loud."

Levi sighed. "I didn't expect to be so aware of your human side," he said simply.

I took half a step back. "Oh, I'm sorry," I said, frowning. I hoped I wasn't causing the other's distress, too. I supposed that was a potential risk of living with vampires, even if I *was* half myself. I didn't want to end up someone's lunch.

"Not I," Richard said. "You look like a snack, but I don't think I want a taste." He pushed off the wall and started to leave the room. "If it makes you feel any better - the only other one in this room who has thought about biting you is Caleb."

Levi shot Caleb a dark look, and he shrugged. "Can't help it, Levi. You and I fed together last time. It's been a minute, okay? Maybe we should all take a trip and get on the same page, so no one has a slip up and kills her, eh?"

I swallowed and glanced at everyone. I hadn't really thought about that. How much safer was I living here than out there?

"Much," Richard assured me before leaving the room.

"Caleb may be right," Kalene said, shaking her head. "I am not particularly hungry, but it would be a good idea. We can go out tonight and get what we need."

"From people?" I asked, a pit forming in my stomach.

"No," Levi answered quickly. "We rarely partake from the source. Like Kalene was saying, we have places we can go. Kind of like blood banks. There are some people who decide to donate blood to our... cause... and it keeps the number of attacks down. Some choose to donate directly, and that's their choice, but most just have blood drawn, get their compensation, and go on their way."

"Are you telling me," I began slowly, "that you guys are basically talking about going to the bar, but for blood?"

"Pretty much," Caleb said. "We go and see what's on tap, get what we need and sometimes bring a little extra emergency stash home, and we're good for a while. When you get old like us, you don't need to feed every day."

"We can bring you, if you'd like," Felicity said, a little mischief dancing in her eyes. She twirled her red hair around a finger, playing innocent, but I could see through her act.

"No," Levi answered abruptly.

"Why not?" I asked, finally looking at him. His eyes seemed a little darker than I recalled. "You said yourself that I should learn about vampire weaknesses. What better way than to walk into a room full of vampires?"

"Because you're not a vampire," Levi said, rubbing his temples. "It sounds like a bad idea."

"Well, I'm half vampire. And you said you can't sense a difference between me and a human, right? So, the other vampires will just think I'm a human." I felt incredibly stupid for pushing the issue, but I was curious more than anything. When would I ever have a chance to go somewhere like that again?

"And you don't think that's a problem? An entire room of vampires thinking you're human?" Levi folded his arms across his chest and regarded me, his jaw clenched.

"You said that humans go there and donate blood, so that's what they'll think is happening." I wasn't backing down, and he could see it in my face.

He threw his hands up and sighed. "Fine, but you stick with me. I don't want you out of my sight."

"We have to wait until dark," Kalene said. "For practicality's sake, the bar doesn't open until the sun goes down. Discretion is more at play than the sun being a bother, but I'll help you get ready later." She walked from the room, and Felicity followed. Caleb glanced at us and ambled from the room without saying a word. Levi and I stood facing each other.

"How bad is it?" I asked, twisting my fingers around each other anxiously.

"How bad is what?" Levi sighed, closing his eyes briefly, almost like he was in pain. Or like he thought I was insufferable.

I shifted from foot to foot. "How hard is it for you to be around me? With my human half all...existing?" If I was making him uncomfortable, I didn't want to make it worse by sticking around him.

"Don't worry, Phoebe. I'm not in danger of attacking you. I just hadn't anticipated being so close to you and being able to hear your blood and putting myself in that predicament, holding you like that…it was my fault. Please don't feel badly. You are in no danger when you are with me." He looked sincere, and I believed him completely.

"Well, maybe we can try this again tomorrow, you know, after you've gotten some blood. But maybe with a bit more instruction and a little less ass whooping?" I chuckled and rubbed the back of my neck.

"Oh, sure," Levi said with a smile. "But don't think you get off, just because this lesson is being put on hold. Come on, we've got other things to do." He grabbed my hand and dragged me from the room and up the stairs. We headed to his room, and I sat on the bed while he puttered around, looking for things.

And so, we sat on his bed, and he showed me various books and talked about vampires. I asked my questions where I had them and often that would lead us to another topic all over again. I learned that we were in a period of relative peace between humans and vampires. For centuries, the humans had been fighting against the supernatural creatures. Learning there were more than just vampires came to a bit of a shock to me, but then again, I supposed it made sense. The Council oversaw the world of vampires. They made the laws that most chose to follow. For the most part, vampires were just regular people with an… affliction they had to deal with. Not all of them were power hungry and not all of them wanted to go on murdering sprees, killing anyone and everyone in their path.

The Council consisted of some of the oldest vampires to date. Aldred, Masci, Idonea, and Nicola. Levi had the misfortune of working with them when they sought to take down Avatrice. He said they were a terrifying group, and, over the years, their views had grown skewed. He didn't think it would be long before someone decided to challenge them, but he hoped he wasn't around to see it.

"So," I began slowly, worried I was about to offend him. "Vampire fangs…."

Levi chuckled. "Where are mine?" he asked, cocking his head to the side. "They're there," he said simply. "It would be impractical to walk around all day with long, sharp teeth sticking out. Doesn't bode well for keeping on the down low."

"But," I said, shaking my head. "Where are they? Where do they go? How do they work?" I fired off my questions and Levi smiled.

He motioned me closer and, wide eyed, I obliged. He smiled, showing his teeth. They looked pretty normal to me. "My canines are sharper than average," he said. "I could do some damage even with them like this," he said, motioning. I suppose he was right. I touched my own canines, wondering for the first time if they were normal. Levi reached out and grabbed my chin gently in his fingers, turning my head slightly. "They do appear to be sharper than normal," he conceded. "But then again, even humans can have somewhat sharp canines."

"But where do yours go?" I asked. He dropped his hand from my face and sighed, leaning back slightly.

"Don't freak out," he told me, eyebrows pulled together. He watched me, as if waiting for me to do exactly that, though he had done nothing out of the ordinary. He opened his mouth again, showing off his teeth. Only this time, I watched as, blink and you'll miss it fast, his canines snapped out, twice as long. I gulped, blinking, and stared in rapt fascination. It was like one second he had regular teeth and in the span of a millisecond, he had fangs.

"Totally not freaking out," I whispered.

Levi chuckled. "We have pockets in our gums where the majority of the fang stays concealed. Within that pocket is a type of venom that we can release at will. So, there is no world in which I could accidentally release the venom, say, during a kiss." He reached out and placed two fingers on my neck. "This is where I would bite," he said conversationally. "If I were intending to drink, and you were willing, I would pierce the skin with my fangs and then release. If you were... ahem, unwilling, I would bite once, quickly, to pierce flesh and then a second time to clamp down. The venom is released to keep the human docile and content. So, it is not an unpleasant experience unless the vampire makes it so."

His fingers were cool on my skin and he was leaning so close, talking softly. I knew he was talking hypothetically, but I couldn't help but imagine us in such a situation. Given my only experience with being bitten was with Avatrice, I had a hard time imagining it being enjoyable in any way.

We were leaning close together, his hand still on my neck, my pulse jumping erratically, when Kalene knocked on the door. We sprang away from each other as she entered almost guiltily. When I cast a nervous glance at Levi, his fangs were concealed once more, as if they had never been.

"Time to get ready!" She said cheerfully, either unaware or unbothered.

Levi climbed off the bed and looked down at himself. He wore dark jeans and a dark t-shirt. "I'm ready," he said dryly. "But I'll leave you ladies to it. And Kalene...don't go overboard." He exited, and Kalene shook her head.

"Even though it's a blood bar, we still want to look good. You wouldn't go to a club dressed just any old way. And I would hate for you to stand out and draw attention." She looked a little like she had a plan going on behind her innocent eyes, and I wasn't sure how much I trusted her. "Shall we?" She motioned to the bathroom, and I followed her, a little reluctantly. I had a feeling she was going to have a fun time playing makeover, and I was going to feel like a life-sized Barbie doll by the time she was finished.

Chapter Twelve
Phoebe

I was right. The girl looking back at me in the mirror hardly looked like me. Her green eyes seemed bigger somehow, her lips fuller. Her hair was perfectly placed, each curl resting intentionally. There were no haphazard strands or loose pieces; I think she used a whole can of hairspray on me. My hair was done up, pinned to perfection, cascading down my back in a half up-do. My body was adorned in a deep midnight blue dress that Kalene claimed complimented my eyes, but I thought she had two other things in mind she was trying to compliment.

I had never put something on my body that was so low cut. But she assured me there would be no slips in this dress. It hugged every curve and came down to just above my knees, a small slit hinting at upper thigh. And she had forced me to put on a pair of black knee-high boots, assuring me they went so perfectly with the dress I simply had to wear them. She swiped red across my lips, dusted my collarbone with a light rose scented perfume, and grinned, stepping back to look at me.

"Beautiful," she said, fairly bouncing on the balls of her feet.

"I don't look... slutty?" I asked, smoothing my hands down the front of the dress. "And my neck isn't too... I don't know, exposed?"

"Nonsense!" Kalene said, waving my concerns away. "Trust me, there will be women wearing a lot less than that there. Besides, you are gorgeous. You should show it off sometimes. Now, I must go get ready, but if he's ready to go, tell Levi that I'll meet you guys there."

She left the room, and I just took a few moments staring at myself in the mirror. My black lined eyes watered, and I blinked hard to keep the tears at bay. I looked so much like my mother with my hair placed just so. I forced a laugh. Mom never would have worn something like this. I recalled the last time I had gone out and shuddered. The party where everything went to shit. If I hadn't gone, would I be in a house full of vampires now? If I hadn't gone, would Angie still be here? I bit the inside of my cheek to keep from crying and turned away from the mirror abruptly.

I turned and left the room, grabbing the little red purse Kalene had loaned me, tossing my wallet and phone inside, and the tube of lipstick she had used on me. I stepped out of Levi's room and caught Felicity's eyes. She scowled at me and turned, almost stomping down the stairs. She was in a little green number that really accentuated her figure. She looked flawless. I followed her downstairs, going in search of Levi. A low whistle sounded, and I turned. Richard and Caleb sat at the kitchen table, both wearing jeans and plain white shirts. "Hot mama," Richard cackled.

Caleb elbowed him hard. "You look great," he said, rolling his eyes. "Kalene loves playing dress up, doesn't she?"

I chuckled and rubbed my bare arm. "Yeah, you could say that. I don't even feel like myself, honestly. I'm definitely a jeans and t-shirt kind of girl."

"You look.... wow." The words came from behind me, and I turned to find Levi in the doorway, watching me. His eyes traveled slowly from the top of my head to my toes, and I shivered. "You should fit right in." He cleared his throat and held his arm out to me. "Shall we?"

I reached out and took his arm, and he pulled me from the kitchen quickly. "Levi?" I asked. "Is something wrong?"

He shook his head, casting a sidelong glance at me. "I wish Kalene had toned it down a little."

I frowned. "Oh... it's too much. I knew it. I'll go change..." I started to pull away from him, but he stopped me.

"No," he said. "I meant it—you look beautiful. But I worry that you won't exactly be inconspicuous. You'll draw attention, so just... stick close to me, okay?" He patted my hand, and we walked out the front door. The night was warm, and I hoped it stayed that way. Kalene had not been so kind as to provide a jacket with this ensemble. "We'll take the car with Richard and Caleb if they would hurry up and get out here. Kalene and Felicity will take Kalene's car. She parks it out back."

"Oh," I said, as he opened the passenger door for me. I carefully climbed in, and he went around to the driver's side. "Is there anything I should know before we get there?" I asked.

Levi glanced at me, his eyes lingering a little too long on my neck. "Just stick close and don't talk to anyone if you can help it."

The back doors opened, and Richard and Caleb slid in. "Exiled to the back," Caleb sighed. "Let's get this train wreck going," he added, patting the back of Levi's seat. With that, Levi fired up the car, and we headed toward town. The ride was silent most of the way and I was too busy trying to keep my thoughts innocuous and quiet to care.

Until I recognized the road we were on. My heart skipped a beat, and Levi glanced at me. "Phoebe?" he asked. "You're white as a ghost. What's wrong? Do I need to pull over?"

"No!" The word came out sharper than I intended. I looked at my lap and my hands were shaking. "Just drive, please."

"Ahhh," Richard said, glancing out the window. "This is where your parents died." My eyes travelled out the window, finding the very spot the car had skidded to a stop after hitting Avatrice.

I heard a soft thud of Caleb punching Richard in the shoulder. "Shut up," he muttered. "That's a little insensitive."

Levi drove faster.

The building he pulled up to looked like any old bar. Neon signs in the window, several beat-up cars parked out front. We all climbed out, and Levi quickly walked to my side. Caleb flanked me on the other side, and Richard walked lazily behind us. We walked inside and a man by the front door looked at us. He quirked an eyebrow and glanced at me. "She's with us," Levi said gruffly.

The man nodded. "You know what you're doing, sweetheart?" He directed his question at me, but didn't take his eyes off the boys.

I swallowed. "Yes, sir," I mumbled. "I know."

He sighed and finally looked at me. "Don't make a mess of her. She's cute." He waved us into the rest of the bar without another word, and we all moved as a unit. Levi found a table in the back of the bar, in the corner, and we all slid in, me against the wall, Levi beside me, Caleb across from me, and Richard in the aisle seat.

I could feel Levi's leg pressed against mine and chanced a peek at him, but he wasn't looking at me. He seemed very tense, but the other two boys seemed at ease. They glanced over their menus, talking amongst themselves quietly. I leaned over. "Don't you need to order something?" I whispered.

He glanced at me. "I will," he responded. I wasn't sure if he was anxious because of me just being there or because he didn't want me to see him drinking blood. I wasn't sure how I would feel about the whole thing when it was actually taking place. For now, it seemed like some far-off thing.

A woman who couldn't have been older than nineteen walked over with a pad of paper and pen. "What'll it be?" she asked, pen poised. She looked at the four of us, her eyes lingering on me a little long. "Three reds and a white?" she asked, eyebrow quirked.

Caleb and Richard ordered, but I wasn't listening. I was watching the girl. She looked so young. Was she human? Vampire? Like me, and somewhere in between? She watched me watch her, never breaking eye contact. I squirmed, finally dropping my eyes. "Levi?" I asked, realizing he still had yet to order anything.

He waved his hand, not looking at the waitress. His eyes swept the room slowly. "I'll have what he's having," he muttered, flicking his fingers toward Caleb. He finally glanced at me again. "Do you want something to drink? Alcohol, soda, water?"

I looked at the table of vampires and thought about the fact that I was in a bar full of vampires, and the idea that my life was spiraling out of control crossed my mind. "Jack and Coke," I said. "Please."

The waitress scribbled it down and left without another word. "Yes," Richard said, leaning across the table. "She was a vampire."

Kalene and Felicity chose that moment to find us both looking stunning. I felt pale in comparison. Felicity forced Richard and Caleb to scoot over, and Kalene pulled a chair over. The waitress returned and took their orders, glancing at me again. When she came back, she had five opaque glasses and one transparent. She set the drinks in front of everyone and, once again, I found her looking at me. But she left without a word, and I looked at the drink in front of me. There was a napkin stuck to the bottom to soak up the condensation from the glass, but I noticed some writing peeking out from beneath the glass. I lifted my drink, took a sip, and looked down at the handwritten note.

A laugh burst out, and I covered my mouth with my hand to silence the sound. The entire table looked at me, and I shook my head. "If I feel like I'm in danger, just order a Bloody Mary," I said, taking a big swig of my drink. "That's hilarious." I tried not to think about the fact that the others were drinking blood out of glasses all around me and flagged the waitress down. I ordered another jack and coke and some cheese sticks. She smiled.

I was three drinks in when Levi stopped me from flagging the waitress down for another. "I think that's enough," he whispered. I looked at him and blinked slowly. I was feeling good, but not too good. I was still aware I was in a room full of vampires, but it seemed a little less scary now, somehow. Levi was leaning close, his arm across the back of the booth, and I could smell his familiar scent. I sighed and leaned back, bumping his arm.

"Fine," I said. "You're right." If I continued on in the same fashion, I would likely end up doing something I would regret. Or I would end up on the floor.

He grunted his approval, and the waitress came and cleared away all of our glasses. She looked at me, and then at Levi, and then back at me. But she didn't speak. When she was gone, I pursed my lips. "I have to use the restroom," I said quietly.

Kalene stood. "I'll take you," she said, holding out her hand. Levi climbed out of the booth and helped me out. "We'll be right back."

"Thank you," Levi said, as she led me through the crowd of people. Several turned to look at us, but no one spoke.

When we got to the bathroom, Kalene checked to make sure we were alone, and then grabbed my shoulders. "You've got to get it together, girl," she said. "I can feel all of your emotions, and I know you've been drinking and are feeling a lot of things, but damn. You're drowning me."

I flinched. "Sorry."

Chapter Thirteen
Levi

I watched the girls walk off to the bathroom before scanning the room thoroughly. I hadn't thought about the possibility of Avatrice being here until we had already walked in the door. But now that Phoebe was here and tipsy, I was feeling protective of her. If something happened here, it would be my fault for allowing her to come. I scowled.

"What's your problem?" Felicity asked.

I shook my head and glanced at her. She was sitting back in the booth, her arms crossed over her chest as she regarded me. "Nothing," I lied.

She scoffed and looked away. "Okay," she said unconvincingly. It was obvious she didn't believe me. It startled me when she kept talking a moment later. "I'm not stupid," she said quietly. "Can we talk?"

I looked at her, surprised. "Yeah," I said, standing. I knew Kalene would get Phoebe back to the table safely. Felicity and I walked off toward the dance floor where the music was a little louder to give us the semblance of privacy. It was hard to have private conversations when Richard was around. "What's up?" I asked, turning to face her. She looked sad.

"I'm not stupid," she said again. "I can see you like her."

I blinked. "Who?" I asked, fairly sure I already knew the answer.

"Phoebe," Felicity said. "You look at her like she's... everything you've ever wanted. We've known each other for so many years, I

97

can't begin to count them. You've known her a couple days and she just... takes my place."

I sighed and pulled her into a hug. "Fee," I said softly. "I love you like a sister. I always have and I always will. I would do anything to protect you, just as I would Kalene and Richard and Caleb."

"But you know that's not what I want," Felicity said, hugging me back tightly. "I really care about you, Levi."

"And I care about you too, but I know it is not in the way you want it to be. It would be unfair of me to lead you on, to make you think we could be something more than what we are. I'm sorry, Felicity. I'm so sorry that you want more from me, but I just can't... I can't give you what you want." I felt like an asshole, even though I was trying my best to be gentle. Was it ever easy breaking someone's heart?

Felicity pulled away from me and sniffled, turning away so I wouldn't see the tears in her eyes. "I know," she whispered. "I've known since I first saw you two together. It's like... almost like you were just made for each other. You guys move and act like you've known each other for ages. There's a chemistry there that we've never had." She shook her head and glanced back at me; her eyes glassy. "I hope she can give you what you want. I would never want to see you hurt, Levi."

I pulled her to me for another hug. "Thank you," I said softly. It was Felicity's way of being nice. She was "giving me up" and giving her blessing for me to pursue Phoebe. I glanced toward the table where Phoebe was sliding into the booth a little clumsily. Was that what I wanted? Did I want to pursue something more with Phoebe?

The answer wasn't so simple.

Felicity gave me a kiss on the cheek and motioned to the table. "Come on," she said. "They'll be wondering what's taking so long. And Levi?"

I glanced at her; eyebrow quirked. "Yes?"

"Spend some time with her. Just the two of you in a way that doesn't have to do with vampires and halflings and Avatrice for just a moment. Let her see you, the person." Felicity shrugged. "Take a chance." With that, she walked off to the table, leaving me standing there a second too long. I followed silently and got to the table just as she was taking her seat.

"Phoebe?" I asked, uncertainly. She looked up at me, her smile making my stomach do a little flip. "Can we...talk?"

She cocked her head to the side but began climbing from the booth. "Sure," she said. "Is everything okay?" She glanced at the others, but when she saw they looked just as confused, she looked back at me. The only one not looking at me, in fact, was Felicity. She already knew. I'd have to do something nice for her, I thought. Get her flowers or something.

"Yeah," I said quickly when I realized I hadn't responded. "Just... come here a second." I held my hand out to her, and she took it slowly, cautiously. It actually pleased me to see that. The alcohol hadn't completely muddled her brain.

We walked back to the spot Felicity and I had been a moment ago. Now that I had her here, somewhat alone, I didn't know what to say. We stood there for a few beats of silence, and she shifted her weight nervously. "Did something happen?" she asked quietly.

I decided it was best to just get it all out there and deal with the consequences later. "Well," I began slowly. "I would like to get to know you better, Phoebe. But I want to get to know you as you, the person. Not you the dhampir. And I want you to know me, the person. I have felt this... unexplainable connection with you since the moment I first met you. I couldn't explain why I came over to you at the party that day. Maybe it was fate, or maybe it was something else. I don't know. I just know that I have a strong desire to know you better and... well...and see where things go with...us." I faltered at the end, but still managed a weak smile. She was staring at me, almost like she was trying to process what I had just said. I was about to open my mouth and probably make things a whole lot worse, when she spoke.

"Okay." She said it softly, but firmly. "I'm glad I'm not crazy." She chuckled and ran her hands down the front of her dress, brushing imaginary lint off the fabric. "I thought it was just because my emotions have been all over the place and I've felt... alone and needy. But I've felt a connection with you, too. And I'm willing to see what happens. I just..." She stopped herself and clamped her lips shut.

"Just what?" I asked, frowning. "I've been around a while. There isn't much you can say to upset me or surprise me, really."

She sighed. "I just don't want either of us to get hurt if it turns out things aren't what they seem between us. I don't know if it's the liquor talking or not, but I worry that I'm just seeking comfort. I'm worried this is all an illusion, and it's going to shatter any minute. My world has been... turned upside down, Levi. A few days ago, I didn't know vampires existed. And now I live with five of them. I'm standing in a vampire bar, talking to a vampire, and I'm worried I'm losing my mind."

"Dance with me," I blurted. When she looked startled, I pressed on. "Let's just take a moment to be you and me. Let everything else fall away and let's do something anyone can do, arguably." I held my hand out to her. "One dance."

She hesitated a moment before taking my hand in hers. I walked her into the center of the dancefloor, ignoring the eyes on my back coming from my family. I swung her into my arms, and she looked up at me, her green eyes troubled. I sighed and brushed a loose curl off her face. "What?" she asked, blushing.

"You look beautiful," I said quietly, swaying to the music as it eased into a slow dance. She felt right in my arms, like that was where she was meant to be. It was crazy, I thought, the way she made me feel. She made me feel like I wasn't a monster, like I stood a chance at living a somewhat normal life. She made me feel like anything was possible.

"Thank you," Phoebe said softly, ducking her head.

"I'm sorry," I said, realizing that while I was enjoying her company, she was grieving. Or, rather, trying not to grieve for my benefit. "I know that you've been through a lot in such a short amount of time. And I want you to know that you don't always have to keep a brave face on. You *are* allowed to grieve for your friend and for the life you've left behind. But I also want you to know that you have a family with us. All of us will be there for you when you need us and you are welcome to stay for as long as you need or want, even if that's forever." It occurred to me that I didn't know what the life span was for an average dhampir.

"I thought this was supposed to be just us," Phoebe said, her eyes brimming with tears. "You know, two normal people having a normal dance in the middle of a normal bar."

I sighed. "You're right," I said, resting my forehead against hers. "I apologize. I let myself get carried away." Again.

"Thank you, though. For everything. I can't imagine going through all of this without you." She cleared her throat, her cheeks turning slightly pink. "All of you."

We slowly spun around the dancefloor, dodging the others who chose to join us. I asked her about her life before and was surprised to find that she not only had her job at the diner, but went to college. It disappointed me to learn she had already missed a few of her classes due to the circumstances. "Do you plan to go back? To work or school?" I asked her. I hadn't given it much thought and wondered if it was just one more thing for her to grieve, the normal part of her life.

She shrugged. "I don't know. My mind isn't really on either of those things, unfortunately. I think I may have to take some time off, maybe from both. Things are just so...crazy." She leaned a little closer to me and I held her a little tighter. "I just don't know if I can really afford to skip out on work."

"Phoebe," I said quietly, slowly coming to the realization that we were still standing together but had stopped dancing. "You know we can take care of you if you need to take some time. We've been around for a while. We can financially support your... sabbatical." I chuckled quietly. I felt anxious as soon as the words left my mouth, worried I had crossed a line. She wasn't someone who *needed* me to take care of her.

Phoebe's arms tightened around me, and she pressed her cheek against my chest. I realized too late that she was crying. I pressed my hand to the back of her head and just held her tightly, not saying a word until she managed to calm herself. I wasn't sure if it was the good or bad kind of tears. She looked up at me and I brushed a stray tear off her face with my thumb, my hand resting against the side of her neck. I could feel her pulse jumping beneath my hand, but it didn't bother me. She looked at me with an unreadable expression, and I suddenly wished I had Richard's abilities. I could have forced her to tell me what was on her mind, but I didn't dare. I wouldn't use her that way. My chest tightened, and I swallowed hard. I wanted so much in that moment. Holding her was enough for now, but I wanted more. I wanted to hold her and kiss her and make her forget about all her worries and fears. But I didn't want to push. I didn't want to scare her, and furthermore, she had been drinking. She was, perhaps, being so open and vulnerable with me because of it. My hand dropped from her throat, and she sighed softly. In relief?

"We should get back," I said quietly. "The others are probably wondering what's taking so long. And besides, we must not forget, this *is* a vampire infested blood bar and you *are* half human."

Phoebe cleared her throat and stepped back from me, shaking her head almost imperceptibly. I frowned. "Right," she said, brushing past me. She walked back to the table at an easy pace, yet I still had the feeling she was running from something. Perhaps running from me. It would be hard for me to blame her.

Kalene visibly jerked when Phoebe arrived at the table, which only worsened my mood. Whatever Phoebe was feeling, she was feeling it heavily if it was pushing into Kalene so suddenly. Richard's face twisted into a scowl as I slid into the booth beside Phoebe and he threw glares at the two of us, but kept his mouth shut. I put some effort into quieting my mind and sent him an apologetic look.

Chapter Fourteen
Phoebe

I was so confused. I felt angry and sad, of course, but feelings of disappointment pushed into my heart. I snuck a look at Levi out of the corner of my eye. What had I been thinking? I had been thinking we were having a moment, growing closer. And that was my first mistake. A relationship was out of the question between us. He was a vampire, and I was a...a... halfling. I didn't hardly even know what that meant. And besides that, we barely knew each other.

But I wanted that to change.

The others talked quietly amongst themselves, but I did not supply anything to the conversation. I was too wrapped up in my own mind. I felt horribly guilty for feeling *anything* for Levi after what had just happened to Angie. I missed her terribly and tears pricked the backs of my eyes, but I refused to let them fall again. I had already allowed myself to come undone in Levi's arms. I couldn't fall apart now. Not again. I wondered what had happened once we called the police. Had they arrived and found Angie? Taken her away? Did her parents know what happened to her?

I looked up as the others rose from the table. Levi turned to me and held his hand out to help me from the booth. I ignored it and climbed out on my own. I brushed imaginary lint from my dress, which suddenly seemed so much shorter than it had back at the house. I turned to Kalene and Felicity. "I'm going to run to the ladies' room before we go."

"I'll come with you," Kalene said brightly.

I held up a hand. "I can handle it," I said. "Thanks though."

I turned on my heel and walked to the bathroom. I closed the door behind me and made sure no one else was in the room before letting the tears fall. I was shaking and crying, trying to keep it quiet lest I attract attention. I looked at myself in the mirror and cringed. I looked a mess. I sniffled and ran the cold water, splashing some onto my face. I looked at myself in the mirror again, swiping my fingers beneath my eyes to remove the little smudges of eyeliner.

I heard the bathroom door open and sighed, pushing off the sink. I had spent enough time away from the others. I turned and felt my blood run cold, my heart lodging in my throat. A strangled cry fell from my lips as I realized the gravity of the situation I had put myself in.

"Hello, little one." Avatrice smiled slowly, the lock on the bathroom door clicking quietly. "What are you doing in here, all alone? Where are your bodyguards?" His eyes scanned the room, as if he expected them to all be hiding in there with me. But I was alone, and it was my own stupid fault. I took a step back, aware that I had no way to escape other than through the door he blocked.

"What do you want?" I asked, my voice coming out much softer than I had meant it to.

He continued to smile at me, his eyes traveling the length of my body slowly. "You'll know in time," he said simply. "I have seen that you've made yourself some new friends since we last met. How long has it been?" He waved his hand, as if to stop me from responding. "Of course, if I had known what you were the night of the... car accident, I would never have let you go, and we wouldn't be here now." Avatrice sighed and took a step closer to me. "You see... I wasn't after you that night. In fact, I barely paid you any mind. I was after your filthy parents." His voice turned into a growl, and I shivered. He took another step closer. "Your father was one of the ones responsible for putting me in prison for a century. I killed him for his transgressions and killed the woman when she interfered. I was crazed with bloodlust... I didn't even realize she was human at first, but she tasted so sweet."

My hands clenched into fists, and my throat burned. I wanted to hurt him. I wanted to kill him. "It was only after I had killed them both that I noticed you. But you were unconscious and not a threat to me. I didn't know who you were, and I didn't care at the time. But later, once I had calmed, I came to the realization that Bradley had gone and done what he put me away for. All my research.... all my attempts to create the perfect race of dhampirs... and he had gone and made one of his own!" Avatrice laughed harshly and suddenly lunged forward. It was a 'blink and you'll miss it' kind of moment, and it was a shock to feel his hands on me. My head cracked against the tile wall of the bathroom as he loomed over me, his chest heaving. "What a fucking hypocrite," he snarled, grabbing me by the throat.

I clawed at his hand; my eyes wide. Was he going to kill me? I flashed back to the last time we met like this and thrashed. I was *not* going to let him bite me again. I knew if he bit me, I might not get away this time. I didn't know if he knew it, but I had an advantage.

Richard! I screamed his name as loud as I could in my mind.

Avatrice must have heard something or sensed it, because suddenly he was gone, and I was on the floor of the women's bathroom. The bathroom door was slightly ajar, and I knew he must have fled from it. I supposed it wasn't in his best interest to have a fight with a Coven of vampires in the women's restroom of the blood bar. Probably smart.

Richard, Levi, and Caleb burst into the women's bathroom. I was breathing shallowly, my hand at my throat, eyes closed, but I heard them enter. "He's gone," I said quietly.

"Who?" Caleb demanded. I opened my eyes to see him looking in each stall, fangs extended.

"Avatrice."

Levi scowled. "He was here?" he demanded, opening the bathroom door and peering out. "I never should have let you come out with us."

Richard held out a hand to me and pulled me to my feet. He brushed my hair back and inspected my neck. "No bite," he said. "Just some bruising."

Levi glared at the floor. "We need to leave," he said. "Let's go, Phoebe." He held out his hand to me and I sighed, taking it reluctantly.

"I did learn something," I whispered.

The three men looked at me as we left the bathroom. We met back up with the girls and they flanked me, pushing the guys away. They looked ready to kill and everyone gave us a wide berth. "You did?" Caleb asked. "What? What did he say?"

I recapped the events of our encounter quickly, not wanting to relive it so soon. Everyone was quiet when I had finished, and no one spoke until we were out of the bar and standing at the cars. "I'll take Phoebe home," Levi said. "Do you two need a ride?" he asked, looking at Richard and Caleb.

They shared a knowing look and shook their heads. "No, we'll take them," Felicity said. She sent me a look that I imagined I was supposed to understand, but I was too tired to try to figure it out. I climbed into the passenger seat of Levi's car without a word and waited for him to get behind the wheel. We sat in silence for several uncomfortable minutes. I was patiently waiting for him to yell at me. To scold me for going off on my own when I knew it was dangerous.

"I'm sorry," Levi finally said. "I shouldn't have let you come. You could have stayed at the house with Kalene. It would have been safer. It was irresponsible of me to bring you here - stupid. I am so sorry to put you in danger."

I looked at him in the dark, his profile illuminated by the dash lights. "No, I don't blame you, Levi," I said softly. "I wanted to come.

It was irresponsible of me to think I could waltz in there and have nothing happen. And really, nothing *did* happen. I'm okay."

We pulled up to the house, and Levi sighed. He turned to face me in the moonlight and reached out, his fingers brushing across my neck and the bruises Avatrice had left behind. "I wouldn't say nothing." He sounded frustrated. "I should have sensed him there. I don't know how he got past all of us."

"He was well shielded in a room *full* of vampires," I said softly. "And you said he was fast. I didn't realize how fast. It was like he knew I had called for help and was just... gone. But he had to have left through the door—it was open. I just never saw him go."

Levi growled softly. "I should have been able to catch him."

I reached out and touched his arm lightly. "Stop," I whispered. "Levi, it's not your fault. Don't blame yourself for it, please. I'm okay. And I came away with it, at least knowing *why* he killed my parents. That was something I didn't have before. So, I guess, in some way, it gave me a little bit of peace."

Levi looked down at my hand on his arm and slowly lifted his hand up to cover mine. It was cool to the touch, but not unpleasant. "Phoebe..." he said, sounding troubled. "I don't want to bring you further into this...world than you are willing to go."

"Well, I am pretty in it now. This man killed my parents, Levi. And now he wants me for... something. I can't imagine it's good. He is the reason my best friend is dead. I am in this. I have to see it through to the end, whatever that may be. And I am so thankful to have met you and your family. You have no idea." I was telling the truth. Whether this ended in my tragic death or Avatrice's, I had to see it through. For my parents and for Angie. I would not let her death go unnoticed. Unavenged.

Levi sighed heavily and climbed from the car. He walked around and opened my car door for me, and I climbed out. We stood there for several moments, not speaking. His hand rested on the roof of the car, his other hand in his pocket. I looked up at him, not sure what to do. Part of me wanted to slip past him and head inside, but part of me wanted to stay there with him and see where this was going.

I waited.

Levi was watching me, like he was waiting to see what *I* would do. After what felt like an eternity, he finally moved. I stepped away from the car and he shut the door with a thud. "We should probably get inside," he said, placing his hand gently on my back, steering me toward the house. He glanced around us rapidly, watching for Avatrice, no doubt.

I nodded. "Yeah..." We both walked to the door, and he pushed it open. Everyone else was already inside and Caleb came looking when the front door opened and closed. He glanced at the two of us, his eyes lingering on the bruises on my neck, and motioned to the kitchen.

"Kalene is making popcorn if you want some. She and Felicity are going to pop in a movie." The offer was directed at me, and I forced a smile.

"Cool. I'm just gonna go get changed into some pajamas really quick, but I'll be back." I threw a glance over my shoulder at Levi before I headed up the stairs and to his bedroom. I slipped out of the boots and sighed. It felt nice to be out of them. I stripped the dress and pulled an oversized shirt over my head like a nightgown and went to the bathroom to wash my face. When I exited back into the bedroom, Levi was there, pacing. His hands were behind his back, and he looked lost in thought. If he wasn't a vampire, I might have thought he hadn't heard me enter. I watched him for a moment before stepping closer.

"Levi?"

He glanced at me and frowned. "Yes, sorry. Didn't mean to bother you. Are you going to watch a movie with Felicity and Kalene?"

I shrugged. "Maybe. Might be nice to do something normal. You know, pretend like everything is okay." I felt self-conscious in my pajamas and tugged at the hem of my shirt, which seemed a lot shorter than I originally thought. I watched his eyes follow the movement and linger on my exposed legs for a moment before he looked away.

"Okay. I'll leave you to it then. Please let me know when you are finished, so I may go to sleep." Levi turned away from me and sat on the edge of the bed. I frowned, realizing that we were commandeering his sleeping space while I was here, in his room.

"Please, don't wait up on our account. If you need to sleep, take the bed, Levi. I can sleep on the couch tonight. I really don't want to put you out or anything. Besides, if I'm going to be staying here, we probably need to come up with something a little more permanent, anyway. You can't sleep on the couch forever." I walked over and sat on the edge of the bed with him, tucking my legs beneath me.

He glanced at me. "Perhaps we can discuss sleeping arrangements in the morning. But thank you, Phoebe. I don't like the idea of you sleeping on the couch, though. Especially not after tonight." He glanced at my neck and grimaced. "It doesn't hurt?"

I shook my head. "Not at all. Don't worry about me so much, Levi. I'm a big girl."

"But still. I could never forgive myself if something were to happen to you in the safety of your own home here with us. I will stay here tonight while you watch your movie, but you will wake me when you come to bed, and I will move to the couch." He spoke like that was final and there was no room for argument.

I nodded, even though I knew that was unlikely. "Sure." I stood and turned toward the door, but I hesitated. Quickly, before I changed my mind, I turned back to him and leaned down, pressing a gentle kiss to his cheek. "Thank you," I said softly, leaning down to look into his eyes. "For everything you've done. It's made this... awful time a little less awful."

The smallest of smiles crossed his face, and, with that, I headed downstairs to find the girls. We settled ourselves down with bowls of popcorn and found a movie we all agreed on. It was a romantic comedy and just what I needed to end the night. I ignored the fact that Kalene kept throwing glances in my direction and tried to focus on the movie, but my mind kept drifting to the vampire upstairs with the blue eyes.

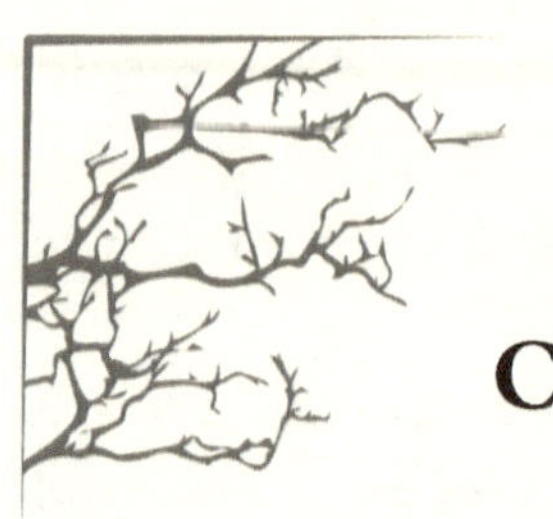

Chapter Fifteen
Phoebe

Kalene and Felicity said their goodnights and headed off to bed after the movie was over. I sat on the couch in the dark for several minutes before climbing to my feet. I checked to make sure the windows and doors were locked and made my way upstairs. Levi was asleep when I entered the room and I sighed softly. I didn't want to wake him; he looked so peaceful. So, instead, I brushed my teeth and climbed into the bed beside him. I tucked myself beneath the covers and curled up, getting cozy. I drifted off to sleep easier than I had anticipated.

I awoke sometime in the morning. The sun was filtering in through the curtains and I could hear Levi's steady breathing beside me. In fact, I could feel his strong arms around me. I looked over my shoulder and found I was snuggled against his chest, and he was holding me. A smile flitted across my face. I felt... safe. I sighed and carefully climbed out of bed and padded across the room to the bathroom. I climbed into the shower, washing the hairspray from the night before out and relaxing beneath the warm water. When I returned to the bedroom, Levi was awake. He looked at me and frowned.

"You didn't wake me up," he said simply.

"No," I said. "I felt badly, so I just slept beside you. I hope that's okay." I frowned, thinking he may not have wanted that. "I hope I didn't offend you. You just looked so peaceful, and I didn't want to disturb you."

He smiled. "Not at all. Thank you for the thoughtfulness. I hope I didn't disturb you in my sleep."

"Nope," I said. "It was fine." I didn't tell him about our accidental morning cuddle session and turned to my bag on the floor. "Shower is free if you need it." I grabbed some clothes and watched him head to the bathroom. While he showered, I dressed and headed downstairs. I found Richard in the living room, reading the newspaper.

"Morning," he said without looking up. "Sleep well?"

"Well enough," I responded, sitting beside him. "How much do you know about Avatrice?" I asked suddenly.

He did glance up then. "Not much," he said. "Just what I've heard from Levi."

I sighed and sat back on the couch, folding my arms across my chest. "I'm going to have to learn more about him. I have to start going on the offensive - find out what he's all about and I might be able to figure out what he wants with me."

"I'll see what I can find," Richard said easily. "Caleb is good with books. Perhaps he can find something as well."

"I didn't mean... thank you," I said, surprised. Richard held a hand up to stop me. I nodded in understanding and went in search of breakfast.

I was eating a bowl of cereal when Levi emerged. He walked into the kitchen, not paying me any attention at first. He moved around, as if looking for something, before finally sitting across from me, empty-handed. He folded his hands in front of him and regarded me for a moment. I lifted an eyebrow in question. "Are you up for a fight?"

I snorted. "Do you mean, am I ready to get my ass beat? I suppose."

Levi chuckled. "I'll go easier on you this time. You need to learn the basics before I just throw stuff at you. Finish your breakfast and we can head out to the backyard to get started." He stood and walked off, and I frowned.

Felicity and Caleb emerged, looking like they had just rolled out of bed. "Morning," Caleb grunted. Felicity halfway lifted her hand in greeting. They both sat at the table heavily.

"Rough night?" I asked.

Felicity yawned. "I'm not much of a morning person," she admitted. "I heard Levi mention taking you outside. Is he planning to torture you?"

"If by torture you mean teach me to fight, then yes," I said with a chuckle. I was almost surprised she was even talking to me. But something about last night had changed. She seemed friendlier than she had before.

"Better not keep your teacher waiting," Caleb said with a smile. "Don't let him run you ragged."

I stood and rinsed my bowl in the sink, bade them farewell, and headed outside. It was beautiful. The morning was crisp, but not cold, and the sun was beginning to warm the earth. I took a moment to just take it all in, looking at the trees that lined the property, the perfectly trimmed grass, the red rose bushes along the back of the house. And then I saw Levi standing in the middle of it all, looking like some kind of avenging angel in the morning light. I remembered he had said that sunlight wouldn't kill him, but it would be uncomfortable, and I frowned, making my way over.

"Are you sure you don't want to do this inside?" I asked, motioning around us.

Levi shrugged. "I'll let you know if I need to go in." He reached out and pulled me closer. "Now, let's begin." I swallowed hard, my heart thumping painfully in my chest. It was all the more embarrassing knowing that he could hear it. I could only hope he didn't think too much about it.

He went over various stances and basic throws. I wasn't sure I would be able to pull any of them off, but I supposed it was handy knowledge to have. He talked about throwing punches and knocking your opponents' feet out from under them. Weak spots and good places to aim for maximum damage. I was covered in sweat several hours later and he still looked perfect. I glared at him with resentment. He was kicking my ass without even laying a hand on me.

"Are you ready to try a practice run?" Levi asked, rubbing the back of his neck. He winced slightly, and I frowned, but he waved away my concern.

"Do I have a choice?" I asked wryly.

He chuckled. "Do one run through and we can go inside and rest."

I blew out a sigh and got into a fighting stance, waiting for him to attack. He moved at less than half speed at first, throwing light punches and halfhearted grabs. As I got better at avoiding those, he sped it up a little. It was harder to avoid and escape, but I did okay. Then he surprised me with a lunge. He caught me around the waist, and it startled me so much, I lost my balance and we both went to the ground. His hand went behind my head to keep me from bouncing it against the ground and he cradled me gently, so the fall wasn't that bad. I was breathing hard and covered in sweat and he was poised above me, our bodies almost touching, his knee on the grass between my legs, one hand behind my head, the other near my shoulder on the ground. He looked down at me, and I couldn't help but admire him. He was the total package, I thought. Handsome, kind, strong, and protective. I lifted my hand slowly, giving him time to move or stop me, but he didn't. My hand rested gently along his jaw, cradling his cheek.

"Phoebe..." He sighed, leaning into my touch slightly. It sounded like a warning, but I ignored it. I lifted my other hand and brushed it through his hair, scraping my nails lightly against his scalp. "Phoebe," he said again.

"Levi." I wasn't sure what I was doing, what *we* were doing. This was a bad idea, all of it. It was insane to be here in the dirt like this, with him. Someone was hunting me for reasons unknown. I was only half human, he was all vampire. We barely knew each other. Yet I didn't squirm when he moved closer. Our bodies were pressed together, and I knew he could feel my heart beating rapidly. He looked at me, eyes scanning my face. Looking for something.

I don't know what he saw there, but I didn't turn away or stop him when his lips came down on mine. His fingers kneaded the back of my neck gently, and my fingers curled loosely into his hair. It felt like electricity sizzled through me. It was gentle and sweet and -

Levi pulled away abruptly as the back door opened and Caleb poked his head out. "How's it.... oh...." He snickered, looking at the two of us. "Didn't know it was *that* kind of training."

Levi climbed to his feet and helped me up. "Stop it," he muttered. He glanced at me, and I blushed. "Take a break," he said. "The sun is... bothering me." He walked away quickly, and I frowned at his back as he walked away.

I felt frustrated, especially when, later that day, Levi sent Caleb to take over my training. I scowled through the whole thing, but he wisely didn't say anything. Levi avoided me the rest of the day and I just felt worse and worse. It was a mistake, I supposed. The kiss never should have happened, and Levi regretted it. Great. I didn't care.

But I did.

Because I hadn't thought it was a mistake. It had felt pretty perfect in the moment, and now I was worried it had ruined everything.

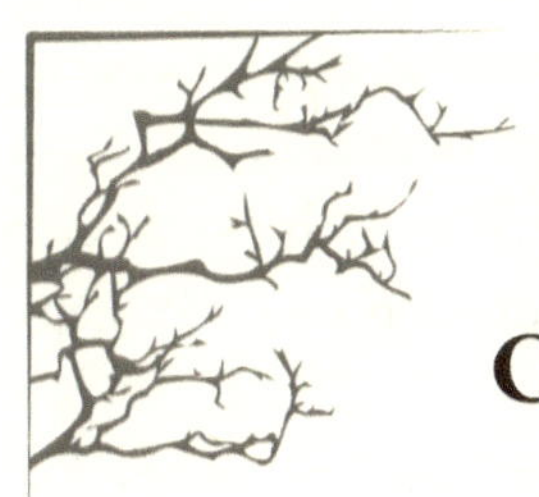

Chapter Sixteen
Levi

I was a complete asshole. I paced the living room, my hands behind my back, face set into a scowl. What had I been thinking? I had been thinking I wanted to kiss her. I growled in frustration. Kalene sat on the couch, feet tucked beneath her, a book in her hands. But she wasn't reading the book. She was watching me while *pretending* to read the book. There was no excuse for my actions, I thought. She was going through so much—had just lost everything, basically—and I was taking advantage.

"You're going to wear a hole in the floor," Kalene said quietly. "What's on your mind?"

I glared at her. "Nothing," I snapped. Just that I'm the biggest piece of shit in the house.

"I don't know about that," Richard drawled, leaning against the doorway. "I probably have you beat. Anyway, Caleb is done tormenting her in the backyard. So, if your aim is to avoid her, you'd better make yourself scarce."

"Avoid her?" Kalene said sharply, throwing a dark look in my direction. "What happened? Why is Caleb training her, anyway?"

"Because he's good at it," I grumbled, my self-loathing only growing. "Why shouldn't he?"

"That's not what I meant," Kalene said, abandoning the book she wasn't reading. She climbed to her feet and stood, hands on hips, regarding me. "What happened?" she asked again.

Richard snickered. "I know," he said in amusement. Of course, he would go looking for answers. Or perhaps he had gleaned the information from Caleb. Perhaps even Phoebe. What was her version of events, I wondered. Was she just as upset as I was? Perhaps even afraid of me.

I pushed past him, toward the front door. I had just opened it when I heard Richard telling Kalene what he knew. I had kissed her and felt terrible about it. I refrained from slamming the door behind me and quickly got into the car and pulled away from the house. *I'll be back later,* I thought, knowing Richard would get the message. I turned the radio on and flipped through the stations, turning the music up as loud as I could stand. I wasn't going to sulk, at least. I was going to get answers.

It had been a long time since I had to track someone, but I figured I would start where I knew he was last. I returned to the blood bar, made my way past the bouncer, and paused in the middle of the room. My eyes scanned every face in sight. No Avatrice. Someone who had been there last night might have seen him. It could give me a lead to follow, at least. I walked back to the front door to speak with the bouncer. It was the same man from before, but I doubted he remembered me.

"Excuse me," I said politely. "I'm looking for someone who was here last night."

"And you think I remember everyone who walks in this door?" he asked gruffly.

"Well, considering he attacked my guest in the women's bathroom last night, it would behoove someone here to remember him." I smiled, but it was not friendly. I pointed to my neck. "Left bruises."

"I assume your guest was human?" the bouncer asked, crossing his arms over his chest. Not wanting to give anything away, I simply nodded. He grunted in response. "Lucky, she didn't get bitten then."

His eyes widened suddenly. "Wait a minute... I remember you. You were with the pretty blonde. She was attacked?"

I nodded. "Yes. She had a couple of drinks and, before we left for the evening, she went to the ladies' room. There, a vampire cornered her and threatened her. He choked her and who knows what else might have happened if I didn't happen to have a mind reader friend with me last night."

The bouncer rubbed the back of his neck. "What did this guy look like? Maybe I will remember him."

I sighed. "His name is Avatrice Loughlin. He has long black hair; probably past his shoulders. His eyes are black... soulless. He is my height, maybe a little taller. Thin, but muscled."

The bouncer's mouth twitched. "Avatrice Loughlin, you say? Isn't that the one who...?"

"Got sent to prison for a century for trying to build an army of half vampire and half humans? The one who killed thousands of innocent humans in his quest to find the one with the perfect traits he sought? The one who slaughtered innocent children born of his crimes that didn't fit the mold he was going for?" I scowled. "Yeah. That's the one."

The bouncer cursed. "That son of a bitch was here? Do me a favor - I'm just the bouncer. Go talk to security. I don't want that guy in here. I hope they can help you more." He paused and frowned. "Why did he attack the girl? He's not thinking about starting again?"

I thought the world stopped turning for a moment. Was that what Avatrice was after? Phoebe was a success in his book. She was walking and talking, had grown into a fine young woman. But what would he want her for? He couldn't use her to create more dhampirs. A dhampir, by definition, is half vampire and half human and, as she was already only half to begin with, her offspring would be only a quarter vampire if fathered by a human and three quarters if fathered by a vampire.

I didn't realize I was growling until the bouncer held his hands up in surrender. Maybe that was it. He could use her to further his experiments; test to see what came out better. More human or more vampire? What other creatures would he try to create? And how many would die in the process? What would become of Phoebe? I couldn't let him get his hands on her, no matter his plans. Avatrice Loughlin had to die. Without saying a word, I turned and hunted down the door that said SECURITY. I banged on the door and a woman answered. She looked up at me and frowned.

"Can I help you?" she asked. She cocked her head to the side, her mouth set in a firm line.

"Yeah, I hope so. I'm looking for someone who was here last night, and I'd be willing to bet you won't be happy he was. Avatrice Loughlin. Does the name mean anything to you?" It was always hard to tell who was around back then, but most vampires had heard the name at least once since their Turning.

She scowled. "Yeah, why? You saying he was here?"

I nodded in response. "And attacked a guest in the women's bathroom. I need to find him and was hoping someone here might be able to help me."

"Fine. I'll see what I can find. It's gonna take some time to sift through the footage and see who he came into contact with last night. I'll work on it. Got a name?" She crossed her arms over her chest.

"Levi," I responded. "You'll call me if you find anything?"

She nodded, pulling her phone out. "Name is Carly," she said. She looked at me expectantly, and I rattled off my phone number. "Cool. If I find anything, I'll let you know." With that, she shut the door in my face.

I sighed. It was a start. I didn't think this lead would pan out very well in my favor, but it was something. I ran my hands through my hair and sighed again. I chatted with some of the waitresses, but none of them remembered seeing him. Of course not. With no one else to talk to, I headed back home. When I arrived, I sat in the car for several minutes. I pressed the heels of my hands against my eyes and groaned before climbing from the car and heading inside.

Chapter Seventeen
Phoebe

I didn't even look up when Levi walked into the house. I wasn't going to beg him for anything. He regretted the kiss, and that was fine, but I wasn't going to be upset about it. Maybe he was right after all. Maybe it was a mistake. Richard, clearing his throat, brought me back to the present. The two of us sat on the floor, cross-legged, opposite each other. He had decided it was time to teach me to block my thoughts from people like him. I half suspected it was because I was a loud thinker, but I appreciated the suggestion, anyway. I didn't know how many other vampires in the world had mind reading abilities, but it would be nice to keep them out if I did encounter them.

"Focus," Richard said sternly. "If you come up against a vampire that can read minds, you're dead no matter what. They'll be able to read your mind to know what you are going to do and react accordingly." He reached out and tapped my forehead with one finger. "Your only chance is to build a sort of block around your mind. Think of it like building a wall between you and me."

I nodded. "Okay," I said. It was easier said than done. I closed my eyes and tried to build a wall mentally, brick by brick. Richard reached out with his mind and easily pushed through. I cringed. "Let me try again."

We did this for another hour before I finally had to call it quits. I had gotten better at building the blocks, and it took him a little more effort to get in. I leaned back and sighed, wiping sweat from my forehead. "You're doing good," Richard told me.

"I don't feel like it." I sighed and climbed to my feet. "You can still read my mind."

"Yes," Richard conceded, standing. "But if you can keep that wall up, I shouldn't be able to hear you in passing. Only if I put in the effort. You'll have to keep working to make sure it's solid and you can keep others with powers like mine out, but you've made some good progress, Phoebe. Eventually, you'll be able to keep me out without conscious effort, at least in passing."

Caleb walked down the stairs then, rubbing his forehead. "I've been staring at articles for the last two hours and my brain is fried. And even worse, I didn't really learn anything new."

I glanced at him. "It was worth a shot."

"What?" Levi asked. I hadn't realized he had stuck around.

Caleb looked at him. "Trying to see if we can find anything new about Avatrice." He was giving Levi a strange look that I didn't understand.

"I see. As it would happen, I've been looking for him. I went back to the bar and asked around. I've got a woman in security reviewing the tapes from yesterday to see what she can see." Levi shrugged his shoulders. "I doubt it will lead us anywhere, but it's a start."

"Good. We need to find out what he wants with Phoebe," Kalene said, breezing into the room. "Do we have any theories?"

"He killed my parents," I said. "Said he didn't know that I was a dhampir at the time. If he had, he would have taken me then. Said he was crazed with bloodlust and didn't even process that my mother was human at the time. He was angry when he figured it out. Said that my father was a... a hypocrite for doing the same thing he had been doing when my father helped get him locked up."

Levi frowned. "I helped too."

I looked at him. "You... helped lock Avatrice up?" The news was a little startling to hear. I had to wrap my head around the fact that Levi may have come into contact with my father once upon a time. Long before my mother came into the picture, of course, but still. It was... difficult to hear.

"Yes. So we will need to be even more careful as we move forward. He wants you, and he likely wants me dead. As for theories... I have one. And it isn't pleasant."

"Well?" Caleb asked. "Don't keep us in suspense."

"I think he wants to continue his experiments using you. He's tried dhampirs. It worked, sort of. But there was a lot of death involved. From what I know of his research, the birth of a dhampir is not a for sure thing. There is a higher chance of the mother dying during childbirth, higher risks of complications. A lot of death followed in his wake, and he ended up with not much to show for it. When his place was searched, they found all his plans and papers, but no children. At least, no live children." Levi lowered his eyes to the floor. "If they didn't die in childbirth, they still were not guaranteed life. If they did not possess the traits he was looking for from birth, he just... killed them."

I pressed a hand over my mouth. "How could he do something like that?" I whispered.

"He's not a nice man," Caleb said, shaking his head. "So, if he's not interested in dhampirs..."

"Yes. After they took him into custody, we didn't find a single living dhampir. So, I think he is moving on to other... fractions. A quarter, three-quarters..." Levi threw a look in my direction. "He just needs a dhampir to get started. And he just so happens to know, roundabouts, where one is."

My blood ran cold, and I curled my arms around my waist. "He wants to use me like some kind of..." I didn't want to finish the thought.

"That's the theory we are going with currently. Until he gives us reason to think anything else. So...be careful. And don't go anywhere alone. One of us should be with you at all times." Levi turned from the room. "I think Kalene and Richard are good choices. Richard can potentially hear Avatrice before he gets close, and Kalene may be able to sense negative emotions nearby." Without another word, he walked from the room.

I frowned toward his back, and Kalene walked over and put her arm around my shoulder. "Let's go for a walk," she said, throwing glances at the other two vampires in the room pointedly. I got the message - she wanted to talk. Privately.

I threw my shoes on and the two of us slipped out the door together. We walked in silence for several minutes before Kalene sighed loudly. "What?" I finally asked.

"I'm not like Richard, you know. I don't know what you're thinking, but I can feel what you're feeling. You've been through a lot in a short amount of time and are doing well, all things considered." Kalene paused and glanced at me. "I understand you're scared. Who wouldn't be? And sad, of course, for all the things you've already lost."

"Angie was my best friend," I said, biting my lip to keep the tears at bay. "She was like a sister to me. We grew up together, and she was *always* there for me. And when she needed me, I... wasn't."

Kalene shook her head. "You can't think like that, Phoebe. You didn't know. How could you have? Her death is not your fault, and I want you to remember that. We will find Avatrice, and he will pay for this. I promise you that. His minion—the other dhampir—is dead. I'm sure that threw a kink in his plans. I don't know where he found another dhampir, especially since Levi said that they found none alive when they took in Avatrice. So, he must have found him naturally. As far as we know, you are the only other dhampir he is after."

I squirmed. "Yeah. Lucky me."

Kalene shook her head. "But that isn't what I wanted to talk to you about. I wanted to talk to you about... well, about Levi."

I bristled. "Oh?" I asked, trying not to seem too interested or upset. Of course, she could probably feel my emotions, so it was a moot point.

"I know about what happened," Kalene said softly, throwing a worried glance at me. "In the backyard." When I didn't speak, she continued. "Don't be too hard on Levi. He's...confused and upset too. I would say you just need to talk to him and clear the air. You both are feeling a lot, especially around each other. Try to get him alone so you can have some sort of privacy and just talk to him, for goodness' sake. Don't let this build up between you two and get worse than it has to be."

I sighed. "Maybe you're right." Because I was confused about the whole thing. And I was hurt by his reaction to it. Maybe I really just needed to sit down with him and get some answers, instead of making them up in my own head.

Chapter Eighteen
Phoebe

Kalene and I headed back inside, and I decided to go and confront Levi head on. She smiled encouragingly at me and flitted off to do who knows what. Caleb and Richard were still in the living room and, as I peered in at them, Richard glanced in my direction and pointed upward. *Thanks,* I thought, and he grunted in response, turning his attention to the television.

I walked slowly up the stairs, putting my mental block in place before giving heavy thought to what I was even going to say. It was a confusing time for everyone, and I didn't want to sound accusatory. I didn't want to sound desperate, either. If Levi had decided he didn't want to see where things went after all, then that was fine. I wasn't going to die. Truthfully, it was probably best for both of us to keep a healthy distance, but I couldn't convince myself that I *actually* believed that. The thought of never seeing Levi again left me feeling cold. Even if we weren't together, I still felt that Levi was meant to be in my life.

The trouble was, I couldn't find him. I assumed he would be in his bedroom, but when I opened the door, the room was empty. The bathroom door was ajar, but he wasn't in there either. I stood with my hands on my hips and pursed my lips. What, had he jumped out the window when he heard me coming? That was fine. He couldn't avoid me forever.

Turns out, he could. I didn't see hide nor hair of Levi for *days*. I was growing stir crazy sitting in the house all day and so I decided I was going to give college another try. I had been going for two semesters, but due to all the craziness going on, I had missed several classes. I had lost a lot of my normal recently, and if I didn't have to give everything up, then I wasn't going to. I got myself dressed and went in search of a bodyguard. I found Caleb in the kitchen doing a crossword puzzle, of all things. "Hey," I said, standing there awkwardly with my hands clasped behind my back.

He glanced up at me and quirked an eyebrow. "Can I help you?" he asked.

I sighed and rocked back on my heels. "I want to go to class."

Caleb stared at me, unblinking for several moments, and I wondered if he understood what I meant. Finally, he heaved a dramatic sigh and rose to his feet. "Fine," he said, but he didn't sound happy about it. "Am I presentable enough for your human school?" he asked, motioning down to himself.

He wore a pair of beat up jeans and a grey pullover sweater, despite the warm weather. I nodded once. "You look handsome," I said.

Caleb snorted and brushed past me, grabbing the car keys. "Thanks," he muttered. He motioned for me to follow, and we left. I hadn't travelled alone with anyone except Levi and it felt weird to be in the car with Caleb, just the two of us. I wondered if I would become afflicted with the same troubles as when around Levi and come to realize it was just a vampire thing. Maybe I wasn't even attracted to Levi. But we made it to campus unscathed, and I didn't feel so much as a belly quiver when his hand brushed mine as I climbed from the car. Caleb was just Caleb. He was handsome and smart, and I was certainly not attracted to him.

Damn.

That meant it *was* Levi.

I had some time to spare, so I showed Caleb around the small community college grounds. He bought me a coffee, and I held his hand to ward off the human girls eyeing him hungrily from all corners of campus. Holding his hand felt like what I imagined it would feel like to hold hands with a sibling, and that was just more proof that I didn't really want. I led him to the building I needed to go to, realizing too late that I didn't bring *any* supplies and Caleb wouldn't be able to come into the classroom with me.

We paused outside the room, and he glanced down the hall. "I'll be... around," he said. "Enjoy your class."

"Don't get into trouble," I said. We made sure to exchange phone numbers just in case, and I slipped into the back row of the classroom, hoping to go unnoticed. Luckily, it was a fairly large class, and I was able to just exist for the majority of it. I bummed a pencil and some paper off my neighbors and took some halfhearted notes, but my heart just wasn't in it. I was much too busy scanning the class, wondering if any of my classmates were vampires. Was the professor? I eyeballed him for the remainder of the class, watching for any too fast movements or subtle signs that could point toward his vampirism, but he seemed like perfectly normal Professor Ted.

When the hour was up, I gathered my meager notes and waited for the rest of the students to file out the door before heading there myself. I stepped out into the hall, expecting Caleb to be waiting for me. I realized quickly that he wasn't there, but neither was anyone else. The hall was eerily empty. I felt a shiver down my back and grabbed my phone, opening my contacts and scrolling to Caleb. My thumb hovered over the CALL button as I felt a hand on my shoulder. I jumped, turning to chastise Caleb for sneaking up on me, but was startled to find it wasn't him.

It wasn't anyone I knew.

"Um... hello?" I asked uncertainly.

The guy standing before me was probably around six feet tall and had sandy brown hair and smart glasses on his nose. He was cute, but I was wary. He smiled sheepishly at me. "Sorry," he said. "I called your name, but I guess you didn't hear me."

I felt embarrassed. He knew my name? Furthermore, he had *called my name,* and I had failed to hear? "No," I blurted. "I'm sorry. I was in my own little world. What can I do for you?" I asked, hoping I didn't sound as skeptical as I felt.

The guy pushed his hand through his hair and shuffled his feet nervously. "I'm Jackson," he began. "We have a few classes together?"

I nodded, feeling terrible for not knowing who he was. "Right," I said, forcing a smile. What did he want? I had a sinking feeling in the pit of my stomach that I knew.

"Well," Jackson said, rubbing the back of his neck. "I just wondered if you would let me take you out sometime?"

I could respect that he said it all at once, just getting it all out there for me. But I couldn't help the wave of sadness that washed over me. There was a time, back before this all started, that I would have been ecstatic to be asked on a date. But I could already picture it. He pulls up to the house full of vampires, three of which are men, and picks me up. We head out to dinner where one of the vampires tails us because I can't go anywhere unsupervised lest Avatrice show up and try to kidnap me. They sit at a nearby table like some kind of chaperone, watching over the date like a hawk. He realizes I'm just a little too weird, and he never wants to see me again.

Or worse yet, Avatrice shows up and *boom!* Now the guy is dead.

Perhaps I was only half vampire, but I was only half human, too. I no longer felt that I belonged to this world. School, dates, petty squabbles. I was too vampire to truly belong, but I was too human to exist in the vampire world. I just... didn't belong anywhere. I opened my mouth, hoping some sort of plausible answer would magically fall out, when I felt an arm slide around my shoulders.

"Ready to go?" Caleb asked, giving me a gentle squeeze.

"Oh," Jackson said, his cheeks turning pink. "Sorry," he said to me. "Forget I said anything. Thanks." He lifted his hand in a wave and fairly sprinted down the hallway to get away. Caleb let his arm drop as soon as he was out of sight. "Was he bothering you?"

I sighed and shook my head. "No," I said, looking back the way he had disappeared. "But you still saved me nevertheless."

"You looked like you were about to throw up," Caleb informed me as we turned and started heading back outside.

"Probably wasn't far from it," I muttered. "He asked me on a date."

Caleb nodded and stuffed his hands in his pockets. "Not your type," he guessed, casting me a sidelong glance.

"I don't know," I admitted, heading back toward the parking lot. "Maybe not."

"Where are you going?" Caleb asked. "I thought you wanted to do this whole college thing today?" He motioned back toward the buildings, his eyebrows pulled together in confusion.

I shook my head and kept walking. "I think I'll switch to online," I said as we reached the car. We climbed inside and Caleb turned to look at me, a serious expression on his face.

"Do I need to go find that guy for you and let him take you on a date? I can be sneaky." He seemed genuine, but I laughed regardless.

"No," I said, motioning for him to start the car. "As nice as he seemed, I just don't think going on a date with a human is a very good idea right now."

"Just a vampire?" Caleb asked, not looking at me as he turned the car out of the parking lot and headed back toward home.

I pursed my lips and refused to answer, staring out the window. That wasn't what I had meant, but he was right. If I wanted to go on a date, a vampire was probably my only option at the moment. Maybe forever. Levi had said that some humans knew about vampires, so maybe I could find one of them and happen to fall in love, but the trouble was, how was I to weed them out? And worse, what if they were a vampire hunter and decided I was just too much vamp to live?

Chapter Nineteen
Phoebe

Caleb and I returned to the house, not speaking any further on the matter. I still needed to speak to Levi, but he was still avoiding me. That was fine. I supposed I needed some more time to sort through everything in my brain. I was so lost and confused. I didn't feel like I could just go back to my normal life after everything that had happened. I couldn't just pretend like everything was fine and I couldn't imagine walking away from the Coven. I almost felt like I was a part of it.

Almost.

But the trouble was, I didn't feel like I truly belonged with the vampires either. I didn't identify with the whole blood drinking, avoiding sunlight when possible thing either. I was both and neither at the same time, and I wasn't sure how I was supposed to live life anymore. Could I just stay with the Coven forever, coexisting with a guy I was pretty sure I had more than just a crush on? Or would we be fated to avoid each other for the rest of our lives?

I got the call from Angie's mom that they were going ahead with the funeral. It had been nearly a week since her... passing and I felt the punch to the gut all the same. I hated the thought of going to see her, knowing Avatrice was still out there. He was responsible for her death. Everyone agreed to come with me, even Levi, but I wasn't sure how I would handle it.

Angie's mom saw me as I entered the building with my small entourage of vampires trailing behind and immediately came over to pull me into a tight hug. I shook with suppressed sobs, and we just stood there for several minutes, holding each other. When we finally pulled away, a tissue was offered to the both of us. "I'm so sorry," I said softly.

Unable to speak, she nodded and turned to greet the next person. Kalene and I walked up to the casket, and a choked cry escaped my lips. I knew her throat had been slit, but whoever took care of her after it had done a great job. You couldn't even tell. Her hair was positioned perfectly, and she was wearing her favorite jacket. My hands shook as I laid my hand over hers for the last time. My lips moved, the words coming out so quietly I knew no human could hear them. But Kalene rubbed my back gently.

"I am so sorry I couldn't be there for you. I wish I had known then what I know now. Maybe you would still be here. I'm sorry, Angie. But the man who did this is gone. I know your parents won't get the justice they want, and I am sorry for that, but just know that justice *was* served. The actual man who killed you died that night. And the man responsible for it will be taken care of." My lips barely moved as I whispered my apology. And when I was finished, I wiped away the remaining tears and went to sit through the funeral with my family.

It was a beautiful ceremony, and many people had wonderful things to say about her. Angie was loved by many and missed by many.

It was remarkably hard to get peace and privacy in a house of vampires, and for the next several weeks, Levi made it a point to *never* be alone with me. I was trying my damnedest to let him have the space he so clearly wanted, but I *had* to clear the air at some point. Richard and I continued our work on my mental blocks, and Caleb took over my training. He was, quite possibly, even more ruthless than Levi, but without the added fun of maybe-flirting. Felicity and Kalene tried to help me maintain my positivity and keep my spirits up by hosting weekly movie nights and encouraging me to partake in some of their girly rituals. We painted each other's nails, talked about the latest gossip, and overall, just became closer as friends. I was surprised to find that Felicity wasn't as bad as I had originally thought. She was quick to get angry, but she typically didn't stay that way. She held no ill will toward me and let grudges slide.

During those few weeks, the police called me. I was so nervous to talk to them, worried I would slip up and say the wrong thing, but when Felicity took me to the police station, it went smoothly. They asked what happened that night and I told them a version of the truth, sticking as close to it as I could.

I was at work that night, working late. I had already talked to Angie earlier in the day and she told me she was staying in. I told her that I had a date after work, and it would likely be very late or early in the morning before I got home. Only, I didn't go home. I ended up going home with my date and I heard the news in the morning. It destroyed me and I felt so responsible. If I had just come home, maybe she wouldn't have been killed. I cried, but they were real tears. I really did feel responsible. The officer seemed to take pity on me and let me go after just a few more minutes of questioning. They told me they would let me know if they found the killer and to call them if I thought of anything else.

I hadn't been to school or work in almost a month, but I was learning more than a college could ever teach me. I did have the intention of doing college online... eventually. I could keep Richard out without even thinking about it in my daily life. It took more of a concentrated effort to force him to stay out when he was actively trying, but most of the time, I could. I still probably couldn't outright fend off a vampire in a legitimate attack, but Caleb assured me I was doing well enough that I might be able to get away or hold on long enough for help to arrive.

Through all of it, Avatrice was there. He didn't approach, never spoke, and always disappeared quickly, but he made it a point to remind me of his presence. He was there at the grocery store every time I went with one of the Coven to restock the fridge. He was there at the blood bar, watching us from across the room, always gone before we could confront him. And, sometimes, he was there, in the woods across from the house, when I stepped out to check the mailbox. I had no proof, of course. It was just a feeling I got that I was being watched from within the darkness. And, while Avatrice was there, Levi was not.

I had all their numbers on speed dial and Kalene had bought me a smart watch so that I always had a means of contacting them with me. And of course, if all else failed, I could try to reach Richard mentally. The further away he was, the harder it was to reach him, but we had started practicing that, too.

Richard had left about twenty minutes ago to head to the park across town. I sat on the couch with Kalene and Felicity, flipping through television channels. Richard would text me when he was far enough away, and I was supposed to try to reach him. When my phone dinged and I checked to make sure it was Richard, I silenced the girls and took a deep breath.

I imagined a spool of thread unraveling in my mind. I sent that thread out, focusing on Richard. The thread bobbed and weaved between other people, searching for its target. I was getting tired. He was further away than we had ever tried before, and I wasn't sure I was going to be able to make it. Finally, after another several minutes of searching for him, my thread hit the target.

Richard.

The text was almost immediate.

Good job! A little quiet, but definitely there. Coming home now - R

I slumped back against the couch. "Did it."

Kalene patted my knee. "You're getting stronger every day! Good job, Phoebe." She was always encouraging me, reminding me that I was doing *great* for someone who didn't know about any of this a few months ago.

I rubbed a hand over my forehead. "Why do you think it's been so quiet? Avatrice hasn't seemed to make any moves lately. I mean, he's around, sure, but he hasn't actually *done* anything."

Felicity shrugged. "You're never alone and, as far as we know, he doesn't know you're here. Or if he does, he knows how incredibly stupid it would be to try to take us all on." She frowned at me. "The thought did cross my mind that he's waiting..."

Kalene shifted uncomfortably. "Watching us? Looking to see who he thinks is the weaker link. Perhaps he is waiting for you to be alone with that person before he makes his move."

"Or he is sizing us up while he gathers up an army." The voice from behind me startled me so badly, I jumped and spun around. Levi leaned in the doorway, a frown marring his features. "It's what I would do." I hadn't heard his voice in weeks. I had only seen him in brief flashes as he ducked and dodged to keep away from me.

I stood and faced him fully. I had a lot of time to think up what I wanted to say and, if Avatrice really was watching us and banding together an army, then I wanted to clear the air before anything happened to anyone. I really cared about all of these vampires - these people. They truly were like family to me, and I hated to see anything happen to them. And, if I was being honest, I was just really tired of Levi avoiding me. He was around, but he never wanted to be alone with me. If we were in a room with another person and that person left, Levi was quick on their heels. It wasn't like I hadn't noticed. He was always on his way out while I was on my way in.

"Levi," I said, a nervous pit forming in my stomach. I felt Kalene's hand on my back, as if giving her silent support. "Can we talk?"

Levi folded his arms across his chest. "Sure," he answered easily. I was surprised, but knew it wasn't that simple.

I shifted from foot to foot. "Privately?"

His demeanor changed subtly. His eyes narrowed, his shoulders stiffened, and his mouth grew tighter. This was the first time I had asked to talk to him specifically, let alone privately. I had to imagine he knew what I wanted to talk about, but would he deny an outright request? We stood there for several minutes, neither of us backing down. Finally, what felt like an eternity later, he sighed. "Shall we go for a walk?"

I had come to learn that 'going for a walk' was the universally agreed upon way for them to have an actually private conversation. Thoughts of Avatrice being out there and watching us made me hesitate, but ultimately, I nodded. I said goodbye to the girls and, for the first time in weeks, Levi and I left the house together. We walked side by side in silence, far enough away that we could not accidentally brush hands, until we had gotten far enough away from the house. He stopped walking and glanced at me; his expression was unreadable. I shifted under his intense gaze and sighed loudly. "You've been avoiding me."

I hadn't meant to say it so bluntly, but there it was. Levi made a noise in the back of his throat. "Hardly. I've seen much of you in the last several weeks, Phoebe. We live in the same house. How does one go about avoiding another in that situation?"

I shrugged and folded my arms across my chest, looking away from him. My eyes found the woods across the road and I scanned habitually, watching for flashes of a ghost. "You may have seen me, but I sure haven't seen much of you. It's easy to avoid someone when you make absolutely sure we are never alone together. This is the first time we've been alone with each other since..."

Levi groaned. "Yes," he said, rubbing the back of his neck. "I never did properly apologize for my indiscretion."

I was dumbfounded. Firstly, how could he have apologized if he wasn't speaking to me, but whatever did he feel the need to apologize for? "Apologize?" I didn't know what he was talking about.

"Yes." He turned to look at me directly as we stood in the middle of the sidewalk. "I want to formally apologize to you, Phoebe. I took advantage and I should not have. You have my deepest and sincerest apologies."

I stared at him, unblinking. I was astounded. "Took advantage? Of me?" I shook my head. "Levi, I don't think you took advantage of me. The kiss was every bit my fault, as it was yours. It was something that just... happened."

"Perhaps," Levi mused. "But you were in a vulnerable state. You were not in a good place to accept my advances, and I should not have even attempted. I was weak and I am sorry. *That* is why I've kept away from you, to the best of my abilities. I can't allow such a thing to happen again."

I held up my hands, as if I could stop him from speaking. "Look, Levi. Let's get one thing straight. I may have been a little vulnerable. I had just lost my best friend and found out I wasn't exactly human. I'm not saying I'm over those things yet, because it's going to take me a long time to come to terms with it all fully, but that shouldn't stop me from living my life. I let myself get swallowed up in the grief of losing my parents and I let myself spiral into a depression. I can't let myself do that again. So, I focus on other things—the mental training with Richard and the physical training with Caleb. Angie wouldn't want me to stop living my life, Levi. And let me assure you, vulnerable or not, I wanted that kiss to happen, and I don't regret it." My cheeks grew hot, but I didn't take it back. It was the truth, after all.

Levi was silent for a long moment. I could almost see him thinking, displayed across his face. If he didn't want to pursue a relationship with me, that was fine. But I would rather him tell me than just ignore me. Suddenly Levi was standing a lot closer, his arm snaking around my waist to pull me against his chest. It was in stark contrast to his behavior the past few weeks, but I couldn't say I minded. He sighed and looked down at me. "Phoebe, I have been miserable staying away from you. This whole time I have been beating myself up for taking advantage of you, worried about what you must think of me. I've been so angry with myself. To hear you say that is... refreshing." He paused and watched me. "I am sorry I've been distant. I assure you; it was the last thing I wanted, but I thought it was needed. I was worried if I let myself get close to you, and be near you, I wouldn't be able to stop myself from wanting to be with you."

I pressed my head against his chest, feeling the ever so slow *thump* of his heart. "Do you?" I asked cautiously. I couldn't look at his face when he answered.

"Do I what?" he asked quietly.

"Do you want to be with me?" I asked, voice nearly a whisper.

I could hear the slow beat of his heart and could feel the rise and fall of his chest with every breath. I could smell the familiar scent of lavender and mint wrapping around me. I felt safe in his arms. "I...do. Do you wish to be with me?" I could hear the hesitation and uncertainty.

I held him a little tighter. "I do." I couldn't deny my feelings any longer. I had more than a crush, and I wanted to see how things played out. I would beat myself up forever if I didn't at least try.

"Then...go out with me, as the humans say. Just the two of us; let me take you on a date. You won't be breaking any rules. I'll play bodyguard this time." Levi pulled back to look at me, a small smile tilting his lips upward. My heart did a little flip in my chest. Was it the perfect time to start a relationship? No. But if it was going to make me happy in the meantime, then I didn't see anything wrong with it. I nodded my head in response and his small smile turned into a full-blown grin.

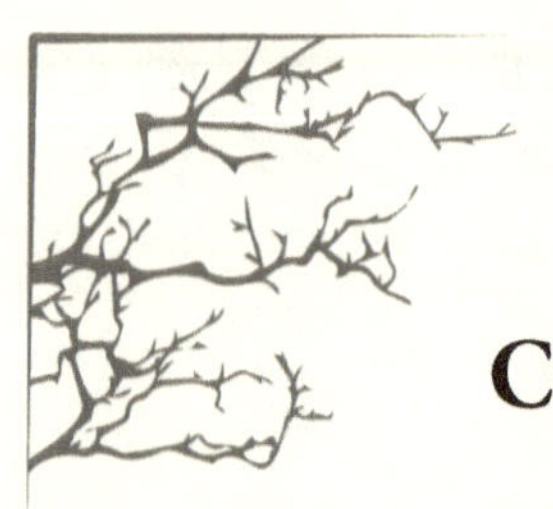

Chapter Twenty
Phoebe

Felicity and Kalene were arguing. They stood on opposite sides of Kalene's room, glaring. "It's a first date," Kalene said in a huff.

"So?" Felicity fired back. "That doesn't mean she has to dress like a schoolteacher, Kay."

Kalene sniffed, offended. "I don't dress like a schoolteacher, do I?" she asked, her lip quivering.

"I think you dress adorably," I supplied. "Very feminine and pretty." I shrank back at the glare Felicity shot at me, but she softened her expression.

"Which do you like better?" she asked, motioning to the two outfits both ladies had put together for my date. Truthfully, I wasn't in love with either. Felicity had picked out a blood red crop top with a pair of skintight leather pants, and a pair of Louboutin's. Her idea was to go for hot, hot, hot. She insisted I needed to wear red lipstick and a choker with little studs on it. Kalene, on the other hand, had chosen a pale yellow summer dress that reached to my calves, paired with a white cardigan and a pair of white strappy sandals. She thought I should wear my hair in a messy bun and go for a pink lipstick.

"What about this?" I suggested, sifting through the pile of clothes on the bed. I grabbed a purple top and a pair of tight jeans. The girls seemed to agree it was at least a cute outfit. A little bit of both styles. I rooted around the mound of shoes on the floor and found a pair of strappy black heels.

"That could work," Felicity said.

"Levi will like anything you wear," Kalene supplied, nodding her head.

"Well," Felicity mused, tucking her hair behind her ear. "He would like it if you wore nothing even better, but that's hardly a first date outfit, now is it?"

I blushed, and Kalene rolled her eyes at her sister. "Let's get you ready. He's chomping at the bit down there," she said, laughing.

Levi
I paced at the base of the stairs, my hands behind my back. The girls had disappeared upstairs what felt like hours ago, and I had gone and quickly gotten ready for my date with Phoebe. I had changed into a pair of dark jeans and a dark blue button up. A quick brush of my hair and stepping into my boots, and I was ready. So, what in the world was taking so long?

I threw another glance up the stairs and sighed. "Your impatience is showing," Caleb said from the living room doorway. "And I don't have to be an Empath to tell you that. They will be down when they are done. And, besides, you know how girls are. They are probably having a great time."

I threw a dark look in his direction. "Why are you always the voice of reason?" I asked my friend.

Caleb chuckled and shrugged his shoulders. "Someone's got to do it." He walked over and patted me on the back before heading up the stairs, presumably to take a shower. As he reached the top, he paused and glanced to his left. He whistled and threw a thumbs up down the stairs at me. And then I wasn't paying any attention to Caleb because Kalene and Felicity were coming down the stairs. My eyes quickly moved past them to find Phoebe, looking beautiful as always.

She blushed slightly when she saw me, and I tried not to grin. She looked great in a pair of jeans that hugged every curve and a flowy purple top that hung off her shoulders. Her blonde curls were left free of constraints, framing her face, brushing softly against her neck as she descended the stairs. My eyes traveled the length of her, starting at the top and working down to her toes, clad in a pair of strappy black heels that I recognized as Felicity's. "Hey," she said softly when she reached the bottom of the stairs. Kalene and Felicity stood on either side of me, watching me, as if gauging my reaction.

"You look beautiful," I said, reaching out and gently brushing a stray curl back off her neck. My eyes lingered a touch too long, and I dragged my attention back to her face. I would need to feed soon. "Are you ready?"

Phoebe smiled brightly and nodded once. "Yes," she said, reaching out and taking my hand in hers. I gave a gentle squeeze and turned toward the door.

"Behave," Kalene said, standing hands on hips. She looked at the two of us and smiled faintly. "But have fun."

Felicity folded her arms across her chest. "Have her back by morning."

"Is that her curfew or mine?" I asked with a chuckle. I led Phoebe to the front door, my hand on the small of her back. "We will be careful."

"If you need something, call," Kalene said sternly. "I don't mean to put a damper on the occasion, but if something happens…"

I nodded once, quickly. "You'll be the first to know." Not entirely true. Richard would likely be the first to know, but Kalene would be the first I called.

With that, I whisked Phoebe out the door and to the car. I opened her door for her and waited until she climbed inside before shutting the door and going around to the driver's side. I climbed behind the wheel and started the car, glancing at Phoebe. She was looking out the window at the front door, a slight frown on her face. I was about to ask what was on her mind when she began speaking, unprompted. "Do you think he's going to be watching us?"

I frowned. "Avatrice?" The thought had crossed my mind, but I hoped it wasn't the case. I hoped tonight would be a pleasant night, just the two of us, with no Avatrice in sight. "I don't know," I said instead. "But rest assured, if he shows up—or any of his lackeys—I *will* protect you."

Phoebe turned her green eyes on me, almost piercing in the night. "I hope it doesn't come to that. I want to enjoy tonight." She smiled a little sadly. "But enough about that! Let's go have a good time. Where are we going, anyway?"

I pulled the car out of our driveway and chuckled. "I thought we could get something to eat for starters. Then we can just see where the night takes us." I reached over and tentatively placed my hand on her knee. "If that's agreeable?"

She nodded. "Sounds great," she said. "As long as we aren't going to my old job to eat," she said with a laugh.

We chatted on the way, and I found it pleasantly surprising that it was so easy. There were no awkward pauses, no scrambling to find the words. We laughed and conversed like we had known each other forever. And when we arrived at the restaurant, I found myself almost wishing we could just stay like that, together in the car. Even so, I climbed out of the car and hurried around to open Phoebe's door before she could. She climbed out and smiled at me. "What?" I asked, feeling a little self-conscious.

"I think you're the only guy who has ever opened my door for me. I like it. Thank you." She slipped her hand into mine and we walked into the restaurant. It was warm and inviting, and we were seated quickly. I sat across from Phoebe and glanced over the menu, barely paying attention. When the waitress returned, we both ordered our drinks and food and were alone together again.

"The waitress thinks you're cute," Phoebe said offhandedly, resting her chin in her hand as she looked at me. "She barely looked at me the whole time she was taking our orders." She smiled, like she thought it was funny.

"Well," I said. "I don't know if that's true, but I don't really care what she thinks about me. Just you."

Phoebe looked startled. "You care what I think about you?"

I smiled. "Of course. I like you, Phoebe. You're funny, smart, kind...to know someone like you can like someone like me; well, I guess that means I can't be all that bad." I waved my hand, as if I could wave away the discussion. The waitress brought our drinks, and I noticed Phoebe was right. She never even looked at her, but made sure to send me her best "winning" smile. I ignored her, not liking to be rude, but she had been rude first. I was clearly on a date. When she returned some minutes later with our food, I reached across the table and took Phoebe's hand in mine, stretched across the far side of the table. She set the food down without a word, and I gave Phoebe's hand a squeeze.

"What was that for?" Phoebe asked, but she was smiling.

"Just wanted to hold your hand," I said, motioning to her plate. "Eat. Enjoy your night." I paused and regarded her for a long moment. "You're beautiful."

Phoebe paused and blushed bright red. She tucked her hair behind her ear and smiled down at her plate. "Thank you," she said quietly.

We ate in amicable silence for a few minutes and when the waitress came to check on us, I ordered us a dessert to share. We laughed and talked over the cake, and I reached over and offered a forkful to her. She snorted with laughter, drawing some of the other patron's attention. I felt my slowly beating heart give a painful thump in my chest. It was as if it were trying to beat faster or jump right out. I wanted to take her into my arms and hold her, but I talked myself out of the rash decision. I paid for our meal and rose, holding my arm out to her. "Shall we move on to the other part of our night?" I asked.

Phoebe took my arm in hers and grinned. "Absolutely. What is it?"

I laughed and wrapped my arm around her, pulling her against my side. "I have no idea!"

Chapter Twenty-One
Phoebe

We climbed back into the car and Levi pulled out of the parking lot, neither of us quite knowing where we were going. That was fine with me. I was enjoying the night and Levi was good company. I slid a sidelong glance over at him and felt my cheeks grow warm. Really good company.

Levi glanced at me and lifted an eyebrow. "What are you thinking?" he asked quietly, returning his eyes to the road.

I twisted my fingers together and shrugged daintily. "I'm having a good time," I said truthfully. "I like spending time with you." I didn't even feel that anxious to be in a vehicle, though my eyes darted to the speedometer for half a second.

"I'm glad," Levi said. "I enjoy your company as well." He smiled in the darkness. "Look," he said, motioning out the passenger side window.

We had made our way to the beach. The night was a little chilly by the water, but I wasn't completely distraught, though snuggling closer to Levi for warmth wasn't going to work. His skin wasn't exactly ice cold, but it was definitely cool—cooler than mine. We headed out to the beach, my borrowed shoes dangling from my fingers. I dug my toes into the sand and sighed. "This is nice," I said, brushing my hair back as it rustled in the breeze.

"Unexpected," Levi answered, keeping his distance from me. I knew he wasn't avoiding me intentionally, but I'm sure he was worried about the cold. I scooted closer to him, anyway. He hesitantly put his arm around me, and the weight was comforting.

We stepped right up to the water, but I didn't dare step a toe into the icy blackness. I looked up at the sky instead and basked in the moonlight. I could feel Levi's eyes on me and had a brief feeling of unease. If he wanted to hurt me, now would be the perfect moment. The beach was deserted—we were completely alone. And here I was, baring my neck with a vampire within arm's reach. I sighed and glanced at Levi. He was looking at me, but not in an 'I want to bite you' sort of way. My unease fled as soon as we locked eyes. He didn't want to hurt me. I could feel that in the electricity darting across the space between us. For a split second, it was like we were connected, and I knew he would never hurt me. I would always be safe with him.

I stepped closer without really thinking. I had to tilt my head back to look at him and he looked down at me. His arm slid around my waist and pulled me flush against his chest. I dropped the shoes to the sand, resting my hands on his chest. "What now?" I said, whisper soft. If he were human, he might not have heard me over the waves. But he wasn't human, and he did hear me.

Levi lowered his head slowly, giving me time to turn away or tell him to stop. But I didn't. And then his lips were on mine, firm but gentle. He held me tightly against him and I reached one hand up to curl loosely in his hair, the other staying on his chest. My pulse jumped beneath my skin and Levi pulled away abruptly, a soft groan escaping his lips. He rested his forehead against mine, his breathing ragged. I gave him several minutes before speaking.

"Are you okay?" I asked gently. I knew so much more about vampires than when we first met, but I still didn't know everything. How hard was it for him to be close to me like this? How long had it been since he had blood?

Levi pulled away and paced, his hands behind his back. "Yes," he answered a little too quickly. He sighed and threw me a glance. "No. Phoebe, I'm sorry. I didn't expect the feeling to be so intense."

"Feeling?" I asked, cocking my head to the side. I could imagine what he was alluding to, but there was still so much I didn't know about him, about vampires.

Levi nodded once. "Yes. For vampires, we bite others for a couple of reasons. Yes, we bite to drink blood, to feed, but there are other instances..." He tore his hands through his hair and continued pacing. "Sometimes we bite for pleasure." He said it in a rush, like he just wanted to get it over with.

I frowned. "So, you want to bite me?" I pursed my lips. "Not to drink my blood, but to... because it would be pleasing to you?" The idea was completely foreign to me, and I wasn't entirely sure how I felt about it. I had experienced it once before, with Avatrice, and it had been anything but pleasurable. The idea of getting bitten by a vampire—even Levi—seemed terrifying and dangerous. Even if his intention wasn't to drink my blood, would he be able to stop himself once he tasted it?

"And you." Levi stopped pacing and faced me fully. "When we bite to feed, we release a type of venom in large amounts. It acts as a sedative almost, to keep them more docile. Or, at least, that's how it is supposed to happen. When Avatrice bit you, you fought back. It was like he hadn't released enough venom, or it wasn't working. Maybe that's the vampire half of you; maybe it doesn't work on you that way." I remained quiet as he talked. "But when we bite for pleasure, we release a much lower amount. It takes away any pain you might feel and leaves the good stuff. It's more like... an aphrodisiac. Everything just feels... better."

If I didn't know any better, I would have said Levi looked thoroughly embarrassed. I knew I was blushing at the thought. Sure, I knew people sometimes partook in love bites when they were getting romantic, but I had never done so myself. And with Levi, it would be a little more than just a love bite. He would break skin and there would be blood. I shivered. "So, what does all of that mean for us?" I asked, before I could convince myself to stay quiet.

Levi rubbed the back of his neck. "It means... hell, I don't know, Phoebe. It means that I want to kiss you, but when I kiss you, I want to bite you and I don't want to scare you away or hurt you. I would never want to hurt you, intentionally or otherwise. Of course, the feeling of wanting to bite someone isn't completely new to me, but I didn't expect it to be so strong with you. It wasn't just something I wanted to do. It felt like something I *needed* to do." He was keeping his distance from me again. It was like he thought if he kept enough distance between us, his feelings would calm.

"So... when you bite someone for *any* reason, they don't turn into a vampire?" I asked, cocking my head to the side. "I guess I never thought about it before. Could I turn into a vampire, already being half?"

Levi sighed. "Not right away," he said. "And I am uncertain if you can become a vampire. We can certainly look into it if it concerns you, but no. To become a vampire, you must be bitten, yes, but that is only the starting process. If you are bitten and nothing else, you will not Turn. However, if you are bitten and then drink the blood of a vampire—even if it is from one who did not bite you—then you will begin to Turn. The process is different for everyone; some go through it quickly, in a matter of hours and others, it may take weeks." Levi had started pacing again. "For example, if I were to bite you tonight and you were human—or if you *are* able to be turned into a full-fledged vampire—you would not Turn unless you drank my blood. Or went home and drank from Caleb or Kalene or any one of the Coven."

I pursed my lips. "So, how long? If you bit me and I went home and mulled it over a bit and decided tomorrow to drink someone's blood, would I still Turn? Is there a time limit?" This was a brand new can of worms I had never considered before, and the possibilities were intriguing.

Levi chuckled. "Assuming you can, yes, there is a window of opportunity. Right away is ideal if you intend to Turn or if the one doing the biting intends it. But you have, perhaps, a few hours to make that decision." He shrugged one shoulder. "I'm sure someone has done the research on it, but I personally have never bitten someone to Turn them, and the specifics have never come up."

A part of my brain was screaming at me. Was I insane? Standing on a deserted beach talking with a vampire about being bitten and Turned into a vampire was not exactly how I wanted to spend my date with Levi. But another part of me was curious. About all of it—the biting, the drinking of blood, and the Turning. However, a part of me was also curious about the other kind of biting. And as I stood opposite Levi and talked about it like it was the most normal thing in the world, I realized that it didn't sound that scary anymore. I wasn't going to Turn into a vampire unless I drank his blood, and I wasn't exactly planning on it. Of course, even if I did, there was no telling if I would actually Turn. I stepped closer to Levi and felt him stiffen. I reached up and cupped his cheek in my hand.

"I know you wouldn't hurt me on purpose, Levi. And I *am* having a good time with you. This has all been very... informative," I said, a small laugh escaping. "I don't want you to think I'm so fragile; though I appreciate you taking the time to explain things to me before just, you know, going for the jugular." I laughed a little louder, the sound laced with self-consciousness, and dropped my hand.

Levi caught it and pressed his lips to my knuckles. "I will try to refrain from going for the jugular," he said, a small smile flitting across his face. His expression suddenly became very serious. "If you do not wish it, I shall refrain from any manner of biting. It isn't always the neck, you know. And biting for pleasure does not involve actually drinking."

"Just... do what feels right," I said offhandedly. "If it should come to that point, we will cross that bridge when we get there." I smiled up at him and swiftly stretched up and pressed a kiss to his lips. His arms were around me in a heartbeat, his lips moving over mine. His arms were strong and sure and never rough. It felt comfortable and right. My heart was pounding in my chest, my fingers biting into the fabric of his shirt, wanting him closer still. He groaned and pulled back slightly; his eyes dark in the moonlight.

"Phoebe," he rasped, but he did not let me go.

"Levi," I said calmly, looking up at him serenely. I felt perfectly peaceful, starkly contrasted against Levi's agitation. I wondered how difficult it was for him to *not* bite me.

"It literally hurts," Levi answered, pressing his forehead against mine. "My fangs ache," he muttered. "It's taking all I have to keep them from extending."

I blinked slowly. Had I spoken out loud? I didn't think so, but Levi had seemingly just answered my thoughts. That was ridiculous, of course. Richard was the mind reader, after all. Levi had no such gifts. Perhaps he had spoken up of his own volition and his words just happened to match up with my thoughts. But soon I began to feel an ache in my mouth, like a dull toothache, and I suddenly had the strangest urge to bite Levi. I had never wanted to bite another person before, and it threw me for a loop. Was this the vampire side of me breaking free? Without any real thought, my lips found Levi's again, and we were tangled together once more. We fell to the sand together, and I had enough presence of mind to know it was going to take days to get all the sand out of every crack and crevice, but I didn't care.

Levi pressed against me, and I knew that he was feeling more than just the urge to bite me. We were in a public place! But...it was deserted. His hands roamed over my body, resting on my hips, and he tore his lips away from mine, breathing heavily. He kissed a trail from my jaw to the base of my throat and a small gasp escaped my lips as I felt his fangs lightly graze my skin. My heart was hammering wildly in my chest, and I was pretty sure he could hear it. "I'm sorry," he rasped.

I pressed harder against him, not thinking about the consequences. His fangs bit a little harder into my flesh, but he still did not break skin. "It's okay," I whispered. The words had just barely left my mouth when I felt Levi bite down. I groaned and tilted my head back a little, curling my arm around his neck. To anyone passing by, we would look like we were just fooling around, but if anyone got too close, they would know something was wrong.

Not wrong. This didn't feel wrong at all. I felt like my body was on fire, in a good way. Everywhere Levi touched came alive, and I wanted him to touch me more. I pressed my hips upward, inviting, bending my knee and pressing it against his side. He growled against my neck and pulled back, his fangs sliding free. A tiny drop of blood dripped from the corner of his mouth, and I reached up and brushed it away with my thumb, drawing his mouth to mine once more. His hand slid up my thigh, teasing.

Levi stopped suddenly and lifted his head. I was almost dizzy, and disappointment flooded my system. He was stopping? Levi pressed a tender kiss to my lips and climbed to his feet, pulling me with him. He brushed his fingers over the puncture marks on my neck and sighed. "We need to go," he said quietly. "Someone is coming."

"Avatrice?" I asked, a frown marring my features. I hoped he wasn't here, ruining everything.

"I don't know," Levi said, dusting sand from my clothes lightly. "But I don't want to stay here and find out." He took my chin in his fingers and brought his lips to mine once more in a kiss that seared me right to the bone and left no room to mistake his desires. When he pulled back, his eyes were dark. A nervous giggle escaped, and he shook his head, smiling. "Come on," he urged, snatching my shoes from the sand and pulling me back toward the car.

155

Chapter Twenty-Two
Phoebe

We hurried back to the car, laughing and brushing sand off our bodies. When we reached the car, Levi pushed me against it and kissed me, hard. I felt it all the way down to my toes. He pressed against me, and I could feel that he was also disappointed with the interruption. I could feel it pressing against my leg. A throaty laugh spilled from my lips, and I sighed. "Do we have to go home?" I whispered, eyes searching. The thought of going back to a full house was less than appealing.

Levi opened the car door for me and I reluctantly climbed inside. When he shut his door, he turned to face me. "I'm not sorry if you're not." He reached out and touched the marks on my neck again. "And, make no mistake, if you'll allow it, I *definitely* want to do it again."

I wasn't sure to which part he was referring, but I didn't care. I smiled and touched his hand. "I'm not sorry," I said quietly. "I had a lot of fun with you tonight. Everything about tonight just felt..."

"Right?" Levi asked. He was smiling, but looked to have something on his mind. If he did, he wasn't sharing. "Come on," he said.

I briefly contemplated if the backseat was big enough for the two of us, but decided against trying anything as I awkwardly slipped my shoes back on. If we were going to sleep with each other, I didn't really want the first time to be in the backseat of a car. But Levi did not head toward home. I smiled privately to myself, and his hand found mine in the dark. We threaded our fingers together and rode in silence until we pulled into the parking lot of a large chain store. I blinked.

"Here?" I asked, confused.

Levi chuckled and killed the engine, climbing from the car. He came around and opened my door, pushing me up against it as soon as I was out and my door was closed. "Why not?" he asked, pressing a tender kiss to my forehead. "Maybe I want to spend more time with you. Maybe," he mused, brushing his knuckles along my jaw. "Maybe I want to spoil you."

He took my hand and led me inside, my heels clicking loudly in the mostly deserted parking lot. Once inside, warm air blasted my face. Levi held my hand the entire time and I couldn't help but feel happy. A brief moment of sadness washed over me, Angie coming back to mind. She would have been so excited for me to know I had found someone. Someone who saw me for me, someone who cared about me, and who believed in me. I cast a glance at Levi and felt my whole body warm. She would have loved him, I mused. "Anything in particular you are looking for?" I asked, as Levi rubbed his thumb across my knuckles.

"No," Levi answered easily. "But it is nice to spend time away from my family. I love them, but I suppose I never realized how much time we spend together. We don't get out much. Not much reason to," he said with a shrug. "But now I have all the reason to. I'm going to take you on all the dates you'll allow," he said with a smile.

"I like the sound of that," I said. And I did. Spending time with Levi alone was amazing. Of course, I loved his family too, but it was different to be with him, just the two of us. It was almost like we were making up for lost time, all those weeks he spent trying to avoid me.

We found our way to the jewelry counter, and I felt my stomach flip. Some of the pieces were pretty but made of cheaper materials. I would have been perfectly happy with a sterling silver piece, but

Levi seemed to have other plans. He moved to the counter, which housed the more expensive sets, and I felt embarrassment wash over me. He let go of my hand briefly, motioning to a few things. I barely saw them. Tears stung the backs of my eyes and I pulled my hair over my shoulder, trying to hide it. Levi glanced at me when I gave less than enthusiastic responses and he frowned, stepping away from the jewelry.

"Phoebe?" he asked, reaching out and taking both of my hands. "What's wrong?"

I shook my head and smiled as tears began welling up in my eyes. "Nothing's wrong," I said softly. "I just don't feel like I deserve all of this," I admitted after a moment of indecision.

Levi shook his head. "You deserve everything," he said. "Phoebe, you've been through a lot, and you have handled it so well. You can tolerate and even *like* my family. And, well, here you are with the likes of me, after all."

I shot him a sharp look. "What's that supposed to mean?" I asked. "Levi, you are *wonderful.*"

He shrugged and laughed a little dryly. "So you say. But this isn't about me, Phoebe. I want to give you something. It doesn't have to be expensive; I don't want to make you uncomfortable."

I nodded. "Okay," I said. "I know you're about as stubborn as they come, and there isn't much point in arguing."

He leaned down and kissed me quickly. "No, I suppose there isn't." He chuckled and turned back to the counter, speaking quietly to the worker. The woman smiled brightly and nodded, reaching into the counter to grab something. Levi took it from her and turned it away so I couldn't see what was inside the box. He closed it with a nod and the woman rang him up, happily passing him the receipt. "Thank you," he said, turning back to me. He took my hand again, tucking the box into his pocket.

"Not even going to let me see?" I asked.

Levi shook his head. "Not yet," he answered. "Come on." He pulled me back the way we had come, toward the exit. It was late, but I didn't want the night to end. I wanted to spend forever, suspended, like this. Just the two of us, pretending we had not a care in the world. We reached the car and Levi stopped me from climbing inside. He brushed my hair back and pulled the box from his pocket.

"There better not be a ring in there," I teased.

Levi shook his head. "No," he said. "Not this time. But I thought it best to let you open it out here, under the moon and stars." He handed the box to me, and I turned it over in my hands a few times before finally cracking it open.

My breath caught in my throat, and I swallowed, blinking hard to keep from crying again. "Levi," I said. "It's beautiful." Nestled inside the box sat a rose gold crescent moon. It hung off the chain upside down, some sort of iridescent whitish stone hanging from its middle.

Levi took the box from my hands and easily removed it from the packaging. "Moonstone," he said conversationally. "A stone of new beginnings." He shrugged when I looked at him. "You learn about a lot of things when, you know," he said, motioning to himself. He slipped the necklace around my throat, clasping it quickly. It was cool against my skin, and it rested gently against my chest. I lifted my hand to touch it softly.

"New beginnings," I said, glancing over my shoulder at him. "I like that."

Levi reached out and touched the marks on my neck. I wondered if anyone inside the store had noticed them beneath my mass of curls, but it was too late to worry about that now. "It's very late and I have to have you back by morning," Levi said, but it sounded like he didn't want to go either. I sighed softly as he opened the car door for me, and I climbed inside. I watched him walk around the front of the car and settle himself behind the wheel.

After a moment, he leaned over, his hand slipping behind my head. He pulled me over the gearshift to him and kissed me. No words were spoken, but I could feel the message all the same. He was there for me, sure and steady, with all the tender sweetness I could ever want. I returned the kiss, hoping he felt the same.

When we arrived back home, we were both slow to leave the car. Eventually, Levi climbed out and came around to open my door. He pressed a final kiss to my lips and brushed my hair back behind my ear gently.

I suddenly was terrified to set foot in the house. There was a mind reader and an empath in there. Between the two of them, everyone was going to find out about what happened. Not that I regretted it, but it was pretty much impossible to keep secrets. Not to mention the conspicuous mark on my neck. I had no good way of hiding it, so I pulled the bulk of my hair over my shoulder on the left side and hoped it would do. Levi snickered and opened the front door before I could say anything.

I swallowed hard and followed him inside. He went to the kitchen and poured me a drink, sliding it across the counter to me. I gulped it down, but nearly choked when the entire household was suddenly in the kitchen, staring at me. I almost felt a breeze from the speed with which they moved, not bothering to hide their curiosity. I felt a blush rise in my cheeks. Richard squinted at me, but I had thrown up the best mental shield I could possibly manage. I felt him trying to get in and gave a push back and he actually took a step back, looking surprised.

"Well, her clothes are all on correctly," Felicity said with a chuckle. "Bummer."

"Is that sand in your hair?" Caleb asked, reaching out as if to touch my curls.

I pulled back and swallowed. "Ended up at the beach," I said swiftly, anxiety forming a pit in my stomach.

"And, what? Fell ass over elbows into the sand?" Caleb lifted an eyebrow knowingly and threw a glance at Levi. His eyes swept him from top to bottom, but Levi looked cool as can be.

"You didn't leave here with that necklace," Kalene said sweetly, glancing between the two of us. "And I'm picking up on a lot of different feelings. Embarrassment, contentment," she said, glancing at Levi pointedly. "Amusement."

I shot her a dark look. "If you are all finished ogling me, I think I'm going to go take a shower." I lifted my chin and turned and heard a startled gasp.

"Levi!" Felicity admonished the other vampire, and I glanced over to see him shrug, his hands tucked into his pockets. I didn't realize what the big deal was until I felt cool fingers brush against my neck.

I jumped, startled. Richard squinted at me again and shook his head. "Does it hurt?"

I blinked. "Does what... hurt?" I asked, realizing too late that they had seen the marks.

He rolled his eyes at me and motioned to my neck. "The bite, stupid." He cut his eyes to Levi, frowning.

I blushed hard and took a quick step away from him. I threw a look at Levi, asking for help, but he was busy fending off Felicity, who had advanced on him, her hands on her hips. Everyone's reaction confused me until I pieced it together.

They thought he drank my blood.

They thought he had hurt me.

My heart warmed at the thought of them all caring about me so much. "You've got it all wrong," I blurted, holding my hands up. I covered the bite with my hand and jumped in with both feet. "I asked him to." Suddenly, all five pairs of eyes were on me, and I cleared my throat. "If you don't mind, I'd rather not get into all the personal details of my... ahem... relationship with Levi, thank you."

I made my escape up the stairs, but heard the low hum of the vampires all speaking quickly over each other. I wasn't going to stick around long enough to get dragged back into it, so I bolted for Levi's room and quickly climbed into the shower. There was the slightest of stinging in my neck as the water ran over the bite, but I was unbothered, knowing it would be healed over in a day or two. I washed and mulled over the night, making sure to keep my mental shields in place, lest Richard decide to peek in. I had been having the best night. The best I'd had in a very long time. Being with Levi made everything calm; made everything seem not so bad. We clicked in a way I had never clicked with someone before. My mind slid back to the moment, just before things got a little heavier, and rubbed a hand across my jaw. My teeth had ached. I had wanted to *bite* Levi. I remembered how he had said that his fangs ached when he wanted to bite me.

But what did it mean?

I had been with other guys before and I had never felt the desire to bite them. I had never felt my teeth hurt like something was trying to burst out of my gums. I was so lost in my own thoughts; I almost didn't hear the light knock on the bathroom door. I shook my head, realizing the water had grown cold, and quickly shut it off and wrapped myself in a towel. I padded over to the door and cracked it open. Levi stood on the other side and smiled faintly at me, a nervous look in his eyes.

"You've been in there a while. I wanted to make sure you were okay after...everything. I... I didn't hurt you, did I?" His eyes slid to my neck, and he shook his head. "It's already healing."

I pushed the door open wider and shook my head quickly. "No, Levi. You didn't hurt me at all, I promise. You were right; it was...great. I just got in my own head a little and lost track of time. Sorry." I didn't even feel that self-conscious standing in a towel in front of him. I walked over to my stuff and found a pair of pajama shorts and a t-shirt. I glanced back at him and lifted an eyebrow. "I had a really good time tonight. Thank you."

Levi rubbed the back of his neck and gave a crooked smile. "Anytime. I'll, uh, leave you to it." He turned toward the door but glanced back at me before he opened it. "If you ever have anymore questions about the vampire stuff, feel free to ask. Any of us."

I smiled as he left. I wasn't sure if he really meant *any* vampire stuff or if he was talking more specifically about the biting, but it still warmed my heart that he was so willing to share his world with me. I know nearly two months ago I had wanted to keep my distance, but things had happened so quickly. Everything was different now and I could hardly imagine my life without all of them in it. Even Richard and I had grown much closer during my time here. Kalene was right, he wasn't so bad. And Felicity could be considered a friend to me now. Being around them had become second nature.

I got dressed and headed downstairs to find everyone piled in the living room. There was an open spot on the couch next to Levi and I smiled. I had a feeling everyone had intentionally left the spot for me. I settled in beside him, tucking my feet beneath me. He draped his arm across the back of the couch behind me, and I felt him shift slightly so that he was touching me and felt my heart flip. He cleared his throat, and I blushed, knowing everyone had probably heard the offending organ stutter. We all just hung out, chatting for a while, some old reruns playing on the tv for background noise. Richard occasionally tried to push into my mind, but I threw him a dark look and strengthened my blocks. He smiled in return, pleased.

I felt... at peace. My mind wandered to Angie and my parents, and I felt a pang of sadness in my heart. I felt a hand on my knee and expected to look up and see Kalene, but it was Levi. He sighed and squeezed. "I know you miss them," he said.

I stared at him, blinking slowly. "What?"

Levi looked back at me, looking equally confused. "Your family... Angie," he said, like I should have known.

Conversation had stopped, and I knew everyone was looking at me. "Levi...you aren't a mind reader too and didn't tell me, are you?" I laughed it off, but I felt a little uneasy.

He shifted. "No. I can't read minds, Phoebe. I mean, I don't suppose I've ever told you about the power I *do* have, though..."

I felt surprised at his words and shifted away from him, feeling apprehension creep into my mind. "Oh?" I asked, trying not to sound suspicious.

"It's a little less passive than Kalene and Richard," Levi began, retracting his hand from my knee. "I suppose the easiest way to say it is just that I can sort of...persuade people without speaking. Encourage people to do things."

A chill raced down my spine, and I clenched my teeth. "Oh?" My words sounded much shriller than I had meant them to. "How... interesting. I mean, I guess the obvious next question is, have you ever used it on me?" My heart was beating painfully in my chest, and I waited for his answer, breath caught in my throat.

Levi winced. "Yes, but—"

I held my hand up to stop him, standing quickly. "When? Tonight?" My words came out in a whisper. Kalene stood and put her hands on my shoulders, as if she were trying to ground my emotions that were probably crashing into her. Even Richard half rose from his seat.

"No!" Levi said sharply, rising to his feet. "Absolutely not. I would *never* do that to you, Phoebe. Or anyone." He held his hands up in surrender. "I've only done it twice. Once the night I brought you here, to find out what you knew about Avatrice. I needed to be sure you weren't working with him. I had to protect my family, Phoebe. And once the night Angie was killed. I just encouraged you to sleep. You had been through an ordeal, and you needed to rest. I swear to you, I have never used it on you any other time. I don't use it on my family without just cause or if I am asked to, and I won't use it on you again. I promise." He sounded so damn sincere.

I heard a small intake of breath behind me from Kalene, and her hands dropped from my shoulders. Levi stepped closer to me and cupped my face in his hands, his blue eyes intense. I looked up at him, unsure of what to expect. "So... what now?" I whispered.

"With your permission, I would like to show you the difference between a suggestion using my power and just a normal suggestion. If I show you this, I swear to you, you'll know I'm telling the truth." Levi was looking down at me so intently, I didn't even realize I was nodding at first.

He dropped his hands and stood back, folding his arms across his chest. "Okay, I normally wouldn't speak out loud, but I will for the purpose of this. So not using my power; sit down." I stared at him. I felt no sudden desire to sit down, so I assumed he must have been telling the truth about not using his power. "Now, with my power; *sit down.*" I felt a little tingle in the back of my mind and felt the urge to plop back onto the couch. I resisted the feeling and felt the tingle increase just a little. I found my legs buckling, and I sat down heavily. He was right; I remembered feeling that before, but I hadn't felt it in a while, and I definitely hadn't felt it tonight.

The feeling of relief was so strong I almost burst into tears. I don't know what I would have done if he had *suggested* anything about tonight. Levi sat beside me again and took my hands in his. "I'm sorry," I mumbled. "I should have trusted you, I just..." I didn't know how to finish.

"I understand," Levi said. "I should have told you sooner, but I hardly ever use it, so I didn't really think about it. I promise, I wasn't intentionally keeping it a secret from you. And I give you my word, I would never *ever* use it to encourage you to do something... like tonight," he said, cutting his eyes to the others in the room.

"But I still have a question," I said, shaking my head. "Twice tonight it seems like you just... know what I'm thinking. Is that part of your... gift? Just knowing things?" It didn't make sense, but then again, I didn't know much about vampires.

"I don't know anything about that," Levi said, eyebrows knitting together. "I certainly can't read minds and I don't just know things," he said with a chuckle.

"Okay. Well, maybe it's just coincidence. I do have another question, while I have you all here. It is, admittedly, a little embarrassing to ask out loud, but here goes." I sighed loudly and looked at my hands in my lap, not wanting to meet anyone's eyes. "Tonight, while we, uh...you know," I said, flicking a glance at Levi and motioned to my neck. "Stuff happened, no details. I felt like...maybe I wanted to...bite back." I picked at my fingernails awkwardly.

There was a long pause. "As in, you wanted to drink his blood and do the whole vampire thing?" Caleb asked carefully.

"First of all, we don't even know if I *can* be Turned, but no. I felt like biting him in the same, uh... way he wanted to bite me." I was blushing furiously by the time I finished speaking, but no one seemed perturbed. I suppose for them it was just a simple fact of life.

"Fascinating," Felicity said, tilting her head to the side. "Perhaps a bit personal, but here we are; did your fangs hurt? Well, your teeth, I mean."

Chapter Twenty-Three
Levi

I was a little startled to hear Phoebe talk so candidly about wanting to bite me. I had to admit; it was surprising but not displeasing. The idea of biting her again was very appealing, but I forced the thoughts away, trying to focus on the conversation at hand.

"Yeah," Phoebe whispered. "They did."

"Well, I suppose it makes sense. You *are* half vampire," I said, rubbing my jaw.

"Maybe so," Phoebe said, shaking her head. She sat cross-legged on the couch and sighed loudly. "But I've been with other guys before and that's never happened."

I stared at her, trying not to show the distaste on my face at the thought of her being with other guys in any manner like how we had been. It was irrational, of course. She didn't even know who I was two months ago, so I couldn't fault her for relationships prior to our meeting. "Perhaps circumstances were simply not the same," I suggested, folding my arms across my chest.

"How do you mean?" Phoebe asked, frowning. Her eyebrows pulled together, and she chewed on her lower lip thoughtfully.

"Maybe it is just as simple as Levi being a vampire," Kalene suggested. "Perhaps the other guys you spoke of were human and so they did not stir the vampire side of you the same way?" She had her head tilted to the side and kept throwing glances in my direction, yet she did not speak further. I knew she must have been picking up on some of my jealousy and so I tried to tamp it down. I liked to think that it was more than just the fact that I was a vampire that caused those feelings to emerge in Phoebe.

"Yeah," Phoebe muttered. "Maybe." She peeked up at me, and a tiny smile flitted across her face before she looked away again. I felt drawn to her. Even sitting in a room full of other vampires—and my own family at that—I wanted to pull her close to me and sink my teeth into her soft skin. I wanted to make her mine, completely. I felt no pull to drink her blood; the thought of doing anything to hurt her was repulsive. I wanted to protect her and to give her everything I could. I felt, in that moment, that I would have done anything she asked of me without hesitation. It was almost as if she had bewitched me. I didn't know if it was possible for dhampirs to have gifts, but I also didn't think she had done anything intentional to me. Everything I was feeling was simply because she was being herself and I found that to be attractive and compelling.

"It's late," Caleb said suddenly. "If you wish, I can look into the matter further and let you know what I learn." He rose to his feet and threw Kalene a pointed look. She rose to her feet in one fluid motion, pulling Felicity up with her. Without a word, Richard stood, and they all disappeared from the room.

I waited until they had all made their way up the stairs, even though I knew it was futile. In this house, it was nearly impossible to have privacy simply because we could all hear too well. Once I heard their bedroom doors shut and all was quiet, I turned to Phoebe to find she was looking at me. "Alone," I said with a chuckle.

She laughed softly. "So, it would seem." She stood and held her hand out to me. Not knowing what she was planning, I took it hesitantly and stood. She led me to the kitchen, and I chuckled when she pulled out the milk and cookies. "A nightcap," she said.

I grabbed two glasses and joined her at the table. "A nightcap of milk and cookies?" I chuckled and took her hand in mine across the table. "How sweet you are."

Phoebe blushed. "What? Would you prefer alcohol?"

I brought her hand to my lips and pressed a kiss to the inside of her wrist, trying to hold back a smile when I felt her pulse jump. "No," I answered honestly. "I can't particularly enjoy the aftereffects; however, you still can. Hardly fair." I released her hand, and she poured us two glasses of milk. I had never really been one to partake in so much eating and drinking since I didn't have to, to survive. It always seemed like a waste of time and money, though I could still enjoy the taste. It was good for pretenses, to keep people from asking questions. But it felt like so much more with Phoebe. I felt like I could be more when I was with her. Life, or undeath, didn't have to be so monotonous when she was with me. Thoughts of going back to school flitted through my mind. Maybe I could do something productive with my time—help people.

"What's on your mind?" Phoebe asked, sitting at the table.

I sat opposite her and leaned on my elbows. "Just thinking," I murmured. "I've been around a while, but I've never really done anything with the time I have," I said.

She smiled. "What would you like to do?" Her eyes were bright as she regarded me, and it took me a long moment to put together my words.

"I don't know," I admitted. "It's hard for people like us to have jobs because, after a few years, people take notice in the fact that we don't age. I would hate for my family to have to uproot themselves because I wanted to play human."

Phoebe stood suddenly and put her arms around my shoulders. "You don't have to play anything," she said softly, kissing the top of my head. "Just be you. I'm sure if you told them you wanted to get a job, a career, they would support you, Levi. Sure, there are some logistics to figure out, but you've got all the time in the world to do it." I loved having her arms around me. She felt safe and comfortable, and it felt right.

"Yeah," I said quietly. I dunked a cookie in the milk and lifted it over my head to her mouth. She took a bite obediently and a few crumbs fell into my lap. We both laughed, and she came around to stand beside me. She brushed a crumb off my shoulder and smiled sweetly, her hand finding mine. I squeezed back ever so gently and stood, pulling her against my chest.

"Not interested in milk and cookies?" Phoebe asked quietly, looking up at me. She looked so delicate. My eyes found the bite marks on her soft neck, and I gently traced over them with my finger. They were nearly gone already. I shook my head carefully, watching her for a reaction. Her heart picked up tempo slightly, but I pretended not to notice.

"Maybe later," I said cautiously. I leaned down and pressed a gentle kiss to her lips, which she returned willingly. I cradled her head and deepened the kiss, pushing her backwards until she bumped into the counter. I lifted her effortlessly, resting her bottom on the granite and positioned myself between her legs, my lips finding her throat. She sighed contentedly, but her hands stilled me. I glanced at her, hoping I had not overstepped or misread the moment. I wanted to be with her, in every way possible, but only if she was ready and willing.

"There is no scenario in which everyone in this house doesn't know what's happening, is there?" she whispered, her hands tracing along my shoulder blades.

I shook my head. "Sadly, no. Not if we stay here. But they are all wise enough to keep their mouths shut. At least to you." I lifted her chin with one finger. "Let me be perfectly clear, Phoebe. *Nothing* has to happen tonight. I don't want you to feel pressure to do anything with me." I wanted her so badly, but if all she wanted was a good cuddle, then that was enough for me.

Phoebe laughed softly. "Isn't it obvious?" she asked. "I want to do... *something* with you." She squeezed her thighs around my hips slightly. "What that means exactly, I don't know yet. I don't know what I'm doing, Levi. With you, with *us*. I'm tired of thinking about everything." She pulled me to her again, pressing her soft lips to mine. I wrapped my arms around her and lifted her up, and she wrapped her legs around me. I groaned and kissed her throat, turning and carrying her effortlessly up the stairs. I listened intently for the others, but if they were awake, they were keeping very still and quiet.

I could appreciate the attempt to at least replicate the idea of privacy. I had to focus on walking when Phoebe started kissing my neck and my jeans grew incredibly restricting and uncomfortable. Her fingers twirled around in my hair as I pushed our bedroom door open. The idea startled me slightly, but it felt right. *Our* bedroom. I carried her to the bed and settled her down against the covers, leaning over her. "Say the word," I whispered, leaning closer. "And I'll stop."

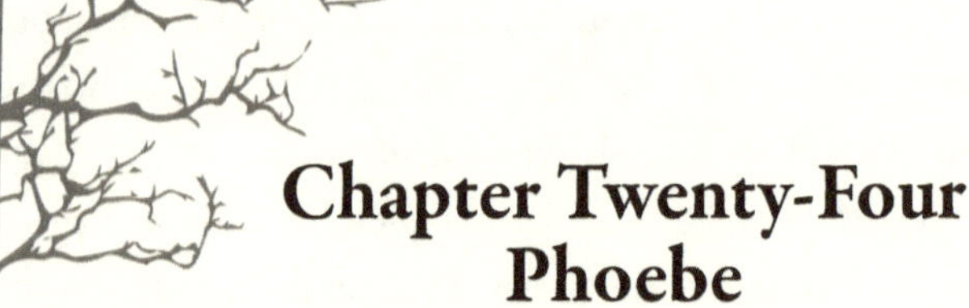

Chapter Twenty-Four
Phoebe

I was not going to talk myself out of this. I wanted Levi, and he *clearly* wanted me. We were two consenting adults—how old was he, anyway? I shook the thought away as Levi's hands skimmed over my body, his fingers brushing beneath the hem of my shirt. I pushed him away just far enough to pull my shirt over my head, exposing my lacey bra underneath. Levi took a moment to look over me, appreciation in his eyes. He removed his own shirt, and I lifted my hands to trace across his chest. He groaned softly and came down again, his lips moving over my neck, my shoulders, my chest.

I reached between us and worked at his jeans, a sigh escaping my lips, when the button finally popped free. In an instant, the jeans joined the other clothes on the floor and Levi was with me again. If I didn't know any better, I wouldn't have noticed his absence. He unbuttoned my jeans and slowly worked them off my hips, tossing them aside. He moved me back farther on the bed, my head resting on the pillows. He rested over me, his breathing slightly erratic, his excitement pressing against my thigh.

"Before we... do anything," he murmured against my ear. "It's a little unnecessary, but I can get a condom. I can't get you pregnant and I haven't been with anyone in... a while." He chuckled dryly.

I pressed a finger to his lips. "I trust you," I whispered. "Remind me to ask about the pregnancy thing when we aren't so... preoccupied." Without another word, I pushed his boxers down and out of the way. He slid my panties off and I graciously removed my own bra. His eyes drank me in, and he took a deep breath.

"Are you sure?" he asked.

I laughed and nodded. "Do I have to spell it out?" I asked. "Levi, I want this. I want *you.*"

He needed no other words. His body covered mine, cool and firm, starkly contrasted to my own soft and rapidly growing warmer body. He nudged my legs apart and kissed me deeply, swallowing my gasp as he pushed inside of me. A moan fell from my lips as he moved, sweet and slow, his lips leaving a path of fire in their wake as he found all of my sensitive spots. He cherished my body as he made love to me and I thought I was going to lose it any minute, but he seemed to know when I was nearing the end and he would change it up to keep me suspended in pleasure. He groaned, his whole body taut. "Phoebe," he whispered, his jaw working.

I clung to him, holding his body against me, my legs wrapping around his waist. "Go ahead," I murmured, voice shaking. "Please."

He needed no other prompting. I felt his teeth pierce my throat and a loud gasp escaped. I almost had enough presence of mind to be embarrassed, knowing the others could probably hear everything, but I didn't care. We moved together, in sync with one another. My teeth ached, and I shuddered, the feeling of his teeth pulling free dangerously exquisite. He kissed me and I could taste my own blood on his lips, which only added more fuel to the fire. I wanted to bite him—no. I *needed* to.

I kissed his throat, feeling his slow pulse pumping. Seemingly of its own accord, my mouth opened wider and without warning, I clamped my teeth down on his neck. To my surprise, I broke skin easily and Levi moaned in wonder and pleasure. He thrust harder, his game of keep away officially over. The bed shook as we moved, our breathing ragged. And we came together in a chorus of gasps and pants.

My body was pleasantly warm as we lay together, a thin sheen of sweat covering my skin. I looked over at him and blinked, my brain uncomprehending. "Phoebe?" Levi asked, noticing my staring.

I reached out and pressed two fingers to his throat. "I bit you," I said.

Levi nodded, a lazy smile spreading across his face. "I know," he said. "I was there, and I do seem to recall." He pulled me more snugly against him, tracing patterns on my bare back.

"No, but... I punctured... I... there... I left *fang marks.*" I said the words in awe, and Levi tilted his head to the side.

"Well," he said casually. "We don't know much about dhampirs. Perhaps, if the circumstances are just right, you can produce fangs." He was looking at me so tenderly, seemingly unbothered by this revelation.

"I hope you don't mind," I whispered, snuggling closer.

"Phoebe. I am *far* from caring. I'm happy you felt comfortable enough to bite me back." Levi leaned over and kissed my temple. "Biting is a perfectly natural reaction to sex."

"I get what you meant," I said gently. "About it feeling more like a need than a want. It was like I just couldn't *not* bite you." My eyelids were growing heavy, and I snuggled into the covers, my hand resting on Levi's chest. This felt right. This felt like home. I fell asleep, our limbs still entangled.

The morning came much too quickly. Levi and I were still curled up together, and he was watching me when I awoke. He kissed me and I smiled lazily against his lips. "Good morning," I whispered.

"Good morning," he said, pushing my hair back off my face. "You're beautiful."

I blushed and rolled over, pushing myself up onto my elbows. "Come on," I said, tapping his chest. "Get dressed and let's go do the walk of shame."

"Walk of shame? I'm not ashamed of *anything* that happened last night. They're the pervs who listened." Levi chuckled as I blushed straight to my roots. I got dressed and dragged a brush through my hair, pausing to inspect the new marks on my neck. They were healing, but still very noticeable. I glanced at Levi's neck as he dressed and sighed. His were still visible too. They likely wouldn't go away until he fed again. The thought of him using me crossed my mind, but I wasn't sure either of us was ready for that.

"Hey. So last night... you said you couldn't get me pregnant." I was hesitant to ask, lest it be an upsetting topic. Because I knew vampires very much could get humans pregnant. Obviously, since my parents had me and dhampirs were a thing at all.

"Oh." Levi sighed and pushed his hand through his hair. "Yeah. Even when I was human," he said with a shrug. "Shooting blanks. When you live forever, you get used to it. So... I hope that's not upsetting to you."

I laughed. "Levi, kids are not even on the radar right now. Should we get to that point, we can always talk about other options." I walked over and kissed him lightly on the lips. "But let's not make an issue where there is none. Now let's go get breakfast before I lose my nerve to leave this room ever again."

Levi snickered and caught my chin with his fingers lightly. He kissed me again, deeper. "We don't have to leave," he said, voice growing husky.

Though tempting, my stomach growled loudly. I snorted and stepped back, putting space between us. "I have a hunger of a different kind," I said.

Levi pouted. "Alright, I guess I need to feed the dhampir." He kissed me again, tenderly, and we slipped out the door together.

It was almost worse than I expected. We entered the room together and everyone turned to look at us, like they were lying in wait. Richard lifted an eyebrow and snickered, turning away at the dark look I threw him.

"Nice matching set," Caleb said, poking my neck as he walked past. "Surprised to see some on him, though, you freak." He hooked a thumb at Levi and gave me a side arm hug. "I feel a little heartbroken," he teased. "I bought you coffee." He pouted slightly, but I knew he was only jesting.

"Leave the poor thing alone," Kalene chided. She sent me an apologetic look. "Try to... um... keep it down next time. And I don't mean the volume. I was about climbing the walls last night."

I blushed furiously, and she chuckled. "I'm so sorry," I whispered, my fingers coming up to cover my mouth. I couldn't possibly get any redder.

Kalene shrugged. "I can't turn my gift off as easily as some people, so it's always on and, yes, horny counts as an emotion." She laughed and shook her head, fanning herself. "Whew!"

"Well," Richard ventured. "From the sounds of it, and the fact that at some point last night your mental blocks went to absolute shit, it was a good night for the two of you, but I got some mental images I never needed to see of my brother."

I turned to Levi. "I'm going to go kill myself now." My cheeks were so red I thought I would burst into flames.

He grabbed my wrist and yanked me against his chest. "Nope," he said, curling an arm around me. "Don't you dare. I like you too much." He nuzzled my neck right there in front of everyone and for a moment, I was afraid he would bite me. His chest rumbled with a laugh. "I have *some* self-control, love."

I rolled my eyes and sighed. "There you go again," I said, resting my head against his chest. I listened to his slow heartbeat and frowned, straightening suddenly. My hand flew to my own chest, and everyone stared at me. My own heartbeat seemed slower than usual.

Chapter Twenty-Five
Phoebe

I sat on the floor of the living room while all the vampires stared at me. "That's... weird, right?" Felicity asked.

Caleb leaned against the wall, rubbing his jaw. "Well," he intoned. "I guess it *could* make sense. She's half human and half vampire and before she got involved in all of this, she was none the wiser about her vampire half. Think about it—she would have known something was up if she wanted to bite people all the time. Maybe, as a dhampir, she can suppress each aspect of her?"

"Like... I can be more one or the other?" I asked. "And now I just seem to be leaning toward the vampire half of me?"

"Maybe," Richard said, nodding. He sat cross-legged in the armchair, leaning forward, his elbows resting on his knees. "It is possible. You've been around us a while and then there was last night, of course." I blushed and looked at the floor. "Don't worry about it, Phoebe. We're all adults here. We'll just... give headphones or earplugs a try if this is going to be a regular occurrence. Or, you know, go get a room."

Felicity scowled at Richard. "She does *not* have to leave to have sex. This is her home too, *Dick*." She sat daintily on the arm of the couch, perched just so. She looked like an angel sitting there, the soft glow of the overhead lights illuminating her dark red hair. She looked like an angry angel, but an angel, nevertheless.

"We are getting off topic here," Levi said, rubbing small circles over his temples. "Is this a bad thing?" he asked. "Can you change back?"

I blinked at him. "Well, I don't feel any different. I still feel like me, Levi. I don't know if it's even a conscious decision to 'change' myself. I didn't do anything last night. It just happened."

He blew out a sigh and stood, coming to sit beside me on the floor. "I didn't mean it that way, Phoebe. We just don't know anything about dhampirs, and I don't want you to get... stuck as one or the other, unless it's what you wanted."

"I don't feel like that's right," I said. "I was born both and neither. I don't think it's possible for me to be exclusively one or the other." I leaned against him and threaded my fingers through his, lifting our hands to look at them. His hands were cool and strong and dwarfed mine. I felt so at peace sitting there on the floor with my family and I could almost pretend that Avatrice wasn't out there, biding his time to get at me. I knew there would be a moment that everything came to a head. He had to be getting impatient, but in that moment, I found that I didn't care. Having this time with these people who cared about me by my side, it wasn't so bad.

Levi's phone rang suddenly, and he blew out a sigh. "Levi," he answered, looking annoyed. "What? When?" He stood swiftly, his posture rigid. "Okay. No, no, I'll be there." He hung up and looked down at me apologetically. "It was the blood bar," he said. "They hadn't seen anything on the tapes from that night he attacked you, but they caught him on the cameras last night."

"Do you need company?" Richard asked. "I can probe the minds around and see what they know."

Levi nodded and was already moving toward the door. "Kalene, Caleb—you come with and get yourselves topped off. If Avatrice is there, it'll help to have backup. Felicity—you stay with Phoebe."

Felicity moved to crouch beside me on the floor, nodding her head. "Got it," she said. "I'll call if there's an issue. Keep us updated and be safe." She looked at each of her siblings and sighed. "Be careful."

I stood awkwardly and watched them walk toward the door. Maybe this was it. Maybe they would be able to find something out about Avatrice and we could find him before he found us. I felt Felicity's hand on my shoulder and gave her a wan smile. When the door closed behind the last of them, we faced each other. "I hate this," I said.

She sighed. "Me too," she admitted. "I hate the idea of my family being in danger and Avatrice *is* dangerous." She scowled and pushed her red locks back. I could see the agitation in the stiffness of her shoulders. "I don't know much about him beyond what Levi has told us, but I know he's bad news."

"Yeah, and he currently has an insane fixation on me. How lucky." I plopped down on the couch and rubbed my eyes. "I just want this to be over."

Felicity held her hand out to me. "Come on," she said. "I noticed the fridge is looking a little bare. I'll keep you safe."

I took her hand and let her pull me to my feet. "You want to leave the house?"

Felicity shrugged. "We are no safer here than we are in public. Arguably, we are *safer* in public. I don't think Avatrice is stupid enough to attack you with an audience." She tugged me toward the door. "Besides, you don't get out enough these days. When this is all over and Avatrice is dead, because we will kill him, we are going to go get a manicure together and get coffee."

I laughed as she pulled me around the back of the house to where Kalene's car was parked. We climbed in and Felicity turned us toward town. "Sounds good to me. But you don't need to drink coffee."

"True," she said, drumming her nails on the steering wheel. I regarded her hands for a moment, realizing I had never paid much attention to the minor details about her. Felicity was deadly. She had a sharp mind and quick wit and she seemed to favor the stiletto nail, effectively arming her with claws at all times. The black color complimented her fair skin, paired nicely with her deep red locks. She was drop dead gorgeous, emphasis on the dead. "I don't *need* coffee, but I can still enjoy the taste and the time-honored past-time of basic bitches."

That elicited a laugh from me, and I shook my head. "Are you saying I'm a basic bitch?"

She slid a sidelong glance at me, her lips quirked into a smile. "You? Definitely." She turned into the grocery store parking lot and turned to face me. "But we can fix that."

I climbed from the car, quirking an eyebrow. "That is the most threatening thing you've ever said to me."

She snickered. "Really?" she asked, as we walked across the parking lot and entered the store, moving around the people coming and going. She kept me within arm's reach as we grabbed a cart. "I can do better." She grinned at me, and I found myself smiling back. Felicity was definitely not all that bad. She was cool and even reminded me of Angie a little. I felt a pang in my chest and felt Felicity's hand on my arm, as if she knew where my thoughts had gone. Or maybe it was simpler than that. Perhaps she just picked up on the change in my breathing or the way my heart stuttered.

"I miss her," I said softly, clenching my hands into fists. "Why did she have to die?"

Felicity pulled me into a hug in the middle of the dairy aisle. "I'm sorry you lost your friend. I wish it hadn't happened, but if you had gotten home sooner, you might have suffered the same fate. That might not be what you want to hear, but you are alive. Miss her, yes. Honor her memory, yes. Let it take you down and defeat you, never."

She gave my hand a pat and turned to the cart and pretended to inspect the various cheeses in front of her, allowing me a moment to gather myself.

Chapter Twenty-Six
Levi

The four of us arrived and walked into the bar together. Richard and I veered off toward the security and Kalene walked off with Caleb to get a drink. I hated leaving Phoebe with only Felicity to protect her, but it could be argued that Fee was the most vicious protector. If someone were stupid enough to make a move, Fee would fight with everything in her to defend Phoebe. But what if Avatrice brought friends?

"Hey, don't think about it," Richard said. "Like you said, er... thought, Felicity is a badass, okay? And she is far from dumb. If she can't fight, she'll get Phoebe out. Besides, they can reach me if there is a problem, and Caleb is the fastest out of all of us. He could be there in no time."

"But Avatrice is faster," I muttered. "I know him better than any of you. He is insanely fast, Richard. That's how he got away from us for so long; he is smart, fast, and deadly. He's been around a long time."

"Yeah, yeah, yeah," Richard muttered, rapping his knuckles on the security door. "We get better with age and all that."

The door swung open and the same woman from before stood before us. She threw a curious look at Richard but said nothing. She stepped aside and let us walk in. I could tell Richard was probing her, but based on the look on her face, she wasn't having it. "Here," she said, thrusting her finger at the screen. "He was here last night. Looks like he was alone, just here to get a drink."

We turned our attention to the monitor and my jaw clenched involuntarily. Avatrice walked leisurely up to the bar and spoke with the woman behind the counter. She laughed, and he smiled. He said something, and she nodded and produced a drink. Avatrice drank it quickly and licked his lips, his eyes sliding toward the camera. My body felt like it was vibrating with rage. He knew he was on camera. He turned away from the woman behind the bar and scanned the crowd. I saw her almost before he did. The woman sitting alone, slumped over in a booth. She looked like she had just donated and was sleeping it off, but she was secluded, and almost out of the camera's sights.

Richard made a disgusted noise in the back of his throat as Avatrice approached her. She lifted her head, her eyes hollow. But she smiled. Avatrice reached out and brushed her hair back off her neck and motioned, speaking to her. She laughed and nodded. "What a sick fuck," Richard grumbled. "She's gonna die. There's no way she has enough left to give."

"A junkie," Carly said, arms crossed. "We see them sometimes. Usually women, but not always, who get a high from the bites. They'll give until there is nothing left just to feel that." She shook her head. "We try to keep them out of here long enough that they can replenish, but some slip through the cracks and there are definitely those that would use her. She's cute."

The three of us watched the video with varying degrees of disgust as Avatrice leaned into the girl. To an inexperienced eye, it could easily be mistaken for a bit of fooling around, but we all knew better. The way her body tensed and then relaxed, the way her hands clutched at him, her head falling back. The way she slumped and Avatrice stood, wiping a hand across his mouth. He looked directly at the camera and quirked an eyebrow, pointing. The video had no sound, but his words were clear enough.

Enjoy her while you can. She's mine.

I snarled and turned around, tearing my hands through my hair. "He's fucking toying with me," I snapped.

Richard knew better than to try to calm me. He took a step back and folded his arms across his chest, giving me space. "So, we kill him," he said simply.

I glared at him. "I would rip his throat out with my teeth if I could. If he puts another *finger* on her..." I groaned and turned back to the monitor, watching Avatrice walk leisurely through the crowd toward the door. He had been alone. I still had no leads. I had nothing. And he knew Phoebe was with me, at least in some capacity. My barely beating heart stopped all together.

"Woah," Carly said, looking at me. "Are you okay, man?" She took a step back as I turned and fairly ripped the door off its hinges.

Richard cursed and followed me, whipping his phone out, fingers dialing quickly. "Come on," he muttered. "Pick up, Fee."

I found Caleb and Kalene at the bar, but they both downed their drinks when they saw me. "We're leaving," I said briskly, throwing money on the counter. "I think this was a setup."

We all hurried from the bar, but Caleb bypassed the car, opting to run. He was gone before I had started the car. "She's not answering," Richard said darkly. "Felicity or Phoebe. Straight to voicemail."

P*hoebe*

We finished the shopping and loaded it into the car. This time, I remembered the coffee. We laughed the entire way home, talking about old boyfriends and bad dates, generally becoming closer as friends. She pulled up in front of the house and cocked her head to the side, frowning. "What's wrong?" I asked nervously.

Felicity was silent for another moment before shaking her head. "I thought I sensed a vampire in there. 'Course, it could be Caleb. He's the fastest runner out of all of us, so Levi might have sent him to check on us. But I'm not sensing it now." She climbed from the car, but her posture was still a little rigid. I grabbed a couple of bags from the trunk and the two of us headed inside. Felicity dropped off the bags she had grabbed in the kitchen and turned. "I'll get the rest if you want to start putting it all away."

I nodded and headed to the kitchen, grabbing freezer and refrigerator food first, so it didn't spoil on the kitchen floor. I was just about to put the eggs away when I felt the most imperceptible change in the room. It was like it grew a little cooler. I turned, eggs in hand, and a gasp escaped my lips. The eggs fell from my hands and shattered across the floor, and I stumbled back against the fridge. "No," I whispered, tears pricking my eyes.

Avatrice lifted an eyebrow, his eyes finding the barely perceptible puncture marks on my neck, and shook his head. "Yes," he said, taking a step toward me.

My whole body shook, my heart hammering in my chest. I felt more human now than I ever had before, fragile, alone, weak. "F-Felicity?" I whimpered.

"Incapacitated." Avatrice moved closer, within arm's reach now. "I'm not a complete monster." He chuckled and reached out faster than I had seen any of my vampires move and grabbed me by the throat. He dragged me against his chest, and I choked and gasped for air. "I just want you." He paused and tilted his head to the side. "Well, and Levi. But I have a feeling he will come to me." He flung me away from him suddenly and I crashed into the kitchen table, the wooden legs splintering beneath the force. I gasped for air and scrambled to my hands and knees, but I wasn't fast enough. Avatrice knelt over me, effortlessly pushing me to the floor and pinning me there. I couldn't move. I could barely breathe. My chest was on fire and tears pricked my eyes.

I was lifted off the floor, and my head fell back, my head swimming. Avatrice slammed my head against the wall, leaving a sizable dent behind and my vision turned black around the edges. He lifted me again and brought my face close to his. "You had to make things difficult," he whispered, stroking my cheek with one hand. "Never matter. Come. We have much to discuss." He carried me effortlessly while I struggled to make my limbs work while simultaneously trying to stay awake.

He carried me through the front door, and my eyes caught a flash of red on the sidewalk. A strangled cry came from my lips and tears fell from my eyes. Beautiful, vivacious Felicity. Reduced to a pile of blood and slashed flesh. Her eyes were closed, and she looked very much dead. She was a vampire, I reminded myself in my panic. She couldn't be dead.

She couldn't be.

As we passed the car, I thought I heard the sound of her phone ringing, but the darkness overtook me, and everything went black.

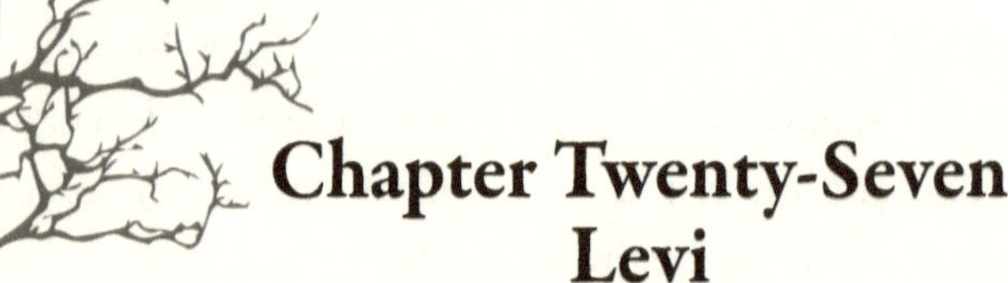

Chapter Twenty-Seven
Levi

Richard's phone rang and he answered quickly. "What?" he asked, voice sharp. "Oh...no..." He closed his eyes and shook his head. "Is she...?"

I shot a sharp look at him, my teeth grinding. I could hear Caleb on the other end, of course, but I didn't want to believe it. Felicity was hurt badly, and Phoebe was gone. I was an idiot. How could I have been so stupid? I played right into his trap. A few moments later, we pulled up to the house. Kalene's car was out front, the trunk wide open. The front door was ajar, and I could smell the blood as soon as I climbed from the car.

Caleb sat in the foyer, Felicity cradled in his lap, his wrist firmly locked in her jaws. It was worse than I thought if she needed blood that badly. Her skin was covered in red slashes, already healing. One of her eyes was swollen shut and purple, but as I watched and as she drank, the purple faded to a greenish hue. Blood caked her hair and clothes. Richard crouched down and brushed her hair back off her face. "Switch," he instructed, and Caleb extracted his wrist from her mouth and Richard slid into his place, wincing slightly as she bit down.

Caleb stood and rubbed his wrist, looking solemn. "There was a fight," he said. "It...doesn't look good for Phoebe." He turned and led me to the kitchen and my eyes took in everything. Broken eggs on the floor, the kitchen table in shambles, several dents in the wall. There was a little spatter of blood and a few strands of hair stuck in the cracks and I leaned closer, staring as if that would change the fact that I knew it was Phoebe's blood, as if I couldn't smell it. I could almost taste it. Her smart watch that Kalene had bought her lay shattered on the floor.

"This is all my fault," I muttered, rubbing a hand down my face. I looked up, frowning. "Wait. Where is Kalene?"

Caleb frowned and glanced around. She hadn't come into the house with us. We headed back outside, glad to see Felicity sitting up on her own as we walked by. Kalene stood on the sidewalk outside, the sun beating down on her harshly. As she stood there, her body began to shake, and she let out a keening wail that threatened to break my undead heart. She collapsed to the sidewalk, wracked with sobs. Her fists came down on the sidewalk, sending spiderweb cracks along the concrete. She punched the ground again and again and Caleb hurried to her side, always the caretaker. He pulled her to her feet and allowed her to hit him when she could no longer hit the cement. Eventually she fell against him, shaking and sobbing quietly. He held her tightly, looking over her head at me. I shook my head. I didn't know what was happening; Felicity was alive, mostly. I didn't dare entertain the thought that she was lamenting about someone else.

After a few more minutes, Kalene took in a deep, shuddering breath. "I'm s-sorry," she hiccupped, swiping her hands over her face. "I got hit w-with all of h-her emotions." She clenched her hands into fists. "She's s-so scared. It's like she l-left behind all of it and it just punched me in the chest, burning my throat. I couldn't shake it. I couldn't let it loose."

Caleb brushed her hair back and kissed the top of her head. "It's alright now," he said gently. "Has that ever happened before? Feeling someone's emotions who isn't around?"

"Once or twice," Kalene whispered. "If the emotions are big enough, strong enough. If I know them well enough." She groaned and clenched her hands into fists. "God, she's *scared*."

"Can you track it?" I asked cautiously.

Kalene shook her head. "It doesn't work like that," she muttered, looking toward the house. "Is Fee...?"

"She's okay," Caleb said. "Richard and I gave her blood. She's okay." He gave her a final hug and stepped back, brushing wrinkles out of his shirt. Kalene pushed her dark hair back and took a deep breath.

"I can't track her, but you probably can," she said, looking at me. I blinked slowly, uncomprehending. Kalene advanced upon me. "I've seen the signs, Levi. The way you are together; the way you've been from the start. Your need to bite her and her need to reciprocate, even at only half vampire. Even your recent uncanny ability to know what she's thinking. I've never seen it in person, but I've read about it. We even talked about it once with her. She's your *Destined*." Kalene shook her head and took my hands in hers. "You were made for each other. Literally. And if you drank her blood, you'd know."

I winced. "I haven't. We've only bitten." But that wasn't really the truth. Even with just a bite, I had gotten a taste and it had been...exquisite. How I had managed to *not* drink from her was unfathomable. I had, on occasion, had blood from the source when I was younger and more impulsive, but I couldn't remember it ever being as good.

Richard and Felicity stepped outside, and she winced, lifting her hand to ward off the sun. Richard twisted his face up. "Gross," he said, looking at me. "I've smelled her blood—never tasted it—but it doesn't smell *that* good. Jesus, Levi."

Kalene was nodding. "I agree. When you brought her here, she was bleeding, Levi. We've all smelled it. But for you, her blood is perfect. And, since she's half vampire, I'd guess if she decided to partake, yours would be too." The thought hadn't crossed my mind that Phoebe might one day wish to drink blood. Or even need to. I shuddered, hating the idea of her being in a situation like Felicity.

"How do I do it?" I asked, facing Kalene. "How do I find her?" I was willing to try anything.

Kalene shook her head. "I don't really know," she admitted. "But supposedly when you find your Destined, you can sense each other. I don't know how far away it works, or if it's just a myth."

I nodded. It was something and worth a shot. I closed my eyes and thought about Phoebe, thinking about her blood. I felt an urge to move, and I let it happen, my body turning slightly to the left. I cocked my head to the side and tried to search for her with my mind, much in the same way Phoebe had been practicing to reach Richard at a distance. No one spoke for several minutes and when I opened my eyes, they all stared at me. "I don't know," I said in frustration. The wind shifted suddenly, blowing against my face and I shivered. "Wait."

"Levi?" Caleb asked tentatively.

"Blood," I said. "On the wind." I started walking without conscious thought. "Phoebe's blood. It's faint, which is good. It means she isn't bleeding profusely. Just a trickle, I think."

"Then what are we waiting for?" Felicity asked, flipping her hair over her shoulder, and inspecting her nails. One was broken and she made a face. "I have a bone to pick. Let's go get our girl."

Chapter Twenty-Eight
Phoebe

I awoke with a groan. I tried to lift my arms and found they were strapped to my sides. I struggled against the binds, my eyes darting around the room. Where was I? I immediately took stock of everything. I was in a room darkened against the sun; curtains drawn. So, I couldn't see outside, but that was okay. I was in some sort of... hospital? I could see IV paraphernalia shoved in the corner of the room, could see the posters on the wall advocating for health. Where was Avatrice?

"Ahh," he said, startling me. I felt hands on my shoulders and gritted my teeth. "So sorry about all of this, love," Avatrice murmured, tracing a finger down my cheek. "Couldn't risk you trying to run on me." He laughed and rounded the table so I could see him. His long black hair was unbound, hanging around his shoulders. "As if you could ever hope to outrun me. We have much to catch up on."

"I don't want anything from you," I spat, struggling against the straps pinning me down. It was no use. All the time Caleb spent training me was for nothing. I was simply no match for a full-fledged vampire with the insane speed Avatrice had.

He seemed unbothered by my struggles. "Perhaps," he mused, tapping a finger against his chin. "But I can tell you more about yourself. I studied dhampirs for a long time. Of course, there are some out in the world, created organically. The occurrences are between a father vampire and mother human, though success rates are low. Oftentimes, the mother is lost upon birth of the child, or the child is simply not viable. There is approximately, based on my research, a thirty percent chance of survival for both parties, and about fifty/fifty of one or the other. So, congratulations, you are part of the thirty percent, love." I glared at him, though he was giving me some valuable knowledge, I supposed. Where else would I learn this information? I hated that I wanted to know more.

"I see I have your interest." He paced the room, and my eyes followed him, straining in the dark. "Once a dhampir is born, they are often raised as human. Most cases of naturally occurring dhampirs result in the vampire parents pretending to be human, at least until a certain age. Usually around puberty, the truth is revealed. Can you imagine a three-year-old who knows they have vampire powers?" He laughed, startling me. "Adorable little monsters."

"Why are you telling me this?" I demanded. I needed to keep him busy, to keep him talking. If I could reach Richard with my mind, I had a chance. But I had no way of knowing how far away he was. I had no idea if I was even still within the city.

"Because it is your right to know. Think what you want of me, Phoebe, but I do not wish you harm. You are a success! A beautiful young dhampir, coming into her vampire capabilities." He smirked. "Do not think I am unaware of the goings on between you and *Levi*." He walked over and traced his finger over my throat. "You let him bite you. Would you allow me the same honor?" He leaned closer, and I flinched, praying he wouldn't. Not again.

I formed the spool of red thread in my mind and sent it out, searching for Richard. By now, I knew how his mind felt, almost as if, when we connected, we were the same person. I popped the cork on my emotions and let them flow. If Kalene was in the area, she wouldn't be able to ignore my big feelings. Waves of anger and fear washed over me, and I consciously pushed them outward, keeping half a mind on the red thread dancing through the world in search of a vampire with green eyes.

"Of course," Avatrice said, almost distracting me, "there will be time for that later. For now, let us just talk." He sat on a stool and scooted closer, resting one elbow on the edge of my bed. "Tell me, have you bitten him back?" I blinked and looked at Avatrice, wondering how to play his game. Tell him the truth or lie? Would he be able to tell I was lying? He chuckled and shook his head and I swallowed hard. "Your human heart gives you away, love. I think yes." He stood and paced some more, hands folded neatly in front of him. "That's alright. I'm not angry. What you did before me is none of my business—not really. We all make mistakes."

"Levi is not a mistake," I blurted. My face heated, and I snapped my mouth shut, hoping I had not just sealed my fate.

"Of course, you wouldn't think so," Avatrice said. "Never mind that. As I was saying—usually around puberty, the dhampir is told of their vampire heritage. You are just a late bloomer, love. Quite alright. Once the dhampir knows of this, it is a glorious thing. You are able to blend in to either crowd, suppressing either of your two halves. Of course, you are never truly human or vampire, always somewhere in between. You seem to have been spending most of your time more closely aligned with your vampire self these past few days." He smiled. "I suppose I should thank Levi for that. But, as you could perhaps guess, you get the good and the bad. When you suppress your vampire side, you are weaker, you age, you require food and nourishment. When you suppress your human side, you are stronger, faster, you do not age. You could live forever if you always suppressed your human side."

"So, I can't be Turned?" I asked quietly.

"No," Avatrice said simply. "Even if I bit you now and forced my blood down your throat, you would not Turn. Your vampire side would simply take over and accept the blood as nourishment."

He shrugged one shoulder. "Believe me, I have tested that theory at length." He sighed and brushed his hair back off his shoulder. "But, like I said, if you suppress your human side, it's almost the same thing."

I tucked that knowledge away for later. "Why do this?" I asked. "Why did you try so hard to create dhampirs if we are such a chance?"

"Hunters." He spoke the word with so much venom, I shivered. "Vampire Hunters have stalked us vampires for as long as I can remember. Always in some form or another and we have never had any real way to defend against them. Yes, we are stronger and faster, but they outnumber us immensely. They are adaptable and, in their large numbers, they created tools to fight us, as if we needed to be fought. As if we were monsters. Most of us aren't all that bad, you know."

I knew of at least five vampires that I thought were pretty good, but Avatrice was not one of them. "You killed my best friend." I spat the words at him, accusatory and angry.

He sighed. "I did no such—"

"Your hand may not have slit her throat, but you killed her all the same. She is *gone* because of *you!*" My voice rose until I was shouting, and tears pricked at the backs of my eyes. "I'll never see her again because of *you.*"

"She was in my way." The words were spoken so coldly, devoid of emotion. Avatrice stepped closer, his black eyes soulless voids staring into my soul. "And I do not take kindly to people standing in my way. My mistake was not doing it myself and I lost one of my dhampirs. Levi and his little *family* have gotten in my way a number of times. I assure you; it will not happen again. I spared the redhead for you, love. Do not take my graciousness for granted." He grabbed my jaw and turned my face toward him. "You will do exactly as I ask, or I will wipe them off the face of the planet."

I scowled. "You didn't lose your dhampir because of my family. *I* killed him," I snapped. "He attacked me in my home, and I defended myself."

Avatrice looked at me for a long time, not blinking, not breathing. His jaw twitched, and I thought he was going to lose it, but his expression smoothed, and he smiled. "Perhaps I underestimated you." He stood and turned away from me. "In any case, I need you." He glanced over my shoulder at me. "You will bear my children."

Chapter Twenty-Nine
Levi

Why was it so difficult to find her? We could only follow the trail of blood so far before it was too faint even for me to pick up. My skin was starting to itch, being out in the sun, but I ignored it. Richard sent me a concerned look, but I ignored that, too. I stood in the middle of the sidewalk, feeling helpless. If she was my soulmate, my *Destined,* then how come I couldn't even find her?

"Wait," Richard said suddenly, tilting his head as if he were listening to something. I opened my mouth to speak, but he silenced me with a look. "It's faint," he said. "And I have no way of communicating back with her, but I can hear her. She will get louder the closer we get. She doesn't seem to have any barriers up, which is good for us, but if Avatrice has any kind of mental manipulation, it could be disastrous for her."

Kalene jumped. "Yes," she said, rubbing her forehead. "I think she is projecting her emotions, too. No holding back. I feel it, like a tickle in my chest."

Great. So, we had two ways of homing in on her with no idea of what direction to go. I felt a hand on my shoulder and looked over at Felicity. "Try again," she said softly. "I don't know how it works or even *if* it works, but right now, it's all we've got. The next best thing is to split up and send Richard one way and Kalene the other and just start looking for her."

"Hospital?" Richard muttered in confusion. He shook his head. "She's... in a hospital?"

"Out here?" Caleb asked, sharply. "There aren't any hospitals on this side of town."

"A clinic maybe?" Felicity suggested. "There is that old walk-in clinic on tenth." She looked at the rest of us and shrugged, walking in that direction. "Any better ideas?"

It was the best thing we had, so we all followed after her. I knew we were heading in the right direction when Richard grunted and covered his ears, as if that would help the sound in his head. "Your girl is *loud*," he muttered. That was a good thing; it meant that we were headed in the right direction and furthermore, it meant she was alive.

A clinic on tenth. *We are on our way, Phoebe. Just hang in there.*

Phoebe

I stared at him. He was going to knock me up and force me to have his children. Suddenly, being strapped to the table seemed much more sinister. I thrashed and squirmed, trying to loosen the straps, but it was no use. "Why?" I finally asked, tears burning my eyes.

Avatrice glanced at me, unconcerned by my struggle. "Because the Hunters must fall," he said simply. "They have mastered the art of hunting vampires, so I sought to create a race of dhampirs that they could not fight. Dhampirs do not... read vampire, so to speak. To me, sitting there, you feel just like a human, yet I know you are half vampire. The Hunters would never be able to tell, and we could stand a chance at fighting them."

I sort of understood his logic, but the way he went about it was horrible and wrong. Forcing women to bear children, knowing it would likely kill one or the other, was horrid. Treating them like some kind of livestock, killing the children that didn't fit the bill. He was beyond just trying to save the vampires from the Hunters. That was just madness. And now, after realizing that didn't work and going to prison for a hundred years, he thought to just start again?

"Do you menstruate regularly?"

The question came so out of left field; I didn't know how to answer. Of course, I wasn't stupid. He wanted to get me pregnant so it would be pertinent information to know when I was likely to have my period. I gritted my teeth and lied. "No," I said. "I have a birth control implant that stops all that," I said. The truth was, I *had* a birth control implant, but had it removed several months ago. I hadn't gotten around to getting back on any other type. I wasn't having sex at the time, so I didn't see much of a need.

Avatrice clicked his tongue. "Alright," he said simply. "Where is it? I shall remove it immediately. How quickly will you menstruate once it is removed?" He shuffled some things around and turned to face me again, holding a scalpel.

I clenched my hands into fists. "I don't know," I said. "I'm not a doctor. Guess it depends on where I am in my cycle currently. I haven't had a period in so long, I don't even know when the next one would be."

He waved a hand and walked toward me. "No matter," he said simply. "I'll be able to tell when it happens. And then we can commence trying to conceive shortly thereafter. Now, which arm?"

I tried to think of some excuse why he couldn't just rip the nonexistent implant from my arm, but had none. I either had to fess up to the lie or let him cut me, searching for something he would never find. *Oh, Richard. Please hurry.*

"Uh, it was in this arm," I said, motioning with my head. "But they move around a lot, so you'll need to locate it with your fingers first." That would buy me some time while he searched for it. "I've had it a while, so who knows where it could be now. Honestly, they say that sometimes they can even move out of the arm completely. That was what made me hesitate to get it but I'm not a pill kind of girl and getting an IUD just seemed so uncomfortable." I was babbling, and he was glaring at me. Could he tell I was full of shit? At least I sounded knowledgeable enough.

Avatrice sighed sharply and set the scalpel aside. Prodding at my arm with his fingers. "What does it feel like?" he demanded.

"About 4 centimeters, they told me. I didn't want to see it before they put it in. But it's a little flexible piece that is about 4 centimeters long." The lies just kept growing. Sooner or later, he would find out the truth, and I wasn't sure how he would react. I just hoped Levi arrived before then.

Avatrice poked and prodded at my arm for several minutes, growing more agitated by the second. I gritted my teeth, preparing for his fury, when he realized he had been duped. He growled and threw a dark look at me. "Perhaps I should just cut your whole arm off?" he asked. "That will solve the problem all together."

He stood and walked back to his table, grabbing a large cleaver. That didn't look like any kind of medical device, and I started thrashing again, screaming at the top of my lungs and mind. *Holy fuck!* This guy was bonkers. He was going to straight up just amputate? I had not seen that coming and I was very unsure what to do now. Should I fess up? Deal with the consequences. Then again, he might decide to cut my arm off as punishment and I was pretty attached to all of my limbs.

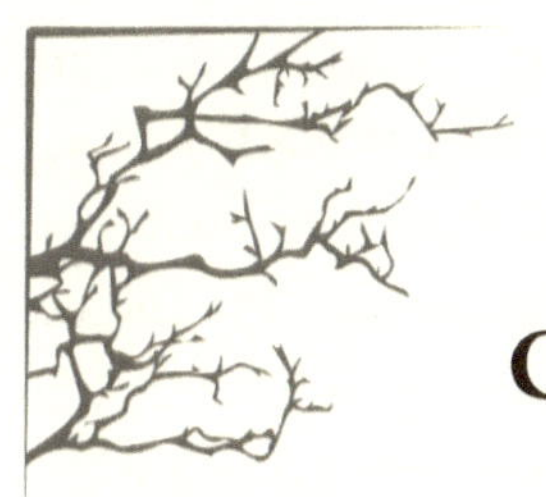

Chapter Thirty
Phoebe

"This will probably hurt," Avatrice said, leaning over me. He grabbed my arm with one hand and placed the cleaver just so.

"Stop!" I screamed. "I was lying. It was a lie! I don't have an implant. I'm not on birth control. Holy shit, please don't cut off my arm!" The words spilled from my mouth without much conscious thought. Avatrice paused and glanced at me, his eyebrow quirking up slowly.

"I wondered when you were going to admit it," he said easily, pulling the cleaver back. "I'm impressed you let it go so far."

I let out a loud breath, my heart hammering in my chest. "You... weren't going to cut off my arm?" I whispered.

Avatrice turned the cleaver this way, and that and sighed. "I probably wouldn't have," he said. "I'd like to keep you as intact as possible."

I was just glad I hadn't pissed myself. But I was still in the same predicament as before; strapped to a table with a guy who wanted to force me to have his babies. I didn't even know if I *wanted* kids, but I knew I didn't want kids with Avatrice. "Look," I said, hoping to reason with him. "You really can't just impregnate people without their consent. That's... well, that's rape."

Avatrice sighed softly and turned away from me, moving things around on a table just out of my sight. "I went to prison for a century, Phoebe. I did atrocious things, I admit. I had a lot of time to think about those things and where I went wrong." He glanced at me. "You might think that one hundred years is not particularly long for a vampire, but I assure you, it is. All that time stuck in one place, inhibitors making me weak. Making me all but *human.*" He said the word with such distaste. He turned to face me again, a syringe in his hand. "My problem the first time was in trusting too many. You might not know this, but your father and I were partners once upon a time."

While he spoke, I wriggled this way and that, trying to loosen the binds. I didn't care so much about what he was saying, just that he kept talking and stayed away from me with that thing. "Partners?" I asked, my eyebrows pulling together.

"Yes, partners. Your father was just as intrigued by the idea of dhampirs as I was. He just chickened out and turned on me when I actually took theory and made it happen." He shrugged one shoulder. "That's business, I suppose, but then he *really* turned on me. Gathered up a group of others who would stand against me. Your precious Levi included." He glared at me. "The Council came. Even I stood no chance against the likes of them."

I had read a little about the Council when I first started learning. I knew they were formidable foes, but I couldn't count on them now. I had to trust that Levi would find me. That the Coven would find me. I prayed that Felicity was okay and that, somehow, my family was on their way to me.

"In any case, I got out several months ago and began tracking down those who wronged me. Levi is the last on my list, lucky dog." Avatrice chuckled and sighed, moving toward me. "I know this isn't ideal," he said, cocking his head to one side as he regarded me.

"Not ideal?" I asked, my heart constricting. "You literally beat the shit out of me, kidnapped me, and are threatening to rape me. Yeah, this is *not ideal.*" The words tasted like venom coming out of my mouth.

"I can give you a choice," Avatrice said, pursing his lips. "Give you some semblance of control over a situation in which you really have no control. I will get what I want, Phoebe. But the choice is yours. I suppose we could do things more...organically. Or we can do it this way," he said, waving the syringe in the air.

I was going to throw up. I felt the bile rising up in my throat and I gagged on it. "Are you fucking serious?" I gasped. I was disgusted and horrified. "Have sex with you or let you inject me with a fucking turkey baster?"

Avatrice shrugged. "While your verbiage isn't accurate, the sentiment is the same. But you are right, for the sake of efficiency, turkey baster it is." He looked me over, tilting his head to the side. "I'll need to do away with your clothes, at least from the waist down." He set the syringe down and turned again and I began thrashing even harder. I felt the straps loosen slightly, but it wasn't enough. When Avatrice turned again, he held a rag in his hands. "Breathe deeply," he said, covering my mouth and nose. I held my breath for as long as I could, struggling against him, screaming for Richard in my mind.

I didn't know how far we were or if they even knew I was in danger. I could only hope he could hear me and that they were on their way. I finally had no choice but to take a breath and the chloroform began its work.

"There now," Avatrice said, stepping back. "It will all be over soon," he said as I finally faded into the darkness.

When I awoke, I was no longer strapped to a table. I was standing up against a wall, my hands bound and wrenched up above my head. My feet were free, but I was also standing in my underwear. I shivered, praying to whoever was listening that he had not done the deed. Tears stung my eyes, and I twisted and thrashed, kicking out, trying to make noise, to knock over anything that could help me.

"Relax," Avatrice said calmly. "Stressing will only make it worse. I don't want to hurt you, but I will if you leave me no other choice." He was on the other side of the room, puttering around with the kind of bed I had seen, and even been on, at the doctor's office. The OBGYN to be specific. It was the kind that had the foot stirrups and I moaned.

"Please," I begged. "Please don't do this." Avatrice ignored me, dragging the bed over. Hot tears coursed down my cheeks, and I rested my head back against the wall. "I'd rather die."

Avatrice glanced at me. "I can't allow that. Any notions of ending your life should be abandoned." He came over and reached up, moving to unchain me. I kicked out, catching him in the chest, and he grunted. Clicking his tongue, he grabbed me by the hair. "Stop," he said darkly, his black eyes narrowed. "Damaging your vessel would not do. I need you to be healthy to carry the baby to term."

I hissed in pain and spat in his face. "Fuck you," I said. If he wouldn't let me go, then I would make it as hard as possible for him to get what he wanted. "I don't want to carry your fucking spawn. And even if you manage to knock me up I hope it fucking dies," I snarled.

Avatrice unchained me, grabbing me by the throat in the same breath. He lifted me up off the floor and I reached up, clawing at his hands, kicking wildly. He carried me effortlessly over to the table and slammed me down, pinning me down. He leaned over, his face dangerously close to mine. "You had your chance," he said, voice deadly. "We do it my way." He moved so fast, even if I had the strength to fight him off, I could never move quickly enough. I found myself strapped to the table, my feet propped up in the stirrups. I screamed. I thrashed, rattling the table.

Please, I thought. *This can't be happening.* I closed my eyes tightly, hearing Avatrice moving around me, humming softly like this was just another fucking Tuesday.

"I can tell you about yourself, you know," he said conversationally. "I've studied dhampirs extensively. While your canines are not as sharp as mine, they are sharper than your average human. And, given proper circumstances, you *can* produce fangs, though your venom is weaker than mine. Or any true vampire. If you were to feed on a human, you would have to release twice the venom to create the sedative effect. You can even drink blood to heal." He glanced at me. "Interesting, no?" I kept screaming until my throat burned, tears searing my eyes. My skin was raw from twisting, trying to loosen my binds. I felt the sticky blood around my wrists, but it wasn't enough.

Chapter Thirty-One
Levi

As we ran, Richard spouted off whatever thoughts he caught from Phoebe. My heart constricted with each plea for help, with each cry for Richard. And every thought begging for *something* to stop had me wanting to vomit. What was he doing to her? I prayed to whoever was listening that she would be alright. I begged God, whom I hadn't spoken to in a very long time, to spare her. May we reach her in time to stop whatever horrible thing Avatrice wanted from her. I could only imagine horrible scenarios, and it made my throat burn.

Richard and Kalene both cried out at the same time, Richard clutching his head and Kalene nearly falling to her knees. And then we all heard it. A scream pierced the air of the all but abandoned neighborhood. I didn't think about the consequences, I just ran, full tilt. And I knew, without a shadow of a doubt, that my brothers and sisters would be right there with me. Richard and Kalene hung back, trying to get their respective powers under control, but Caleb and Felicity flanked me on either side.

"Plan?" Caleb asked, his expression dangerous.

"Don't have one," I said. "Kill Avatrice." The most important thing was saving Phoebe. I hoped she hadn't been hurt, and I hoped we were in time to save her. I didn't know how I would live with myself if she were hurt, or worse.

"Good plan," Felicity said with a humorless laugh. "When we get there, Caleb, you get Phoebe. You're the fastest, and you need to get her away from him. Levi and I will take on Avatrice. Maybe together we can do... something. He caught me off guard before and it *won't* happen again. I'm ready this time."

We both grunted our approval and ran faster. The screams kept coming, slicing through me, nearly causing physical pain. We were nearly there when I smelled the blood. I growled, crashing through the door to the clinic. I knew he would sense us coming, so there was no point in trying to be quiet. We needed to be fast. The smell grew stronger, and the screams were wreaking havoc on my ears. I took some comfort in the fact that it was probably worse for Avatrice, being so close to her. The three of us barreled down to the basement level, my feet barely touching the stairs. Every second that ticked by was agonizing.

The screaming turned to wracking sobs just before we crashed through the door. I didn't want to think about what was happening to her, but in an instant, my eyes took in everything. Avatrice leaning over Phoebe, naked from the waist down, strapped to a gurney, tears coursing down her face. He held a syringe in one hand, his other pressing down on Phoebe's stomach. He glanced back at us, as if completely unconcerned, and I realized he was not worried.

He didn't have goons blocking the door because he truly thought he was unstoppable. He believed he could beat us, no matter how many of us came to her rescue. My gut twisted, imagining all the sick things he may have done to her. I didn't even want to think about what was in the syringe.

"Levi!" Her voice was strained and hoarse, probably from screaming, but it still sounded beautiful to my ears. She was alive. We would deal with the rest, but all that mattered was getting her safe.

I lunged, hoping to catch him off guard, but Avatrice sidestepped easily, leaving me scrambling to leap over Phoebe or crash right into her. I whirled around in time to see Phoebe thrashing. Avatrice clicked his tongue and shoved Felicity in the chest as she attacked him, sending her sprawling. She groaned as she pushed herself to her hands and knees, shaking her head. Caleb eyed Avatrice warily, not as eager to jump into the fight. His goal was to free Phoebe. I had to get Avatrice's attention back on me.

"Avatrice!" The name tasted like ash. *"Leave them alone."* The suggestion was probably the strongest I had ever given, and yet, Avatrice remained unperturbed.

"Silly boy," he said, shaking his head. "You will never be the same caliber as me." His eyes narrowed, and he turned to face me fully, giving Caleb the chance he needed. He moved as fast as he was able, skidding across the room, slamming into the table Phoebe was laid up on. Caleb began ripping at the binds holding her down, bending down to use his teeth to tear them to shreds. His goal was fast, not pretty. *"Enough."*

The word was spoken so softly, and yet I felt the power of it. There was no way. Caleb stilled, his eyes darting to me. "Oh fuck," he muttered, his body stiff. As if he were unable to move.

I felt the suggestion threaten to take hold of me, and I growled. I pushed back, trying not to let myself think about this turn of events. He wasn't worried about taking us on because he had the same gift as me, but he was much older and had far more time to perfect it. Whereas I barely used mine. I felt the command trying to take hold of my mind, but I shut it out the way Richard had taught Phoebe. If I had known he possessed the ability to Compel, I would have planned more. I would have... done what?

Phoebe squirmed on the table, ripping one arm free from where Caleb had managed to do enough damage. She twisted and began clawing at the other binds. Felicity was still on the floor. Had she been affected too?

Avatrice took a step toward me. *"You will stop this nonsense,"* he said darkly. *"The others will leave us alone."*

Felicity began climbing to her feet, but I could see she was struggling against the commands given. I had to do something, fast, before he just Compelled everyone to abandon Phoebe. I shook off his command, worried that he would manage to get his hold firm over me. *"No."* The word was like ice. "You *will stop. Get on the ground."*

It was like a battle of wills, each of us trying to command the other. I may not have been able to actually sway him, but just acting like I could take him on was enough to wound his pride and he turned the full force of his powers on me, freeing Caleb and Felicity from his control. In an instant, Caleb had Phoebe free. He pushed her behind him and she scrambled to grab her clothes from the floor, yanking on her underthings haphazardly.

I hit my knees, hard. I hissed, struggling against his power. "Go!" I snarled, balling my hands into fists.

"Levi!" Phoebe sounded scared.

I shook my head, gritting my teeth. I had promised her I would never use my powers against her, but I had to break that promise now. I needed her to be safe. *"Go!"*

Caleb grabbed Phoebe by the arm and started dragging her toward the door. Even if she was able to deflect my command, Caleb would get her to leave. Avatrice roared, the first chink in his armor, and whirled to direct his powers at her once more. Felicity was there, putting herself in between them, throwing a punch that connected solidly with his jaw. As her punch landed, Phoebe and Caleb faded from view. I knew they hadn't made it out of the room yet and I had to smile. Felicity had distracted him long enough to cast an Illusion on the entire room, hiding them from sight. His head snapped to the side and, as I staggered to my feet, I felt pride. He grabbed her by the throat and threw her to the side. I was there in an instant, wrapping my arm around his neck from behind. I would rip his head clean off if I had to.

Felicity climbed to her feet and jumped at the two of us, fangs bared. She bit down hard on his shoulder, ripping and tearing. Blood dribbled down her face and neck, but Avatrice seemed unbothered. He bucked me off, and I hit the ground hard. He backhanded Felicity hard enough that I heard a loud crack, and she cried out in pain. I scrambled to my feet and just managed to knock him off kilter before he brought his boot down on her head. She had been through a lot today—I didn't want her close to death again if I could help it.

Avatrice turned his attention on me, and I realized he must have been using his powers to keep Felicity docile because she had yet to attack again. Smart move. But I wondered how many he could control at once? Richard and Kalene were due to arrive any minute. Would Felicity's illusion hide them as well? With Caleb and Phoebe out of the room, I felt I could better focus on the task at hand, knowing she was safe for now. I knew she wasn't far, as I could still smell her. Not her blood, I realized, but her own unique scent. Like vanilla and honey, I mused.

We circled each other, two predators locked in battle. I knew he likely thought he would take me out and go after Phoebe again. He was still confident. Of course, I still had an ace up my sleeve. I wondered if he was aware of Richard's abilities as the man himself came barreling through the door. His arrival seemed to snap Felicity out of it, and they descended.

Avatrice lunged at me, catching me around the waist. We crashed through the gurney Phoebe had been on, fangs tearing flesh, punches landing, but I barely felt the pain. And then Richard was there, in all of our minds simultaneously. I took comfort in his presence. He knew what our moves were almost before we did. Avatrice had me pinned, sitting on my chest, his claws around my throat.

But still I smiled.

Felicity came up behind him, grabbing his arms and wrenching them back, his hands coming loose from my throat. With his arms pinned, Richard moved, grabbing a cleaver off a table nearby. And, with a mighty swing, he lopped Avatrice's head clean off. Or, at least, he tried.

Richard heaved a sigh, yanked the cleaver free of Avatrice's throat and I reached up, grabbing his head in my hands and, as promised, I ripped it right off his shoulders. It rolled across the floor, where Felicity stopped it with her booted foot. She gave a snarl of distaste and kicked it away from her. Avatrice's body fell to the side; but I wanted to be sure. I plunged my hand through his chest and ripped out his barely beating heart, and I watched it give a few more pitiful pumps before crushing it between my fingers.

"Everyone okay?" Richard asked, looking at the two of us.

I nodded. "Beat up, but breathing." I glanced around, my stomach clenching tightly. What had he been up to? "Where is Kalene?"

"In the hall," Richard answered. "Helping Caleb hold Phoebe together. Or hold her back from coming in here. It's all a little garbled."

"Felicity, Richard, take care of this mess. I need to see Phoebe." I strode from the room before they could respond, finally beginning to feel the pain. Avatrice had done a number on me. My right eye was swollen shut, my lip split open, and I was pretty sure my left arm was broken. Nothing a little blood couldn't fix. I found Caleb, Kalene, and Phoebe halfway down the hall. As soon as she saw me, Phoebe burst into tears. Caleb and Kalene let her go and she flew down the hall, throwing herself into my arms. I grunted in pain, but I refused to let her go. Her small body shook with horrible sobs, and I was afraid of speaking. I needed to know what happened, but at her discretion.

Chapter Thirty-Two
Phoebe

I knew everyone wanted answers, but I wasn't ready to give them. Levi was hurt, I was hurt. In more ways than one. My stomach ached constantly, the state of my nerves probably permanently fucking up my digestive system. I couldn't even think about eating food. Caleb and Kalene made sure we were okay enough to get home, and Levi assured them we were. I wasn't convinced, but they left to go make a run to the blood bar, grabbing some to go orders for everyone.

Levi put his good arm around me, pulling me close. "Can you walk?" he asked. I nodded my head silently and the two of us shuffled slowly back toward the house. It took us a long time, and I wondered if it was because Levi was too injured or if he wanted to let me process what had happened. I wasn't even sure I was ready to think about it. How would he feel once he knew? I peeked up at him and winced. His face was banged up pretty badly, and I wondered what we must have looked like walking down the street, clinging to one another. I would be surprised if we didn't get stopped by the cops.

But we made it back to the house, and we settled on the couch together. Without a word, I laid on my side, curling up in his lap. Levi sighed softly and began gently stroking my hair. "I am so sorry," he said, voice tight. I peeked up at him, but he was staring straight ahead, his jaw clenched. "I never should have left your side. Avatrice was just waiting for the perfect moment." He rubbed a hand down his face, wincing. "But you don't want to talk about that."

I shook my head, settling back down. I did not want to talk about that at all. I closed my eyes, trying to enjoy the gentle touch of his hands in my hair, but my stomach twisted, and I felt bile rise up in my throat again remembering Avatrice's hands on me. I lurched up off the couch and just managed to get to the kitchen sink. I heard the front door open as I deposited the contents of my guts into the stainless steel basin and quickly turned the water on to wash it down and rinsed my mouth out. My whole body hurt.

Kalene was there when I turned around, holding a glass of water and two small white pills. "For the pain," she said softly. She held them out to me, and I took them silently, downing the pills in one gulp. I didn't ask what they were, and I didn't care. I hoped they were strong. "Why don't we go get you cleaned up while Levi drinks?" she asked.

I glanced around her into the living room where Caleb was passing a Styrofoam cup to Levi, presumably filled with blood. My stomach threatened to turn again, and I looked away, nodding silently at Kalene's suggestion. She helped me up the stairs and into Levi's room. She didn't push and the energy she was giving felt so motherly, it made me want to cry. Of course, everything made me want to cry. I wasn't sure how to exist and I thought the best course of action was to just let myself be numb for a while. Maybe I could ask Levi to just make me forget.

Kalene helped me into the bathroom and turned on the shower. "Hot?" she asked. I nodded, and she cranked it up. "Do you want me to help you?" I nodded again. Gently, and without comment, Kalene helped me strip off the torn and dirty clothes. She made no comment on my naked body as she helped me step under the scalding spray. "I'll throw these out," she said softly. She turned as if to leave and I reached out, grabbing her, my eyes wide and filling with tears. "Oh, honey," she whispered, dropping the clothes and sitting on the edge of the tub.

Water splashed everywhere with the curtain wide open, and Kalene was getting soaked, but she didn't seem to mind. I sat on the floor of the shower, letting the water wash over me. Maybe it could burn his touch off. After several moments of just sitting there, Kalene sighed softly and reached over. She turned off the shower and plugged up the tub, allowing it to fill around me. And as it filled, she grabbed the shampoo and began washing my hair. Her touch was so gentle, and I couldn't bring myself to be embarrassed.

"I know you don't want to talk, and you don't have to. You can shut Richard out, and I will tell him not to go looking, in fact. Nothing is expected of you, Phoebe. You don't have to do or say anything, for however long you need." Kalene rinsed my hair, being careful not to get soap in my eyes. "The bad man has been taken care of and Levi will be here for you every step of the way, no matter what comes next."

I felt the tears sliding down my face, but neither of us commented on it. She grabbed a washcloth and gently washed my body, giving me notice every time before touching me. I had a feeling she knew. I felt like a child, but I wasn't sure I could take care of myself. Not right now. And Kalene didn't mind. She talked about nonsensical things, mentioning movies she wanted to see and places she wanted to go. She talked about anything under the sun, but she never once expected me to respond. I was grateful.

Once she was finished washing me up, she stood. "I'll get you some fresh clothes." She drained the tub and handed me a plush white towel. I slowly climbed to my feet and wrapped it around myself as she headed into the bedroom and grabbed me a pair of soft pajama pants and an oversized t-shirt. She returned and helped me dress, grabbing a brush and running it gently through my hair. She braided it down my back, humming softly. "Do you want to just get in bed or head back downstairs?" she asked.

I wrapped my arms around myself and nodded my head toward the bedroom door. Downstairs.

Kalene wrapped an arm around me, and we descended the stairs. Everyone was home by the time we came down. Felicity stood with her arms folded across her chest, leaning one hip against the arm of the couch. Caleb paced the room while Levi and Richard sat on the couch. Richard jumped up when he saw me and motioned for me to take his seat. I smiled faintly and went to sit, tentatively lying back down, curling up in Levi's lap. He hesitated before gently stroking his hand over my hair again.

"Feel better?" he asked quietly. I shrugged one shoulder, not really sure. He didn't push the issue and for that I was grateful.

"Well," Felicity said carefully. "The...*issue* has been taken care of. He won't be bothering us anymore."

Good.

Richard glanced at me, his expression concerned. "Phoebe?" he asked. "Are you okay?"

Not really.

"Do you want to talk?" Richard asked. "I know you went through something pretty traumatic..."

No. The thought came vehemently.

"Fair enough," Richard said, nodding. "You can have all the space you need." He motioned around the room. "No one will press."

"We're here for you, love," Levi said tenderly. "Always."

Chapter Thirty-Three

P_hoebe_

I didn't speak for three days. I was in survival mode, and I barely ate, barely slept, and when I did, I often awoke screaming. Levi was always there, comforting me. He was careful not to touch me too much, and I was grateful for his care. But I knew they were dying to know what had happened, and I knew Levi couldn't rest with the uncertainty. And so, I climbed from bed and got showered for the first time in three days, brushed my teeth, dressed in real clothes, and slowly walked downstairs. Everyone always spoke rapidly, in hushed tones, and they often fell silent when I came into a room.

This was no different.

Kalene came over with a plate of food and handed it to me. "Eat," she said gently.

"Thank you." The words were whispered and sounded strangled, but still, she smiled. The first words I had spoken in days and, after the way she had cared for me, it felt right that they were spoken to her. I sat at the table across from Levi and began eating, forcing myself to take bite after bite, despite the food tasting of cardboard. When I had cleared my plate, I reached across the table and took his hand in mine. It was also the first time in days that I had initiated any sort of contact.

"Good morning, beautiful," Levi said, giving my hand a gentle squeeze. He had been so patient, and I knew I needed to tell him what happened, but the thought of speaking the words sent my mind in a tailspin. I forgot to shield from Richard and, based on the way the glass in his hand shattered, I knew he must have heard at least something. He turned around quickly, washing the blood from his hands, and cleared his throat.

"Sorry," he muttered. "I...uh..."

"Heard?" I whispered. "Sorry."

"No," Richard said quickly, turning to look at me, his eyes flashing angrily. "*Fuck,* Phoebe. Jesus," he said, pushing his hands through his hair. "I mean... *fuck.*" He shook his head. "No wonder you didn't want to talk about it."

Levi looked concerned, his eyes flashing between Richard and I. "What?" he demanded. It seemed he was done waiting. And it was time to tell them. And so, I did. It was painful and slow, and I had to stop several times to cry or to let Levi cool off. When I had finally spoken the last of it, there was a heavy silence that fell over the room. It felt uncomfortable and I just knew Levi was trying to keep his temper under control. It wouldn't do anyone any good. Avatrice was dead. He had gotten what was coming to him, but it felt hollow.

It would feel even more so if I missed my period.

I didn't want to think about that now. I stood and took my plate to the sink, washing it slowly and methodically. Things would get back to normal, eventually. Or, at least, what I had come to know as normal in the last few months.

"What will you do now?" Levi asked, coming up behind me. He took the plate from me, dried it, and returned it to the cabinet.

I glanced at him, frowning. "I suppose just try to get on with life," I said. "I have a lot to... deal with, mentally. I've been through so much in not a lot of time. I just... I need familiarity," I said. I turned to face him, wrapping my arms around my middle. "I need *you.*"

Levi let out a breath, and I realized he must have thought I was planning to leave. I wasn't going anywhere. I stepped forward and leaned into his chest. He carefully wrapped his arms around me, and I sighed. "You have me," he said softly.

"Good," I whispered. "This is home."

Things really did go back to semi-normal. I still had nightmares, but Levi was there to wipe away my tears and help me settle. He continued to help me train, getting better to hopefully be better able to defend myself if something were to happen. Three weeks went by, and I began growing anxious. There had been no sign of my period.

I was pacing the living room, chewing on my lower lip, trying to decide if I was freaking out over nothing. It could just be late. I went through a very stressful situation, so it was plausible. Then again if I *was* pregnant the thought that it was Levi's crossed my mind. I knew he said he *couldn't,* but maybe he was wrong. Was I ready to be a mother? If I was pregnant and it turned out to belong to Avatrice, what would I do? I didn't think I would be able to keep it.

My phone rang suddenly, causing me to jump. I scrambled to find it, and after a moment of hesitation, answered. Tears burned my eyes after a quick conversation, and I plopped back on the couch as Levi came looking for me. I had been a little distant, worried about how he would react if things turned out to be bad. "That was Angie's mom," I said softly. He came to sit beside me, resting his hand comfortably on my knee. "Her headstone finally came in. I should go see her."

"I'll go with you," Levi said gently. "We all will."

Days passed, and my period had still not arrived. My stomach twisted into knots as I sat on the toilet, a pregnancy test in my shaking hands. I was nearly a week and a half late already and I had to know. Levi had gone with Richard and Caleb to get something to drink, and the girls stayed back with me. They both sat outside the bathroom, waiting for me.

I did what I needed to do and set the test down on the counter. My heart beat painfully in my chest and I swear it was the longest five minutes of my life. I heard the front door open and close, and I cursed, knowing the guys had returned home and would likely come searching for us to send Kalene and Felicity off to get theirs. I paced the bathroom, wringing my hands, casting nervous glances at the test. I threw up the thickest of mental blocks I could muster, determined to keep this quiet. I had to be the one to tell Levi if it came back positive.

My phone beeped, signaling that it had been five minutes, and I took a shaky breath. I stepped back up to the sink and looked at myself in the mirror. I had dark circles beneath my eyes and my face looked thinner. I needed to take better care of myself. I closed my eyes, took another deep breath, and looked down.

There was a gentle knock on the door. "Phoebe?" Kalene asked.

"What does it say?" Felicity demanded. I opened the door. They both sprung to their feet, having been sitting on the floor.

"It's negative?" Kalene asked hopefully.

"Positive?" Felicity hedged, making an anxious face. I motioned for them to go take a look and, when they both stepped into the bathroom, I hurried downstairs, my heart beating painfully in my chest. I saw Levi standing in the foyer, talking with Caleb. He looked up when he saw me coming down the stairs and flashed me a smile. I descended the rest of the stairs rapidly, throwing myself into his arms. He caught me easily, holding me tightly. When he dropped me back down to my feet, I stretched up on my toes and kissed him. It was the first time we had kissed since everything happened and I knew it had surprised him. I hadn't known I was going to do it, but I was happy. Happier than I had been in a while.

"Thank god," Richard said, giving me a knowing look.

"What?" Levi asked, tucking my hair behind my ear. He hadn't known I was going to take a pregnancy test. I fidgeted anxiously.

"I took a test," I said quietly. "My period is over a week late," I said.

Levi frowned, his eyebrows pulling together. "Phoebe, you know I can't..." he stopped, looking more and more upset by the second.

I took his hands in mine and shook my head. "It was negative," I blurted. "I'm not pregnant, Levi."

The realization flashed across his face, and he grabbed me again, pressing his lips to mine. I wrapped my arms around his neck, kissing him until I couldn't breathe. I slowly began to fall apart, and he pressed my back against the wall, resting his forehead against mine. I hadn't realized how terrified I was until I had gotten my answer. I was so relieved to not be pregnant, but things weren't quite over yet. I would be anxious until my period came, giving me that extra confirmation. In the meantime, I knew my family would be there for me, whatever I needed.

"Always," Levi said, lifting my chin and kissing me tenderly. This is where I belonged. Vampire... human... it didn't matter.

I belonged.

Chapter Thirty-Four
Phoebe

I needed to go see Angie. I had put it off long enough. So much had happened, and I wanted to tell my best friend about it, even if she wasn't really there. Clad in a black dress and boots, I stepped out of the car, tears already threatening to run down my cheeks. Levi climbed out after me and took my hand. Kalenc and Felicity climbed from the back seat. Richard and Caleb had elected to come separately, and I saw that they were already waiting for us. We made our way toward the grave and I felt my stomach clench, but Levi was there, taking my hand and giving a reassuring squeeze.

I crouched down in front of her grave and blew out a soft breath. "Hey, Angie," I whispered. "A lot has happened since you left." The cemetery was pretty empty and, with my vampire guards, I unleashed everything I had been through in the past months. I didn't feel embarrassed or shy as I detailed my experiences with each of the vampires I had grown to love deeply. Everyone gave me space, pretending not to hear me and, when I inevitably started crying, a tissue was slipped into my hand wordlessly. I couldn't have been more thankful for these people, but I truly wished I could share everything with Angie. I knew she wasn't really there, buried beneath my feet, but I took solace in the fact that I believed she could hear me from wherever she was.

It wasn't until I slowly rose to my feet, emotions spent, that everyone started acting a little strangely. Levi grabbed my hand a little tighter than usual and everyone closed ranks, shielding me. From what, I didn't know.

"Hunters," Richard hissed in my ear. "There, there, and there," he said, motioning with his eyes. I followed his line of sight and could pick out the people he was referring to. There was a man in a suit with his hands clasped behind his back, eyes darting around every few seconds standing a few graves over. Across from him, on the other side of the cemetery, was a woman with curly black hair. She wore a knee-length black dress and a black jacket that could easily hide a weapon. And to our left stood another woman with blonde hair whisked into a bun. She wore slacks and a jacket similar to the other woman. A nervous chill raced down my spine.

"Why are they here?" I whispered.

"From what I can tell, they caught wind of Angie's case and thought it sounded sketchy. So, my guess is they either came to dig her up and take a look or they know what we are and followed us." Richard's eyes focused on the raven-haired woman for a beat longer than the rest.

"Wait," I said, voice barely audible. I knew they could hear me. "Can they *tell* that you are... ahem. You know?"

"I don't know yet," Richard muttered. "None of them have given us much thought. Wait," he said, frowning.

My eyes darted around to the three people, but I couldn't see anything worth getting worked up over. The man was on the phone and the two women had their heads bowed respectfully, it seemed. "What is it?" Caleb asked.

"The woman over there, she keeps looking this way. Barely. She's being very discrete, but her thoughts give her away. I just can't tell if it's because she suspects us or because she thinks one of us is hot." He snickered suddenly. "Me. She thinks I'm hot. Nice."

"Richard," Kalene chastened. "This is a cemetery—stop laughing."

"Oh, shit," he muttered, his humor gone. "She knows."

I stiffened. "She knows about you?" I asked, glancing discreetly at the raven-haired woman. She seemed to be looking in our direction, but trying to look like she wasn't.

"Yeah. I think she figured it out. Not sure how. Thermal tech, maybe? Checking the heat signatures. You'd read human, so they are probably thinking you are a victim. Shit. She's going to come over here." Richard ran a hand through his hair and turned to Felicity, as if they were talking.

The raven-haired woman approached a moment later. "Hi," she said, a tentative smile on her face. "Did you know the victim?" she asked, motioning toward Angie's grave.

I frowned. "Angie?" I asked. "Yeah. She was my best friend."

The woman nodded. "I'm so sorry," she said, sounding genuine. "And you all?"

"Just here for support," Levi answered coolly, giving my hand a squeeze. "Are you with the police?"

She chuckled. "No, no. Private investigator," she lied easily. "Just looking for other angles, you know? Hoping to find her killer." Her eyes swept the group, lingering on me.

"I told the police everything I know," I lied. "But I hope you are able to find her killer. Her family deserves that." The lie was sour on my tongue, but I hoped it was believable.

The woman nodded her head. "Right," she said. "Well, sorry to bother you." She turned and walked back to her post, a phone to her ear before she even made it back. She watched us for the rest of our time there, not even trying to hide it. Once I had said my final goodbyes, Caleb passed me a bouquet of flowers, and I stepped up and placed them at the grave. With a final glance toward the Hunters, we all headed back to our cars. The trio was not far behind.

"Kalene, Felicity—you go ahead and take your car. Just get out of here," Richard muttered. "Phoebe, get in Levi's car."

I did as I was told but cracked the window so I could hear what was being said. "Hello again," the same woman from before said as Kalene pulled away, Felicity watching us out the passenger window.

"Hello," Caleb answered cordially. "What can we do for you?"

The man scowled. "Let's go ahead and cut the act," he said. "We know what you are."

Caleb feigned ignorance. "Concerned citizens morally supporting a friend in her time of need?" he asked, hand over his barely beating heart.

"Vampires." The blonde woman spoke so bluntly, it startled me. I almost laughed, but I knew how serious this could have been.

Richard took a step forward. "Don't even think about starting something here," he said. "We have done nothing wrong. We are really just here because Angie was a friend to Phoebe." He hooked his thumb at me, and I waved dumbly. "We live peacefully."

"You still drink blood," the man muttered.

"Yes," Levi supplied. "From each other or the blood bar in town. Animals in a pinch. We do not feed directly from the source. You have no quarrel with my family."

"Don't feed from the source?" the blonde woman asked. She pointed at me. "Then what do you need her for?"

"Oh, Phoebe?" Levi asked. "She's not human."

That seemed to startle all three of the Hunters. "Then what is she?" the raven-haired woman asked, staring at me. "She doesn't run hot enough to be a werewolf, and I've never heard of vampires and werewolves interacting nicely."

"Not a werewolf," Caleb said simply. "You are half correct in assuming she is human."

"And half incorrect," Richard supplied.

All three of them stared at me, working it out in their minds. I could see Richard squirm and wondered if they were being loud. I tried twice as hard to shield my own thoughts so I wouldn't add to his discomfort. "A dhampir?" the raven-haired woman said after a minute. "That's... rare."

"Yeah, she's pretty special," Levi said, coughing to hide a laugh. "So, as you can see, we are doing nothing wrong. We bear no ill will toward you and I ask that you not harm my family."

"For now," the man said. "We will be keeping an eye on you." He turned his back on us. "Miranda, Jessica—let's go." The three walked off and Caleb let out a loud breath.

"That was tense," Richard muttered. "Don't know that I like them keeping tabs on us."

"It was bound to happen," Levi muttered, climbing into the car. "We probably have Avatrice to thank for that." We headed back to the house, where Felicity and Kalene were waiting with popcorn and a movie.

We piled into the house and claimed spots on the couch and chairs. I curled up next to Levi, resting my head against his chest. I made sure my mental blocks were up and thought for a long moment, drumming my fingers against his thigh. "Hey, Levi?" I asked.

"Hm?" he asked, looking down at me, tracing circles on my back. I chewed on my lower lip, and he frowned. A lot had happened recently, and I didn't want him to think I was just saying it to say it. I really meant it. Kalene let out a happy squeak and slapped a hand over her mouth when I shot her a dark look.

"I love you," I said, when I looked back at Levi. I laughed softly. "Ask Kalene."

The vampire was bouncing in her seat, her eyes huge and excited. Levi grabbed my chin and lifted my face to his. "Well," he said softly. "I suppose it is an excellent thing."

"What?" I asked, confused.

He lowered his mouth to mine, kissing me sweetly. "That I love you too."

Things might have been complete shit the last few months, but at least something good came of it. I was determined to live a relatively normal and happy life. I had a wonderful family, the man I loved at my side, and best of all, I was *definitely* not pregnant. What more could a girl want?

Don't miss out!

Visit the website below and you can sign up to receive emails whenever Jennifer Noel Dennis publishes a new book. There's no charge and no obligation.

https://books2read.com/r/B-A-BMUW-ADGFC

BOOKS 2 READ

Connecting independent readers to independent writers.

www.ingramcontent.com/pod-product-compliance
Lightning Source LLC
Chambersburg PA
CBHW020326160726
47992CB00004B/1721